VENDETTA

Center Point
Large Print

Also by Lisa Harris and available from
Center Point Large Print:

Southern Crimes series:
  Dangerous Passage
  Hidden Agenda

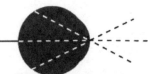

The Nikki Boyd Files, #1

VENDETTA

LISA HARRIS

CENTER POINT LARGE PRINT
THORNDIKE, MAINE

This Center Point Large Print edition is published
in the year 2015 by arrangement with Revell,
a division of Baker Publishing Group.

The text of this Large Print edition is unabridged.
In other aspects, this book may vary from the original edition.
Printed in the United States of America on permanent paper.
Set in 16-point Times New Roman type.

ISBN: 978-1-62899-761-3

Library of Congress Cataloging-in-Publication Data

Harris, Lisa, 1969–
  Vendetta : the Nikki Boyd files / Lisa Harris. —
  Center Point Large Print edition.
    pages cm
  Summary: "Missing Persons Task Force detective Nikki Boyd's search
for a missing girl takes a chillingly personal turn and she begins to feel
that she is not the hunter at all—but actually the one being hunted"
    —Provided by publisher.
  ISBN 978-1-62899-761-3 (library binding : alk. paper)
  1. Large type books. I. Title.
  PS3608.A78315V46 2015b
  813'.6—dc23

                                                        2015028540

You can make many plans,
but the Lord's purpose will prevail.
—Proverbs 19:21

1

Northeast Tennessee near the Obed River

The initial step off the sheer face of a three-hundred-plus-foot drop was always the most terrifying. Nikki Boyd leaned back into her harness as far as she could, locked her knees, then peered over the edge of the sandstone cliff that dropped into the ravine below. The terror faded, followed by a shot of pure adrenaline as she kicked off and plunged over the edge.

Legs horizontal to the rock face, Nikki shimmied down the side of the cliff, kicking loose a few rocks along the way. The stress of the past few weeks began to dissipate into the crisp morning air. A day climbing and rappelling with Tyler Grant had definitely been the right thing to do. They'd come, not to dismiss memories of Katie's death, but to celebrate her life. Which was exactly what they were doing.

Halfway down, Nikki glanced up, then slowed to a stop. The rope had shifted and now ran over a sharp edge of the cliff wall. She caught her toes against a narrow ledge and fought to catch her balance. While perhaps not common, it was possible to sever a weighted rope on a descent.

"You okay?" Tyler hollered down at her.

"The rope moved and it's running over a sharp edge."

She'd been told by more than one experienced climber that they hated rappelling because it was the most dangerous part of the day. And this was why. No matter how much training and preparation, no matter how many times she checked her equipment, things could still go wrong. And it just took one mistake. But all she needed to do was unweight the rope and move it to a safer place.

"Can you move it?" Tyler asked.

"I'm trying."

"You're going to have to take some of your weight off the rope."

"Like I said, I'm trying."

Her gloved fingers held on to a crack in the rock face while she searched for another crack for her feet. Her fingers cramped. A trail of blood dripped down her arm. She didn't even remember scraping it. Her feet finally found a narrow crevice, alleviating her weight on the rope enough to give it some slack. All she needed to do now was redirect the rope's path.

Simple.

But she couldn't get enough leverage to unweight the rope.

"Nikki?"

"Just a minute . . ." Sweat beaded across her forehead as she stood on her tiptoes, her fingertips pressed back into the crack, heart pounding against her chest.

She'd heard plenty of stories about things like this happening. Freak accidents against the side of a sheer cliff. Climbers plunging to their deaths. *You know this isn't how I want to die, Jesus . . .*

And certainly not today. Not on the anniversary of Katie's death. She glanced at the ground below, then felt her breath catch. If she couldn't move the rope to a safer spot, it could snap above her.

"Nikki?" Tyler shouted from the top of the cliff. "What's happening?"

She drew in another breath. "I'm okay, but I'm having trouble moving the rope."

She hung balanced on the ledge, trying to figure out what to do. Accidents like this weren't all that common, but as with any sport, there were always variables you couldn't count on. She shifted her gaze to the ground. Two months ago, a college student had plunged to his death near here. The steep, rocky terrain made it a popular spot for risk takers.

She pushed the thought aside. What she needed to do was focus on solving the problem. Theoretically she knew what to do, but she was going to need both hands. Which was a problem. Currently, with her right hand holding the rope behind her to keep her from sliding down, she'd need to run the end around her legs a few times in order to secure it. But that was a move even an experienced rappeller would hesitate performing. Unless—

"Stay put, Nikki, I'm coming to you."

"I can figure this out."

"Stay put," he ordered. "I'm coming down."

"Okay, just be careful."

A handful of small rocks bounced off her helmet as Tyler descended toward her on a separate rope.

"How was your date last night with Ryan?" he called down to her.

Her date? Was he serious?

She never should have told Tyler about Ryan. Now he was simply trying to distract her. Trying to get her to focus her thoughts away from the fear and panic. Panic because she was stuck on a narrow ledge a hundred-plus feet off the ground with the potential of a severed rope. And with it the reminder of how quickly life could spiral out of control.

"The date went fine," she finally answered.

She could hear him making his way down the sheer cliff above her. His feet scattered another volley of pebbles.

"Fine doesn't tell me anything," he countered. "Give me some details. Last night was your third date with Mr. Perfect. You've got to have something interesting to share."

Details? He really wanted details while she was hanging off the side of a cliff praying she wasn't about to plunge to her death?

A cramp gripped her calf as her fingers dug deeper into the rock crevice above her. She tried to wiggle her leg without losing her footing on the ledge. There honestly wasn't much to tell. Ryan was six foot three and looked like a model straight off a Banana Republic ad. On top of that, he made a great living, owned his own house, and was completely debt free.

None of those things, though, was the real reason she'd agreed to a second and third date. She'd half expected him to be a snob, but surprisingly, he wasn't. At all. Instead, he was down-to-earth, complimented her without making her feel he wanted something in return, and treated her like she was the only one in the room when they were together. She'd never met another guy quite like him—except perhaps Tyler.

Which was why Tyler had dubbed him "Mr. Perfect" the first time she'd told him she'd gone out with a guy set up by one of her mother's friends at church. Making it to the third date was something of a record for her—as of late anyway. But despite Ryan's "perfection," she still wasn't completely convinced he was perfect for *her*. Everyone—including her mother—had already made the decision she'd finally found Mr. Right in Mr. Perfect. But making that decision for herself felt a lot like taking that first step off the cliff. A shot of terror along with a huge rush of adrenaline.

A sharp pain jetted through her head, and Nikki realized she was clenching her jaw. She took in a deep breath and forced herself to relax. "He's not perfect, and there's nothing new I want to share with you."

Tyler laughed as he dropped next to where she hung and stopped. "The guy owns his own company, runs half marathons for fun, and supports orphans in Africa."

"So he's a good guy. That doesn't mean I'm planning on—I don't know—*marrying* him."

"Yet."

Nikki frowned. No, those were her mother's plans. Besides, talking with Tyler about her date was . . . well . . . awkward.

"One of us needs a bit of a boost in the romance department, and since I'm not going there, that leaves you," he said.

She caught a flicker of pain in his voice. How did you start dating again after losing the love of your life? She wasn't even going to ask that question.

"There's a slightly deeper ledge six inches to your right for your feet. It will give you some extra support, but I think the simplest solution at this point is to transfer you to my rope."

Nikki drew in a deep breath as she felt for the

ledge, then managed to shove her toes into the crack.

"What did the two of you do?" he asked.

She watched while he locked off his belay device and ran the bottom of his rope through hers, grateful for his special ops training.

"We went to dinner and the symphony."

"And . . ."

"That was it. Dinner, good food, and interesting conversation."

"Do you like him?"

She hesitated. "He's nice. A gentleman."

"Like I said. Mr. Perfect, though I'm not sure that *nice* is what a guy wants to hear."

"Then what does he want to hear?" Nikki wiggled her toes while still trying to keep her balance. The cramp had spread from her calf to the arch of her foot.

"That he's intriguing . . . intelligent . . . funny . . . a bit romantic."

"He brought me flowers," she said. Somehow he'd found out she loved wildflowers and had brought her a bouquet.

"But no fireworks yet?" Tyler asked.

"I'm just getting to know him."

For Tyler and Katie, it had been love at first sight. She'd never believed in the notion until the day they'd met. But that wasn't exactly her own experience. Her longest relationship— two and a half years—had ended in a nasty breakup. Not exactly a scenario she wanted to repeat.

Like the scenario she was dealing with right now.

"You're good to go," Tyler said finally. "Ease down slowly."

Nikki tightened her fingers on the rope as she made her way down the rest of the cliff with Tyler following. She skidded down the slight incline at the bottom of the rock, then disconnected from the rope.

"Let's not try that again," she said, thankful her feet were finally once again on solid ground.

"You're telling me. You okay?"

She brushed the dust from her pants, then peeled off her gloves. "I think my ego's more bruised than I am. I anchored the rope in the wrong spot."

"Sometimes you do everything right and it still isn't enough."

She caught the sadness in his eyes as they began collecting the equipment. Why was that statement always so hard to accept?

"You're sure you're okay?" he asked again.

She held out her hands, unable to stop them from shaking. "I'll admit, that was a bit sobering."

He pulled her against his chest while she tried to let go of the fear that had surrounded her only moments before. She snuggled into his shoulder. His heart was beating as fast as hers. She looked up at his familiar brown eyes and short, military cut hair and felt his day-old beard brush lightly against her cheek. His arms tightened around her shoulders, making her feel safe and protected.

He knew as well as she did that sometimes doing everything right simply wasn't enough.

But thankfully, today hadn't ended in tragedy.

"As long as you're okay," he said, "that's all that matters."

She let out a soft swoosh of air. She didn't want today to hold another reminder of what could go wrong. How in one fragile moment life could suddenly slip away and be gone forever. But that fact wasn't something either of them could ever forget.

"Thank you." Her heart rate was beginning to slow to normal. "You saved my life, you know."

He brushed away a strand of her shoulder-length blond hair that had fallen across her cheek, then took a step backward. "Being here with you today has made me realize—not for the first time—that I'm the one who needs to thank you."

"For what?"

"For coming with me today." He squeezed her hand before pulling off his helmet. "For everything you've done for Liam and me. I'm honestly not sure I would have gotten through the last year without you."

"I miss her too. Maybe that's why I'm feeling so distracted today."

Nikki felt the tears well in her eyes and tried to blink them back. She'd promised herself she'd be strong for Tyler. Blubbering like a baby wasn't keeping that promise. But while the pain had dulled even a year later, sometimes the loss still felt like it had happened yesterday. Sometimes she still heard Katie's voice. Heard the phone ring and expected it to be her, until she remembered that Katie would never call again. But as much as she missed her best friend, her grief was nothing compared to what Tyler and Liam had gone through.

"You ready to call it quits for the day?" he asked.

"Are you kidding?" Nikki blinked back the rest of her tears and smiled. "We've barely started. I didn't wake up before dawn to give up and go back home again before breakfast."

They'd planned this day for months. A day out of the city, near the place where they'd sprinkled Katie's ashes. A day to celebrate Katie's life. She would have wanted them to be here today.

"How about a break then?" he asked. "Your hands are still shaking."

Nikki pressed her palms against her sides. "I could use some coffee. And if you're hungry, my mom packed breakfast to go along with the thermos she sent with us."

"I love your mom." Tyler smiled as he started

for the trail leading away from the cliffs. "But the smell drove me crazy the entire trip here."

"Me too, and there's plenty."

There always was. Boyds' BBQ in downtown Nashville had been in the family for three generations, and Nikki's mom never missed an opportunity to ensure her daughter stayed well fed.

"How about we take care of that scrape on your arm first," Tyler said. "Then we can eat some of your mom's breakfast and get at this again."

Nikki nodded, then glanced at the gash where she'd noticed the blood earlier. "You know you don't have to baby me."

He smiled at her and shook his head. "You've always been there for me, Nikki. Just let me do the same thing for you."

Five minutes later, she sat on the tailgate of Tyler's pickup truck in the parking lot while he pulled out the first-aid kit and started cleaning her wound. He washed away the trail of blood caked with dirt from the mountainside, then covered it with an antibacterial spray.

Nikki winced.

"You're worse than Liam," he teased.

"Funny, but that stuff—whatever it is—stings. Remember you're going to school to be a psychologist, not a doctor, Mr. Grant."

"I think I can handle this assignment, Special Agent Boyd."

She laughed, thankful that most of the panic was finally wearing off, because she still had her eye on conquering a couple of climbing routes that had gotten the best of her the last time she was here. Today, she was determined to stay focused and make it to the top of at least one of them.

Her phone rang, and she pulled it out of her back pocket.

She glanced at the caller ID. Unknown. "I should ignore it, but it could be my sister-in-law trying to get ahold of me. She was supposed to go see her obstetrician this morning."

"Anything wrong?"

"Maybe. She's only got a couple weeks before her due date, but she started bleeding last night."

Which had Nikki worried. She'd watched Matt and Jamie navigate an emotional roller coaster through eight years of infertility and three miscarriages. This pregnancy finally promised the first grandbaby of the family, and just last week they'd finished the nursery. If anything went wrong now . . .

"Go ahead." Tyler pressed a butterfly Band-Aid over her cut. "I've got my phone on in case Liam needs me. You'd better answer."

Nikki nodded and took the call.

"Agent Boyd." The voice of her boss, Tom Carter, took Nikki by surprise. "How is the great outdoors treating you?"

She glanced at Tyler, who'd started putting the first-aid supplies back into the plastic case. "I'm fine, sir, thanks."

"Good. Listen, I hate to put a wrinkle in your day, but I have a favor to ask of you."

Nikki frowned. Saying no to her boss was somehow harder than saying no to her mother. "I'm here with Tyler Grant, sir, we're—"

"I remember you mentioned you were going climbing." He paused. "Today's the anniversary of his wife's death, right?"

"Yeah."

"How's he doing?"

Tyler had met her boss during a joint military training exercise designed to increase the military's ability to function in an urban setting. According to Carter, he'd been highly impressed with Tyler's skills and instincts.

"He's okay. We're having a good time. The weather's perfect." There was no use mentioning she'd been clinging to the side of a cliff a few minutes ago, afraid for her life. "What's the favor, sir?"

"I just got a call from a friend. Actually, I went to university with his father, and we stayed close until he died. The son's name is Kyle Ellison. He's not far from where you are with his sixteen-year-old sister, celebrating her birthday over the weekend. Problem is, she went out for a walk this morning and didn't return."

Nikki glanced at her watch. It was just past eight. "Has he called the local authorities?"

"Not yet. He's convinced she probably just wandered off the path to get a closer look at some wildlife and sprained her ankle, something like that. He called me for advice."

"How long has she been gone?"

"He's not sure. She was gone when he got up, around seven."

Which meant they were already looking at a minimum of two hours ago, and maybe longer.

There was another pause on the line before her boss spoke again. "Listen, all I'm asking is for you to look into it for me. I'll text you the address of the private cabin where they're staying. Interview the brother and the girl's friends, then pass it on to the local law enforcement if you need to. The boy's scared."

"Okay. I'll see what I can do."

Nikki hung up the phone and glanced down at her climbing clothes. With her tan, lightweight climbing pants, orange T-shirt, and hiking shoes, she wasn't exactly dressed for the job, but it would have to do for now.

She jumped down from the tailgate. "That was my boss."

"What did he want?" Tyler asked.

She hesitated. "A favor."

"He wants you to work a case."

Nikki nodded, trying to read Tyler's expression.

"It shouldn't take long. A quick interview about a missing girl who's probably just lost out here somewhere."

"I don't mind." He shot her a smile. "As long as I get some of your mama's cooking as soon as we're done."

Nikki laughed, hoping he truly didn't mind. She'd already begun sorting through the limited information she had. Because with missing persons cases, time was never on their side. If the girl *had* been abducted, at a mile a minute she could easily be across the state border by now. But hopefully the girl's brother was right. She'd simply gone out walking and gotten lost or turned her ankle. Most kids who went missing were found.

Nikki tossed Tyler the truck keys that he'd laid on the tailgate. "They're staying in a private cabin not far from here. I'll pull up the directions on my phone while you drive."

The familiar feeling of guilt swirled through her as she slid into the truck and fastened her seat belt. Because not knowing what's happening to someone you love can be the hardest thing in the world to handle. And something she understood far too well.

2

Nikki shelved the guilt and worry as Tyler followed the narrow country road toward the cabin. The first forty-eight hours of a missing person investigation were the most crucial. Technology, including public alerts and cooperation between law enforcement agencies, had enabled officers to solve cases quicker. Especially when a possible abduction was indicated. Tyler slowed down as he drove onto the shaded drive in front of the address her boss had texted her.

Nikki pocketed her phone. "That's got to be it."

The two-story cabin sat back from the road, its large front window overlooking the scenic view. The nearest neighbor had to be at least a mile away.

Tyler let out a low whistle as they exited the truck and started up the gravel drive. "Someone's got a bit of money to throw around. It's undeniably a step or two up from camping." He stopped halfway up the driveway when she didn't respond. "You okay with this?"

"Definitely. It's my job." She glanced at him, willing herself to remain impartial and professional. It *was* her job. Bringing her own baggage with her wasn't an option.

A young man stepped out onto the front porch and into the early morning sun. Late twenties with a slender build, he wore blue jeans and a long-sleeved gray polo shirt.

"You must be the detective?" he said, worry lines creasing his forehead.

Nikki held out her hand. "Special Agent Nikki Boyd. I work with your father's friend Tom Carter, with the state's Missing Persons Task Force. This is Tyler Grant. We were out rappelling when Agent Carter called me."

"Kyle Ellison," he said, shaking her hand. "He told me you were going to come by. I can't tell you how much I appreciate it, though my gut tells me I'm probably making a mountain out of a molehill here."

"It's always better to report something like this right away on the off chance you're wrong," Nikki said.

"That's exactly what he told me. Why don't you both come in?" He stepped back into the house, holding the door open for them. "Do you want some coffee? I just put a fresh pot on."

A hint of cinnamon mingled with the scent of pine as they stepped into the large open space that included the living room, dining room, and kitchen.

"Coffee would be nice," Nikki said.

"I agree," Tyler added. "Thanks."

Kyle grabbed magazines, DVD cases, and empty microwave popcorn bags from the leather couch and offered them a seat before heading to the kitchen. Nikki took in the details of the room. The inside of the cabin was warm with its massive stone fireplace and vaulted ceilings. There were a few pieces of local artwork on the wall, some colorful pillows on the couches, but few personal touches. Which meant that more than likely the house was a rental property used by tourists throughout the year.

"This place is beautiful," Tyler said.

"Yeah, it is." Kyle grabbed two mugs from the cupboard and filled them from the coffeepot.

"Is it yours?" Nikki slid into one of the leather couches next to Tyler.

"Are you kidding?" Kyle laughed as he handed them their coffees and sat down across from them. "I don't make this kind of money. When Bridget asked to have her birthday out here, I spoke with a friend of mine who let me have it for the weekend. I figured a girl's sixteenth birthday only comes around once in a lifetime. I wanted it to be special. No roughing it."

"What did you plan to do while you were here?" Nikki asked.

"Bridget loves the outdoors. She wanted to bring a couple of her friends up here, do some hiking. We're supposed to go white-water rafting today."

"Can I ask you why you didn't call the local police first, Mr. Ellison?"

"Please, call me Kyle." He leaned forward and clasped his hands together. "I thought about calling the police, but like I said, I was afraid I was overreacting. Bridget's . . . well . . . she's a typical teen, and you know how teenagers are. She flies off the handle, then five minutes later, I'm the best brother in the world. She told her friends she was going for a walk, and to be honest, I have no reason not to believe that's exactly what she's doing."

"Except for the fact that it's been a couple of hours now, and she hasn't come home," Nikki said, praying he was right.

Kyle shifted in his chair. "Yes. And she's not answering her cell, which really isn't like her."

"When was the last time you saw her?" Nikki asked.

"Late last night. The girls stayed up late watching movies. I crashed somewhere around one this morning, I guess, after playing games on my computer. The girls were upstairs in one of the rooms. I tried to stay out of the way. Everything seemed fine when I went to bed."

"Did you go out and look for her this morning?" Nikki took a sip of the coffee, thankful it was strong, the way she liked it.

"The girls and I spent an hour searching the trails nearby before calling Agent Carter."

"What about a fight? Any problems with you or her friends?" Tyler asked.

"No. She seemed to be having a good time."

Nikki glanced at Tyler, then back to Kyle. "There must be some reason you think it might be more than simply an early morning walk for you to decide to involve the authorities."

"No . . . yes . . . I don't know." Kyle stood up, walked to the window, and stared out across the sunlit field. "Bridget and I have had our differences over the years, but she's my sister, and I love her. I panicked when I found out she'd been gone so long. All I could think to do was call my dad's old friend."

Nikki would buy his explanation. For now. But she couldn't ignore the fact that far more children were abducted by family members than nonfamily members. She couldn't dismiss the possibility that Kyle knew more than he was admitting.

"Has Bridget ever run away before?"

"She's gotten mad a couple of times and run off in a huff, but never for long. She went through a rough patch a few months ago, but things have actually been going better lately. She's finishing her sophomore year of high school, excels in sports, and has a few close friends." Kyle shook his head, still staring out the window. "I work a lot, which I know isn't good, but I really don't have a choice. And things have been going well between us . . . or so I thought."

Nikki studied Kyle's behavior—hands fisted at his sides, jaw taut, breathing faster than normal —but it was from her own experience that she could deduce what he was thinking. Assuming he was innocent, he was walking backward along the morning's timeframe in his mind. Wondering if he'd missed a warning sign. Wondering if he'd missed something crucial that could have avoided this situation. Asking himself over and over if Bridget's life was in danger.

"Kyle." Nikki leaned forward. "Why don't you sit down and tell us everything that happened over the past twenty-four hours. The sooner we can find out exactly what happened, the better."

"Okay . . ." Kyle pulled himself away from the window and sat back down in his chair. "We . . . we got here yesterday evening around six. Today's a school holiday, so it gave us an extra-long weekend. Bridget invited a couple of friends to celebrate her birthday with her—Mia Foster and Chloe Rogers."

"Did you stop on the way here?"

"Just for an early dinner. Once we arrived, we went for a short hike before dark, then planned what we wanted to do today. After that, the girls just hung out in their room for the rest of the evening. Bridget seemed . . . happy."

"When did you notice she was missing?"

Kyle's fingers gripped the sides of the chair.

"I got up this morning around seven, and noticed that the alarm to the house was turned off. Nothing seemed to be missing or out of place, so I went to check on the girls. That's when I discovered she was gone."

"And the girls? What do they know?"

Kyle shrugged. "Apparently Bridget told them she wanted to watch the sunrise and was going out for a walk."

"What time?"

"They weren't sure but said it was still pretty dark. Five . . . maybe closer to six? They fell back asleep and didn't wake up until I went to check on them."

"What about her things? Are they still here?"

"As far as I could tell. Everything but her phone."

"And you said you tried to call her?"

"Of course." Kyle frowned. He was getting agitated again. "I called a couple dozen times, but she didn't answer. Which isn't like Bridget, trust me. The girl's phone is like another appendage. She never goes anywhere without it. If she's not texting, she's posting selfies."

Tyler cupped his coffee mug between his hands. "What about your parents? Are they around?"

"I've been her legal guardian for the past year. Our mother . . ." Kyle's gaze dropped. "She's an addict and emotionally unstable. She walked out a couple years ago. That's when I realized I needed to step in."

"And your father?" Nikki asked. "I understand he passed away."

"Died of a heart attack five years ago. I think that's what set my mother off into a downward spiral. She really never recovered after his death."

"I'm sorry."

"Yeah, me too. It's not exactly been smooth sailing. Agent Carter has helped me, even with my getting custody of Bridget, but . . . I don't know. I love my mother, but Bridget and I are better off without her in our lives." Kyle stared at his hands now clenched in his lap. "I'm sorry. I realize I'm a bit high-strung at the moment. I just never expected to be the father figure to a teen. Now this . . . I don't know what to do."

Despite his distress, Nikki needed to press forward. "What do you do for a living?"

"I work in the IT department at Zamcore Pharmaceuticals in Nashville."

"What exactly do you do there?"

"I analyze and install programs, repair and maintain servers, you name it. If it's broken, I troubleshoot the problem."

"Any enemies?"

"Enemies?" Kyle shook his head. "It's not exactly a high-profile job."

"These are just routine questions we need to ask," Nikki said. "I do think we need to call in the local authorities and start an official search for your sister." She caught the panic in Kyle's eyes. "If we start with the assumption she's lost or hurt, the local authorities will be best equipped to organize a ground search of the area."

He caught Nikki's gaze. "What if that assumption is wrong? What if someone did take her?"

"Is there any reason for us to believe that?" she asked.

"No . . . I don't think so. It's just that I'm responsible for my sister. I can't just . . . lose her."

She set her coffee cup down on the end table. "I don't know what happened to your sister, but I'll be honest with you. At this point, without more information, an abduction isn't something we can completely dismiss. Not yet, anyway. But the good news is that stranger abductions are far rarer than the media likes to portray. Statistically, parents are the most dangerous kidnappers, and that doesn't seem likely in this case. For teen-agers—if this simply isn't just a case of her getting lost—we can't rule out the possibility that she's run away."

Kyle's eyes narrowed. "Why would Bridget run away? We get along okay for the most part. I pay for everything, plus she gets an allowance. If anything, I'm too easy on her."

"We have to look at all the possibilities."

"Wait a minute." Kyle shook his head. "You think . . . you think I had something to do with this?"

Nikki kept her voice level. "I don't know enough to make a judgment about what happened, but in a situation like this, we have to look at all the options. Which sometimes means we have to ask hard questions."

"Like if I had something to do with her disappearance." Kyle stood and shoved his hands into his jeans pockets, his brow furrowing in anger. "You know . . . you have no idea what I'm going through. My sister's missing. I'm responsible for her, and now you're blaming me."

Nikki felt the punch to her gut.

"No one's blaming you." Tyler leaned forward. "And actually, she does know what you're going through."

Nikki glanced at Tyler and felt a surge of resentment. Keeping her emotions separate was difficult but necessary. It was what allowed her to do her job. Now Kyle was looking at her, clearly waiting for an explanation. An explanation she didn't want to give him.

She took a deep breath, then forced herself to hold his gaze and give him the answer he was waiting for. "My sister disappeared ten years ago."

"Really? Wow . . . I'm sorry." Kyle sat back down, clasping his hands together in front of him. "Did you ever find her?"

Her hand went automatically to the heart necklace where she kept Sarah's photo, wondering what she'd look like today if she walked through the door. "Not yet."

Kyle shook his head. "I'm sorry."

Ten years, and she'd yet to give up hope that Sarah was still alive. Never completely let go of the fact that her sister's disappearance was her fault. She'd watched her parents over the years as they struggled after Sarah's abduction to put the shattered pieces of their lives back together —if that were even possible. Not with the gaping hole Sarah had left. Because it wasn't over yet. And Nikki wasn't sure it would ever be over.

"What that means is that I know that one of the hardest things a person can face is not knowing where a loved one is. Which is also why I will make sure everything is done to find her, even if that means asking tough questions." Nikki waited for his nod. "It also means that we need to get the local authorities involved. The good news is that the majority of missing persons are found within a matter of hours."

She wasn't going to tell him the other statistics. All she could do for the moment was pray that Bridget really had gone out for a bit of fresh air and taken a wrong turn.

"We'll need to talk with the other girls," she continued. "I also need Bridget's phone number so we can start trying to trace her cell, and any photos of her you might have."

"Of course. There's tons of pictures of her on her Facebook account."

Kyle gave her Bridget's number while he got up and grabbed his iPad from the kitchen counter. A minute later, he found her Facebook page. With long blond hair and bright blue eyes, Bridget smiled up at Nikki. There were dozens of selfies and group photos with friends. A couple with her and her brother.

On the sidebar of her account were places she'd visited. Where she went to school. Her favorite sports teams, movies, TV shows, and books. Her entire life on one tidy page.

Nikki scrolled down Bridget's timeline through the dozens of recent birthday messages from friends. "She looks happy."

"I think she is. You can download them from her account, then email them to yourself." Kyle motioned to the stairs leading up to the second floor. "In the meantime I'll go get the girls."

Nikki leaned against the back of the couch, a photo of Bridget staring up at her. The sun streamed through the window, leaving floating patterns of light on the hardwood floor. She would forever link the first day of spring and the scent of mowed grass with her sister's disappearance.

"You shouldn't have brought up my sister," she said to Tyler, her gaze still focused on the computer screen as she quickly downloaded the first photo.

"You needed a way to connect—"

"I don't want a way to connect." She looked up at him. "Not that way."

The urgency of the situation began to build as she downloaded a second photo, but for a moment she was there again. Standing on the curb in front of the school in the sunshine waiting for her sister. It had been warmer than normal that afternoon. The sound of a lawn mower filled the air. Nikki had checked her watch . . . again. She was late, all because of a pair of shoes she'd impulsively decided to buy at the nearby mall. She'd assumed Sarah would wait the extra few minutes it took to try them on and ring them up with the cashier. But when she arrived, Sarah was nowhere to be found. Nikki had questioned everyone she could think of who might know where Sarah was. Then came the desperate 911 call. Hours later, the police interviewed the last person known to have seen Sarah. Another sophomore girl who'd seen her get into a black sedan ten minutes after the last period bell had rung.

No one ever saw Sarah again.

She downloaded one more of Bridget's recent photos onto Kyle's iPad, then emailed copies to herself, refusing to get lost in the past. When Nikki joined the force, she'd trained herself to separate the emotions of her past from her work. She used her experiences to help motivate herself to ensure that other families didn't go through what her family had gone through. She'd researched every serial killer and kidnapping case across the state over the past twenty years, noting and memorizing every detail, including the Polaroid photo Sarah's abductor had left behind. But she preferred to keep those pieces of her past to herself.

Her phone rang, interrupting her thoughts. It was her boss again.

"Have you spoken to Kyle yet?" he asked.

"Yes. We're here now. I'm recommending we bring in the local police to start a search of the area. I've already sent Jack and Gwen the information I have so far so they can run a trace on the girl's phone and see what else they can find out."

"Use Tyler if you need to until I can get you some backup. With his background he's got plenty of relevant experience."

She glanced at Tyler as she hung up the phone. Her boss was right. Today wouldn't be the first time she'd turned to him for advice. Tyler had gained his experience fighting terrorism in three separate tours as a part of a special ops team in the Middle East. Which meant his input—especially in the face of a crisis—was nearly always right on target.

His hand grasped hers. "You were right. I shouldn't have stepped in." His fingers pressed against her palm. Warm. Reassuring.

She shook her head. "I'm the one who should be sorry."

"Don't be. Today's one of those days that's thrown both of us off-balance."

She couldn't let herself forget that she wasn't the only one dealing with the past.

"What do you think?" he asked. "About Kyle."

"He's nervous, distracted, defensive, but all those things are understandable considering the situation. We need to hear what the girls have to say. And we need to get a team out here on the ground looking for her as soon as possible."

He released her hand. "I agree. Why don't you go ahead and start questioning the girls as soon as they're ready? I could call the local authorities and get a team out here."

Nikki nodded. All they needed to do was stay until the local police arrived, then she and Tyler would be free to leave.

She grabbed her cell phone again as Tyler headed for the front door, then punched in a call to Jack Spencer. For over eight years, she'd made her way through the ranks in the local police department until her promotion to the governor's missing persons task force. Learning to depend on her team had become second nature.

"Jack, this is Nikki," she said as soon as he answered.

She quickly filled him in on the details and asked him to report Bridget was missing to all

36

local agencies, as well as putting a trace on her phone.

Nikki ended the call as Mia and Chloe walked down the stairs in front of Kyle, hesitating in the middle of the living room. They exchanged looks, then sat down on the couch across from Nikki.

Kyle made the introductions, pointing to the girls as he spoke. "This is Chloe and this is Mia. Bridget's best friends."

Nikki shook their hands, then took a second to study the girls. Mia had shoulder-length blond hair and wore black jeans and a pink, zippered hoodie. Chloe was a few inches taller with darker skin and long black hair pulled back into a braid. Both looked scared.

"I need to ask both of you some questions about Bridget."

"Of course," Mia said, glancing again at Chloe. "But before you start, there's something we need to tell you."

"Okay."

"Bridget didn't just go out for a walk this morning." Mia drew in a sharp breath before continuing. "She met a guy online a couple months ago. She planned this entire weekend so she could meet him."

3

Nikki felt the air rush from her lungs as her mind worked through the ramifications of the girls' confession. While it was possible that Bridget had come to meet an innocent guy she'd fallen for, online predators targeted both boys and girls of all ages. Most were master manipulators who looked especially for the emotionally vulnerable. They knew how to befriend their victims. To empathize with them while building trust. And they were everywhere.

"Who is he?" Nikki asked. The urgency germinating inside her had just skyrocketed, because the odds that they were still looking at a lost hiker had substantially diminished.

"What?" Kyle crossed the room until he was standing in front of the girls. "Why didn't you guys tell me that this morning when we were out looking for her?"

Mia picked at a broken nail, tears forming in her eyes. "We didn't think it was a big deal. Not until now, anyway. Bridget made us promise not to tell you."

Chloe chewed at her bottom lip. "They were just going to meet. We figured she'd be back by now."

"Who is he? Wait . . ." Kyle's voice rose. "It's that Jacob . . . somebody, isn't it?"

Chloe shook her head. "She dumped Jacob a few weeks ago."

"Then who in the world is this guy?"

"Kyle . . ." Nikki held up her hand. "I need you to stay calm. Why don't you go make another pot of coffee while I talk to the girls. I promise we'll get to the bottom of this, but right now we've got to keep cool heads about it."

Kyle hesitated for a moment, the vein in his neck pulsing, then strode away.

Nikki turned back to the girls once he'd stepped out of the living room. "I need the two of you to start from the beginning and tell me everything you know about this guy she was planning to meet as quickly as you can."

Chloe nodded. "Like Mia said, she met him online."

Nikki's gut clenched. Sometimes missing persons cases revolved around random strangers plucking a person off the street, but more often than not, once they began peeling back layers, the truth was much closer to home.

Chloe looked to Mia, then dropped her gaze. "She didn't really talk about him that much. But honestly, you have to believe us. We didn't know she was planning on meeting him here this weekend. At least not at first."

"Do you know how easy it is for a predator to

set up a false account? A false ID and photos?" Nikki asked. "You have no idea who's really behind his profile."

"Not this guy. We do know he was sweet and charming. Bridget trusts him completely."

"And so because he was sweet and charming online, he has to be a sweet and charming guy in real life." Nikki frowned, holding back a wave of anger. What she'd really like to do was throttle some sense into the girls.

"You should read some of the things he wrote her." Mia fiddled with the zipper of her hoodie. "He was always complimenting her. Telling her how pretty she was. He's got a couple of younger sisters. Showed her photos of him and his family. She really liked him."

"And they were planning to meet this morning?"

"She told us about it last night and we swore we'd keep her secret. It sounded so . . . romantic. Like some prince straight out of a fairy tale. They just wanted to meet and talk. I've never seen Bridget so happy." Mia started sobbing. "We thought—"

"For now, let's go on the assumption she did go to meet a guy, and he's everything he says he is." Nikki worked to rein in her anger. "Tell me what the plan was."

"They were going to meet here for her birthday," Chloe said. "It's why she asked her brother to come here."

"Why here?" Nikki asked.

"I don't know." Mia shrugged. "They both like outdoor stuff. He said it would be romantic."

Nikki listened to the girls' confession. Their original theory of Bridget simply having gone out for a walk and gotten lost had just been completely shot down. Clearly Bridget had never had any plans for an innocent walk in the woods.

"What's his name?" Nikki asked.

"Sean . . . I don't remember his last name," Chloe said. "He even told her he knew some producers in Nashville. Kyle doesn't like the idea, but Bridget wants to get into the music business one day. She's pretty into country music. Sean promised he could get her an audition."

How many clichés had this guy used?

Nikki woke up the screen of Kyle's iPad that was still in her lap so Bridget's Facebook page stared up at her. She'd seen it all before on Instagram profiles and Facebook statuses. Girls falling prey to predators who fed on their desire to be loved and cared for. While parents with all their good intentions were out earning a living, their children were sucked up in a world of instant messaging and social media. And while moms and dads thought everything was fine, their kids had managed to completely disconnect from their parents and instead were connecting with strangers. Lonely girls, lured by promises of love and acceptance by strangers to replace the holes in their own lives.

She went to the top of Bridget's timeline and touched the screen to open up the friends' search box, then typed the name Sean. One name popped up.

Sean Logan.

Mia leaned forward and glanced at his photo. "That's him."

Nikki clicked through to his profile page. His cover photo was of him and a couple of other guys hiking. She clicked through his photos and "about" page. On the surface, everything looked legitimate. From where he went to high school to places he'd lived, to his favorite movies and basketball teams. It was all there, along with a few dozen random photos.

Nikki turned to Kyle, who walked back into the living room as the smell of percolating coffee began filling the space. "Did you know anything about this guy?"

Kyle stared at the page. "Do you think I would've brought her here if I'd known she was planning to run off with some stranger?"

"He wasn't a stranger, and they're not planning to run off," Mia insisted. "They'd been friends for a couple of months. They chatted every day. They just wanted to meet."

"A couple of months?" Kyle's frown deepened. "Why didn't she ever mention him to me?"

Mia's gaze dropped. "She knew you'd over-react."

"Overreact to her seeing a guy secretly that she'd only met on the internet? Of course I'd overreact."

A sick feeling spread through Nikki's gut. She pulled out her phone and typed a text to Jack with the information he'd need to do a complete background check on Sean Logan. Because this was the potential setup for every parent's nightmare. Girls believing they'd found their Prince Charming who would save them from school or home. Except they weren't princes or even charming once the truth came out.

Kyle sat down beside Nikki on the couch. "You're not buying the Romeo and Juliet, star-crossed lovers scenario, are you?"

Nikki sent the message. "We don't have enough information to make a judgment yet. But we'll find out."

"Then what about putting out an AMBER Alert in the meantime? Isn't that what normally happens next?"

Nikki shook her head, feeling his frustration, but there were procedures in place for a reason. "There are specific guidelines that have to be followed before an AMBER Alert is issued."

"You're telling me this situation doesn't meet the criteria?"

"Not yet. The primary one being that we have yet to confirm an abduction."

"Bridget's been gone for what . . . at least three . . . maybe four hours. That's not confirmation enough?"

"All we know right now is that she went to see a guy she met online. We have no proof her life is at risk."

"So what does that mean?" Kyle asked, his voice rising. "That it will take finding my sister dead somewhere before anyone takes this seriously?"

Nikki bit back a sharp response hovering on the tip of her tongue. She knew Kyle's words weren't meant as an attack on her. Helping families negotiate the tangled web of emotions was one of the toughest aspects of her job.

"I assure you we are taking this situation extremely seriously. But to abuse the system would only end up weakening the effectiveness of the alert."

"It's just that . . ." Kyle stood back up, clenching his fists at his sides. "Tell me what our chances are of finding her if this guy isn't who he said he is."

"I can't answer that," Nikki said.

"Then what am I supposed to do?" he asked. "I can't just sit here doing nothing."

"Good, because I'm going to need your help. All of your help."

Mia drummed her pink nails against her leg. "Tell us what we can do."

"A couple of officers will be here any minute. They will be equipped to coordinate a ground search of the area, but we also need to get the word out as quickly as we can. And we'll need a complete rundown of Bridget's information. I'll give you the website of a checklist, but write down everything you can think of, like height, weight, age, hair color, distinguishing marks, and what she was wearing when she left this morning as well as anything she might have taken with her."

Chloe leaned forward and nodded. "We can do that."

"Great. Get started. As soon as you get that together, I'll have my teammates send out the bulletin to all missing persons databases."

Kyle pointed to the kitchen. "There's a notebook over there by the telephone."

Nikki wrote down the address for the website, then turned to Kyle. "What kind of support do you have, Kyle? Extended family . . . friends . . . church?"

Kyle was pacing again. "The last time I went to church was probably junior high."

"Friends? Family?" Nikki asked.

"She's in Nashville right now, but my girl-friend could help," Kyle suggested. "She works for a local television station and could easily handle coordinating whatever needs to be done from there."

"Perfect. Once that list is together, we're going to need short clips for local media that can be used to break into their regularly scheduled programs. Some officers feel like the media will only get in the way, but I believe it helps. The more eyes we have looking for your sister—the more her photo is out there—the better our odds of bringing her home quickly and safely."

Nikki turned to the two girls, who were already at the dining room table with the pen and paper. "Chloe and Mia, keep at that list, but you also need to contact your parents. The last thing you're going to want is their finding out about this on the morning news."

She could see the fear in their eyes as the reality of the situation sank in. And feel the fear in her own heart as she realized that each second that passed meant Bridget could be that much farther away.

"I need to go update Tyler, but I'll be back in a minute."

Nikki grabbed a couple of Tylenol from her bag, downed them with the rest of her lukewarm coffee to stave off the headache that was coming on, then walked out onto the front porch, where Tyler was just hanging up a call. Morning sunshine spread across the open field in front of the cabin, though she didn't miss the dark clouds that had begun to gather along the horizon. They mirrored exactly how she was feeling inside.

"The girls confessed that Bridget set up this weekend to see a boy she met online," Nikki began.

"A boy?" Tyler gave her his full attention.

"His name is Sean Logan. I sent Jack the information so he can do a background check. We need to find out if this guy's legit."

"Because if she didn't simply get lost out there . . ."

"Yeah . . ." She sighed. "And we need to know where to start looking."

"If this does turn out to be an abduction," he said, "at least we've got the ball rolling. I've contacted the local police department. They're sending out some officers now who will coordinate with your team as well as the Morgan County Sheriff's Department for a ground search."

"Good. The sooner we get a team out, the better our chances of finding her." Nikki searched his expression, needing to know what he was feeling beneath the urgency of the moment. "Thank you. For everything. This day was sup-posed to be about you and remembering Katie."

Tyler stuffed the phone into his pocket. "You don't have anything to be sorry about. There's a girl's life at stake here, and you, more than anyone else I know, realize that time isn't on your side. However innocent this situation might turn out to be, we need to find her."

"We?" Nikki shook her head. She wasn't going to involve him in this. Not today. "You need to go home—"

"No, I don't." He ran his hand down her arm, then squeezed her fingertips. "You're going to need volunteers, and I want to stay and help. I've just spoken to my mother. Liam's doing fine," he continued without giving her a chance to lodge her complaints, still holding her hand. "They're getting ready to go to the zoo."

"Tyler—"

"You always need volunteers in cases like this, and I'm volunteering. Besides, we weren't going to get back until tonight anyway. He and I have plans to go zip-lining tomorrow, and in the meantime, my mom promised to spoil him rotten today. Trust me. He won't even miss me."

She smiled up at him, knowing he should leave her to deal with this on her own. She just didn't know how to accept him giving up today, of all days, for a stranger. "You're sure . . . ?"

"Very sure."

Nikki let out a sigh. "Thank you."

His gaze softened as he let go of her hand. "Katie always believed in you and what you did. If she were here today, I know she'd want the very best to be out there looking for Bridget, and she'd be one of the first volunteers out there with you. Just tell me what else I can do."

"Okay."

She wanted—needed—him with her today, but she also understood the significance of what today meant. And the importance of him needing a distraction. After Katie's death, she'd seen how work and school had become a natural escape for him. But Nikki also didn't miss the hint of sadness in his eyes. She'd make sure she made up their missed day later.

The sound of an engine rumbled in the distance.

"They're here," Tyler said.

Two squad cars from the local police department pulled into the driveway in front of the cabin, and four uniformed officers stepped out.

Nikki met them on the porch and made the introductions. "Thank you for responding so quickly. We'll set up a temporary command site here, where we can get you up to speed, but I want a search team out looking for her ASAP."

Nikki ushered them into the cabin, praying that the pain medicine she'd just taken would take the edge off the headache starting to pulse around her temples as they began coordinating a solid plan.

"For now, I want us to move ahead with the assumption that Bridget left of her own free will," she said. "We'll leave the ground search of the area to the local authorities since you know the terrain far better than we do, but I want checkpoints set up on all major roads going out of the area in case this turns out to be an abduction."

Nikki's phone rang beside her on the table.

"I need to take this, but go ahead and finish working out the details of the search team, so we can get a team out looking for her now." Nikki answered the call, then walked into the kitchen to dump out the rest of her coffee and get a refill. "Please tell me you have something, Jack."

"I do, but you're not going to like it," Jack began. "I was able to track down the love interest."

"And . . ."

"Sean Logan doesn't exist."

She leaned against the island and felt her pulse speed up. "What do you mean, he doesn't exist?"

"Logan's a fake Facebook profile. I was able to trace the photos to a Joey Matthews from Buffalo, New York. The profile photo's at least two decades old *and* the guy's deceased."

Nikki tried to absorb the information. "So our suspect's using a stolen identity."

"And that's not all," Jack continued. "Using phone records, I've started tracking down his cell phone movements. I'm pretty sure he was stalking her."

The pain in her temples radiated down Nikki's jawline as she took in the news. Her missing persons case just became an abduction.

4

Nikki pocketed her phone while Jack's words swirled around her. She walked across the room to where the men were coordinating the ground search.

"We've got the details lined up and are heading out now," Sergeant Michaels said, picking up his car keys off the table.

"Good, because I just got off the phone with Jack Spencer, one of my teammates," she said. "I have some new information about Sean Logan."

"What did you find out?" Kyle took a step forward.

She studied Kyle's reaction as she gave Jack's update—understanding the roller coaster he was experiencing right now. Far too often, in cases like these, it felt as though they were starting over at square one. Over and over again.

The sergeant hesitated. "And the ground search?"

"I still want you out there immediately," Nikki said. "My team will keep you updated with what we find."

"You've got it," the sergeant said, heading out the door with the other men.

"Wait a minute." Kyle gripped the back of one

of the dining room chairs as the men left, his knuckles white. "How do you know he's been stalking her?"

"Jack believes he's been using the GPS tracking in the photos she's been posting on Facebook and other social media sites," Nikki said.

"Tracking her photos?" Chloe walked up to the end of the table, her eyes wide with fear.

Jack's explanation over the phone had been chilling, but Nikki had learned that sugarcoating the truth—and sheltering the family—was never the right answer. Even in a situation like this.

"With some basic knowledge of technology," she began, "people can take your online photos— the ones you put up on Facebook and Instagram and other places—and pinpoint your location. Whether it's a football game, hanging out at a restaurant . . . or your bedroom."

Chloe shook her head. "And track you? How?"

"It's simpler than you might think," Nikki said. "Photos are tagged using mapping and geotags that in turn translate to actual addresses and maps."

"So a selfie taken on my phone and posted is a way for someone to find exactly where I live?" Mia asked.

"Basically, yes. The only way around that is to turn off your smartphone camera's GPS."

Kyle combed his fingers through his hair. "Which clearly Bridget didn't do."

With the advantages of technology had come a number of threats most people never stopped to think about. And the potential results were frightening.

Kyle glanced at Mia and Chloe. "So this guy Sean . . . who is he really?"

"We don't know that yet," Nikki answered. "He was using a false identity complete with a false name and photos."

"He seemed so . . . nice. So normal." Mia sat down beside Chloe on one of the dining room chairs, her eyes flooded with tears.

"That's what they do," Nikki said. "It's like a game to them."

Chloe brushed the tears with the back of her hand, then hiccupped. "Bridget had no idea he was lying to her. She really, really liked him and thought . . . All she wanted to do was meet him in person."

A choice that very well could cost her her life.

"What we have to assume now is that he took her against her will. My teammates, Special Agents Jack Spencer and Gwen McKenna, are currently at a community event two hours away and are leaving now with our mobile command post that we'll set up here."

"How could she have done something like this?" Kyle toppled the chair over, sending it crashing against the floor. "How am I supposed to fix this?"

Nikki asked Tyler and the officers to stay with the girls, then turned to Kyle. "Why don't we go outside for a minute and get some fresh air?"

Three months on the job had yet to fully prepare her for the emotional side of what she had to do. She knew what she needed to tell him. Knew that now more than ever he was going to have to keep it together. But as of this moment, normal didn't exist.

Outside, he smacked his hands against the railing. "I'm sorry, I just don't know how to handle this."

"I understand, but I need you to stay focused. For Bridget's sake."

"Focused? How? We have no idea where she is. No idea where to begin looking. The only thing we actually do know is that some crazy person manipulated her and now she's missing. We don't even know what direction she went, or if she's even alive for that matter."

"Which is why we keep doing exactly what we have been doing. We keep asking questions and looking. We're going to expand the search. Make sure all law enforcement as well as airports and bus stations have been advised she's missing and have her picture. I need you to help me do that. We need to get the word out. The more people who see her photo, the better chance of us finding her."

Kyle stared out across the empty field where

the storm clouds were darkening in the distance. "Every day I go to work and I fix problems. That's what I do. If the company's network is down, I fix it. If something crashes, I fix it. But this . . . I don't know how to fix this."

Nikki hesitated, wanting to choose her words carefully. But Tyler had been right. If she wanted to connect, there was only one place to go. "I blamed myself when my sister disappeared. Ten years later, I still struggle with that same guilt."

Kyle turned around and looked at her. "How did you deal with that guilt then, because clearly I'm not doing a good job. It's hard enough trying to raise a teenage girl on my own, but now this. I don't know how to do this."

"No one is ever prepared for losing someone they love. You feel lost and out of control. And when they're missing, it isn't a problem you can simply fix with some formula."

"Like computer data." Kyle rubbed his temples. "What gets me the most is that I was supposed to be the one who kept her safe, but I didn't even know about this boy. How could I have missed that?"

"Because as much as we love and try to protect those around us, sometimes we do miss things. And sometimes there's nothing we can do."

The words sliced through her. It was something she'd had to learn to live with every time the guilt surfaced.

"Nikki?" Tyler stepped out on the porch. "Sorry to interrupt, but we just got a call from the Gatlinburg Police Department."

"Gatlinburg?" Kyle asked. "That's almost a two-hour drive from here."

"Two officers discovered an abandoned car on the outskirts of town. They called it in and found out the car was stolen late last night."

"Do they think Bridget was in it?"

Nikki didn't miss the expectation in Kyle's voice as he asked the question, but she knew that not every lead was a step in the right direction. All they could do was pray that this one was.

"It's possible." Tyler handed Kyle the cell phone he held. "I need you to look at this photo. The description of Bridget that was sent out to the local authorities a little while ago included a pink beanie. Do you recognize this?"

"The hat? Yes . . . Bridget has one just like that. Was it in the car?"

"Yes."

"It could be a coincidence—"

"No." Tyler shook his head. "She was there."

"With traffic, Gatlinburg's a good two hours away." Nikki glanced at her watch. "We don't have that kind of time."

"One of the officers just told me that the highway patrol's aviation unit has a helicopter in the area," Tyler said. "They can get you there in thirty minutes."

Kyle stepped in front of her. "I want to go with you. If she's there, I need to be there . . . please."

Nikki had waited in her parents' living room that afternoon. Waited while the police spoke to each of them. Waited for them to come back with news of Sarah's safe return. But they never had. And even all these years later the waiting had never gotten any easier.

"I can't make any promises, but I'll see what I can do."

Forty-five minutes later, Nikki stood with Tyler beside the 2001 silver Ford Focus on the outskirts of Gatlinburg where local law enforcement had discovered the abandoned vehicle. After the Tennessee Highway Patrol had flown them in, Sergeant James from the nearby precinct had driven them to the scene.

Beyond the rail lining the winding road, green tree-lined mountains rose up in the distance. Like the Obed River area, the Smoky Mountains were one of her favorite places to get away to. Outdoor enthusiasts like herself could enjoy hiking, sightseeing, fishing, and camping. Gatlinburg was known as one of the main entrances into the Great Smoky Mountains National Park.

Officer Walker handed her an evidence bag. "This is the hat. It was found jammed between the two backseats."

"Any signs of a struggle?" Nikki asked.

"None."

"What about the car's owner?"

Officer Walker glanced at her notes. "His name's Frank Turner. He called this morning and reported it missing from his driveway."

"Anything else inside the car?" Nikki asked.

"Just trash from a fast-food restaurant, and the owner said he hates fast food." Officer Walker set her hands on her hips. "We're doing a background check on the man just in case, but I don't think we're going to find anything there."

Nikki nodded. "See if you can track down the restaurant where he bought breakfast and find video surveillance with the car. We need to identify the driver."

"Will do. We brought a fingerprint kit to the scene and have already dusted for prints. It will take awhile before we get any results, but we'll submit them to our records division as well as AFIS and see if we can come up with any matches. Who knows? Maybe we'll get lucky."

"I hope so." But by then it might be too late for Bridget.

Nikki took a step back from the car, thankful that Kyle had decided to wait with Chloe and Mia until their parents arrived. Because for all they knew, they could be simply on another wild-goose chase. But something told her it was far more than that. Bridget was out here. Some-where. And they needed to find her.

Nikki walked across the gravel road, stopping beside Tyler. "Go over this with me. Why would he abandon the car? There are no flat tires, no obvious signs of car trouble."

"If he had Bridget when he stopped here," Tyler said, "which we are assuming he did, he might have been worried about the police blocks and the fact that this car was stolen."

"So he did what?" she asked. "Tried to walk out of here?"

"It's possible. Maybe he lives nearby. Or has a friend nearby."

This wasn't the first time she'd come to Tyler with a problem. He knew how to look at things out of the box. Which was what she needed right now, because predators didn't follow the rules. Which meant she couldn't simply look at the obvious.

"Here's what I don't understand. Everything he's done so far seems to have been methodical and planned. From stalking Bridget, to setting up and starting an online relationship, to plan-ning a place and time for them to meet."

"True."

"But after doing all of that, why end up panicking and dumping the car?"

Tyler folded his arms across his chest and leaned against the rail. "Maybe you need to consider then that this *was* part of his plan."

"Okay." She worked through her theory as they spoke. "He uses technology to stalk Bridget. He would have anticipated the fact that once Kyle and the girls realized she hadn't simply gone out for a walk that they would contact the local police. And taking that a step further, he'd have known that the local police—and even the state authorities—would get involved in the situation."

"Which would mean roadblocks, photos on the local news, and a possible AMBER Alert."

"Exactly," she said.

"It makes sense that Bridget didn't suspect this guy was a fraud, but it didn't take Jack long to completely blow the guy's cover."

"All he needed was time to get away." Which was exactly what he'd done. "There could have been another car."

And maybe even a partner.

Nikki looked out across the trees and walked through the profile assessments she'd studied. "Obviously, he's charming. On the outside, this guy could be your next-door neighbor. The kind that buys ice cream for your kids in the summer and Girl Scout cookies from the neighbor. Everyone likes him. Everyone wants to be his friend, because he can be charming, but only if that's what he wants you to see. He's manipulative, cunning, smart, and has a temper. He needs to dominate women. Traits similar to a serial abductor or killer."

Similar to her sister's abductor.

Nikki's cell phone rang and she grabbed it out of her back pocket.

Jack.

"What have you got?" she asked.

"We've changed routes and are headed to you now. Bridget's phone just turned back on. I can't get a call through, but I did manage to track it via GPS."

"Where is it?"

"Two miles from where you are. Just inside the entrance to the national park."

5

Nikki ended the call with Jack a minute later, then headed back toward the officers who were wrapping up the scene. "We've got another possible lead. Bridget's phone signal just popped back onto the grid."

"Where?" Tyler asked.

Nikki glanced at the map Jack had sent to her phone. "According to the GPS coordinates, she's close to the Gatlinburg entrance of the park, somewhere around the visitor center."

Officer Walker nodded. "We can be there in a couple of minutes. Parker . . . Yates . . . make sure this car gets towed into evidence, then meet us there. I'll notify the park rangers and let them know we're on our way."

Nikki hesitated. "And since there's a good possibility our guy is armed, I want all tourists cleared out of the immediate area in case this turns into a hostage situation."

She turned back to Tyler as she slid into the backseat of the squad car, nerves strung tight. Her mind continued to work through the possible scenarios as they sped down the two-lane, tree-lined road toward the park's entrance. "I need to get inside this guy's head, Tyler. How did he miss the fact that she left her hat? And that she has a phone? He knows too much about technology to do something stupid like allowing the police to track him."

Tyler's fingers drummed against the seat on the empty space between them. "All you need in a case like this is one bad move. He thinks he's smart, but you're the one who's always telling me they're never as smart as they think they are." He ran his hand down the side of her arm, then hesitated before pulling away. "You need to be careful going in there. If this guy's armed . . ."

"I know." Nikki's nerves bristled.

"What does your gut tell you, Nikki?"

"Just how little we know. We have a profile of a young man that's complete fiction, which essentially means we know nothing beyond what we can speculate. I'm also wondering why he'd take her to a crowded place like a visitor center. The only reason that makes sense is that abductors tend to take their victims somewhere familiar. Maybe that's the reason he decided to take her inside the park."

Nikki had hiked the trails through the Smoky Mountains dozens of times. Beyond the marked routes of mountainous terrain were endless varieties of plants. Rhododendron and mountain laurel amid weathered rocks, hundreds of species of flowering plants, and other shrubs so thick you couldn't even get through them.

And on top of that, the Smoky Mountains held

half a million acres of wilderness and hundreds of miles of hiking trails. Phone service was poor. There were dozens of small towns and scenic routes. They'd have better luck trying to find a needle in a haystack.

"So for now we'll assume he's familiar with the park," Nikki continued as they approached the entrance. "He decides to take her inside, thinking they can get lost. A perfect place to disappear."

"Or dump a body," Tyler threw out. At her look he shrugged. "Sorry, but I'm just being realistic."

She wasn't ready to go there. Not yet. "Let's assume she's still alive for now. She manages to leave her phone near the visitor center because she knows we'll track it? She clearly proved resourceful with the hat earlier."

"But why dump the phone? Why not just keep it with her if she knows it can be tracked?"

"I don't know." Nikki frowned, her mind searching for a plausible answer. "Maybe she was afraid he was about to discover she still had it? She finds an opportunity to turn on the phone and call for help, and he almost catches her so she dumps it."

Tyler leaned back against the seat. "Let's go with the idea that he's here because the place is familiar."

"Yes," she said.

"Then who is he? A park ranger? An avid hiker? Maybe an eco-friendly guru?"

"Or even a volunteer."

"Which is the problem," he said. "That doesn't exactly narrow down your suspects. Beyond the permanent and seasonal personnel that run the park, you have hundreds of volunteers and more than nine million visitors a year."

Nikki's frown deepened as the sergeant pulled into the parking lot. Tyler was right. The scenarios were only guesses based on what little evidence they had gathered. What they needed was an eyewitness. Someone who could positively put Bridget at a specific place at a specific time.

Nikki joined the rangers, the search and rescue team, and local police officers outside the visitor center at the park entrance, while Tyler waited on the perimeter. She undid the side straps of the bulletproof vest one of the officers had handed her and slipped it over her head. The incident commander, Ranger Jerry Anderson, briefed them on the layout of the visitor center they'd already evacuated before dividing them into teams.

Her pulse accelerated. No matter how many times she did this, there was always the inevitable adrenaline rush of that first step inside. The anticipation of not knowing what was on the other side of the door.

Like the initial step off the edge of a sheer cliff.

She stepped through the glass doors of the building seconds later, gun raised, heart beating, focus narrowed. The inside of the building was well lit, as she made her way past the information desk, map kiosk, and theater entrance. Past signs, exhibits, and a huge map of the park.

Please let us find her, God . . .

The normally crowded gift shop was empty as she followed her team inside. Books, maps, DVDs, and all the typical souvenirs sat for sale on neat rows. She searched the aisles systematically, looking for every possible hiding place. But there was no sign of the phone. No sign of Bridget.

"Clear."

"Clear."

"Clear."

Officers called out their status one by one, then regrouped back in the lobby next to the information desk.

Nikki drummed her fingers across the countertop, frustrated, as she waited to get Jack back on her cell. "She's not here, Jack."

"Her phone still hasn't moved."

"Then why can't we find it?"

"I don't know. She might not be there, but the phone is. Keep looking."

She hung up, then turned back to the incident commander. "We need to do another search of this building. The phone is here somewhere. And

I want a team interviewing everyone you just evacuated. They can hand out flyers with her photo so we can see if anyone remembers seeing her. And that includes everyone who comes through that entrance from now on. I want everyone to see her face."

Anderson nodded as one of the officers emerged from the other end of the building carrying a trash can. "We found a cell phone."

Nikki pulled on her rappelling gloves, took the phone, and pressed one of the keys. A selfie of Bridget smiled up at her. This was her phone. Her link with the world. The one link she'd never simply drop in a trash can.

"I want this place swept, video surveillance gone through, anything you can get me. We need an ID on our abductor." She was back on the phone with Jack seconds later. "What's your ETA?"

"Thirty . . . forty minutes tops."

"Okay, we need to expand the search. I want you to double-check that Bridget's name is on every possible missing persons list, with an update of her possible location. Send it to every agency in the state, including the FBI, and the state's missing children's clearinghouse. As soon as you get here, we'll regroup."

As soon as she hung up with Jack, another call came through.

"Nikki?"

Nikki paused, then turned away from the officers. "Mom? Hey . . . is everything okay?"

"No, it's not . . . It's Jamie."

Nikki's heart raced, but this time not from the adrenaline of the search. Her sister-in-law had waited too long for this baby. If anything went wrong now . . . "What's going on?"

"I know this is your day with Tyler, but there's been a complication with her pregnancy."

Nikki pressed the phone tighter against her ear and moved to the far end of the counter, away from the noise, so she could better hear what her mother was saying. "What happened?"

"The doctor said it's a placental abruption."

"What exactly does that mean . . . a placental abruption?"

"The placenta has partially peeled away from the inner wall of the uterus."

"And Jamie and the baby?"

"They've checked Jamie into the hospital and are monitoring her closely. If the abruption progresses, they'll have to do an immediate C-section, or . . . or they could lose the baby."

No, God . . . no . . . no . . . no . . .

"I'm on my way there now," her mom continued. "Jamie's mom is driving in and should be here in an hour or so. I didn't know if I should call you—"

"Of course you should have called me." Nikki pressed her hand against the counter, going through her options. "My boss pulled me onto a case this morning. There's a girl missing."

"Oh, Nikki . . ."

Nikki heard the emotion in her mother's voice. Ten years hadn't come close to erasing the memories of the day Sarah went missing. Even all these years later they never forgot Sarah's birthday. The empty chair at the Thanksgiving table. Or the fact that she hadn't graduated from high school or college. So many milestones of Sarah's life they'd missed. And she'd never stopped praying, searching, or hoping that one day they'd be able to bring her sister home.

"Let me call you back as soon as my team gets here. I could be back in Nashville by this afternoon—"

"It's okay, Nikki. I know that girl needs you right now. Her family needs you . . ."

Nikki felt the tug of duty. Toward Tyler . . . Bridget . . . and now Jamie.

"As soon as I talk to my team, I'll be able to let you know how soon I can get away."

"Okay. And I'll keep you updated."

Nikki hung up and stared across the room.

Why does everything have to happen at once, God? Because this day can't end this way. Not with Bridget still missing. Not with Matt and Jamie losing another baby. And Tyler—

"What's going on?"

Nikki looked up at Tyler and shook her head.

Until two nights ago, the pregnancy had been uneventful. Jamie had called her, worried about a few cramps, but her obstetrician had assured her there was nothing to worry about. And now she was facing losing another baby?

Nikki traced her fingers around the patterns on the countertop of the information desk. "It's Jamie. She's in the hospital. The placenta has partially separated from the uterus. There's a chance she could lose the baby, Tyler."

He placed his hand on hers. "Then you need to be there."

"I know." Nikki rubbed the back of her neck. "But I need to be here too." She tried to sort through the facts of the situation without letting emotions cloud her thinking, but instead, an overwhelming fatigue washed through her. She'd expected today to be emotional. What she hadn't expected was feeling as if her emotions had been completely shattered into tiny shards.

She pressed her lips together. "My mother's on her way to the hospital right now. Jamie's mom is driving in from Memphis. If I went, there's nothing I could do, but here—"

"I think you're wrong, and you'd regret it later. I know how close your family is."

Nikki stared across the open space of the visitor center. Like every family she knew, hers had its own drama, but Tyler was right. They were close, and she needed to be there. Dinner on Sunday nights at her parents' restaurant, birthday parties, Thanksgiving, Christmas, and yearly extended family reunions had helped to make her family close-knit.

She nodded, turning her hand over and squeezing Tyler's. "You're right. My team will be here any minute. They're capable of finding Bridget without me. And I'll have my phone if they need me."

"I'll find us a ride back to Obed, then I'll drive you back to Nashville."

She nodded her thanks. "About today . . . again. I know I've already said it, but I really am sorry. Nothing went the way we planned."

"And I've already said you have nothing to be sorry about. I wanted to spend the day with you —someone who cared about Katie as much as I did. You were her best friend. I told you before, I wouldn't have made it through this last year without you, and I meant it."

The day Katie married Tyler, she'd told Nikki she was the luckiest girl in the world. They'd experienced the normal ups and downs of typical newlyweds, but even through their first years of marriage, Katie had never stopped teasing Nikki about how she needed to find someone like Tyler. Because he made her happy, protected, and complete. For Katie, a girl who'd grown up in a broken home, Tyler had become her knight in shining armor.

Nikki massaged her neck. The tension head-ache was back and now settling into the muscles of her back. "I'll let you drive us home, if you let me treat you and Liam to dinner."

At least she'd be closer if her family needed her. And at the same time be there for Tyler.

"I'll be okay, Nikki."

She knew he was right, but when she looked into his eyes, she didn't miss the flicker of pain. Grief pressed against her chest. He might be okay, but she also knew how he still slept in the guest bedroom. How he hadn't finished remodeling the master bathroom. She knew about Liam's nightmares. His fear of water, even taking a bath. Neither of them had set foot on the *Isabella* since the accident. A couple of months ago, she'd finally convinced him to start turning the baby's nursery into a playroom for Liam. They stripped off the pink wallpaper and packed away the unused baby gifts before painting the room in bright yellow and lime green, adding book-shelves, and setting up a tepee she'd found online.

For a man who'd spent so much time defending his country, he hadn't been able to escape the scars Katie's and their baby's deaths had left behind. Sometimes pain stacked up, its weight crushing. Lifting it off to put life back together felt impossible.

"Nikki?"

She nodded, the decision made. "Let me go speak to the other officers, then as soon as Jack and Gwen get here, I'll be ready to go."

Tyler squeezed her hand. "We'll leave as soon as you're ready."

She slipped quickly back into her professional mode. Organizing. Directing. Trying to ensure everything that could be done was being done. Once volunteers started to trickle in, they'd need to be briefed. Tasks would be assigned in order of importance, then added to as new leads were uncovered. They needed to move quickly, but if Bridget was in the park, they were going to be up against thousands of acres of daunting wilder-ness.

"Agent Boyd?" Ranger Anderson was walking toward her. "You're going to want to see this. One of the rangers found this in the women's restroom."

"What is it?" Tyler asked.

Nikki felt her heart stop as she picked up the photo in the evidence bag. She didn't have to ask that question. It was a Polaroid photo of Bridget.

"Someone must have dropped it."

She shook her head. It wasn't dropped. It was *his* signature. One she hadn't seen at a crime scene for ten years.

"Nikki, what's wrong?" Tyler asked.

Nikki turned around slowly, the photograph in

her hands. No one used Polaroid cameras anymore. But he had.

Her mind flashed to another crime scene, the last time she'd seen his signature. Yellow tape surrounding the forested area. Officers working, cameras flashing. The crunch of the pinecones under her shoes. The smell of decaying flesh in the distance, the rain against her cheek . . . Each and every nuance of that afternoon had been embedded into her brain. None of those memories had completely faded away.

"Nikki?" Tyler asked.

"I know who's behind this."

"Who?"

She'd been hired by the Tennessee Bureau of Investigation because she'd memorized each and every abductor's signature. She'd studied every detail and pattern. Anything that might one day help her discover the identity of her sister's abductor. Anything she could do to stop the same thing from happening to someone else's daughter.

They were all looking at her. Waiting for her answer. Waiting for her to tell them what she knew about the significance of the photo.

Instead she stood there, the photo frozen in her hand. Terrified. Terrified he was out there, mocking her. Stalking her. Except that couldn't be true. *He* didn't know her. Didn't know she'd been looking for him for the past decade. Didn't know she'd dedicated her life to saving girls like the one he'd stolen from her family.

"I'm sorry, I need some air."

Nikki escaped through the front door of the visitor center. Officers were interviewing tourists and handing out flyers with Bridget's photo. She had to find a way to get ahold of her emotions. Calm down and stay focused. Six hours had passed since Bridget had gone missing, and she knew if it was *him,* the chances of her being alive continued to diminish. Because she had no name, no current description . . . nothing. She slowly inhaled and counted to four while holding her breath. When they'd agreed to hire her for their newly expanded missing persons task force, she'd assured herself she could keep her pro-fessional and personal worlds separate.

One, two, three, four.

She slowly breathed out. Until now, she'd managed to find a way to remove herself from her cases. But she'd feared it would come to this one day. The day when the past collided with the present. She leaned against the stone wall of the building and stared out across the manicured flower beds and wooded area beyond them. But all she could see was Bridget's photo.

Sarah's abductor was back.

6

"Nikki?"

Nikki heard Tyler's voice and realized he was standing beside her.

"What's going on? You froze back there."

She looked up and caught his gaze, battling to come up with an explanation she could give him. "I know. I'm sorry."

"Don't be sorry. I don't know of many officers who don't get at least somewhat personally involved in their cases, and for you, this hits even closer to home. Tell me what's going on."

She shook her head, not knowing where to begin.

Not knowing how to process what she'd just seen. Because what she held in her hands had to be nothing more than a coincidence. Or at least that was what she wanted to believe. The alternative was too frightening.

"Remember what they taught you at the academy." He braced his hands against her shoulders. "Take deep, slow breaths. Count to four. Hold it—"

"I'm trying."

She was trying, but her mind couldn't focus. For ten years she'd looked for the man who'd taken her sister, and somehow she'd stumbled upon him in the middle of the Smoky Mountains on a random case. How was that possible?

"Why did that photo spook you?"

"It proves Bridget was here," she said finally. "And that she was abducted by a predator."

"Okay, but that's not all, is it?"

"No." She drew in another slow breath, waiting for her mind to clear. "I know who has Bridget."

"How can you know that, Nikki?"

"There hasn't been any sign of him for years, but he's back, Tyler." She took another deep breath, still trying desperately to control the panic mushrooming inside her. "The man who kidnapped Sarah."

"Whoa . . ." Tyler took a step back and dropped his hands to his sides. "Don't you think you're jumping to conclusions?"

Nikki shook her head.

"Then tell me how that photo links this case to your sister's case," he said.

"He left Polaroid photos of the girls at his crime scenes. Six times. Six girls from 2002 to 2006. Sarah was the fifth girl he took."

"Does anything else about this case seem familiar?"

"He stalked them before he took them, which was why the police believe they weren't just random abductions of opportunity. In four out of the six disappearances, people gave similar descriptions of a man who became known as the Angel Abductor."

She kneaded the back of her neck with her fingertips, her temples pounding as she spoke.

"Headache back?"

She nodded.

"Give me a second." He returned with a bottle of water and a couple of pain relievers. "I know the basic facts about your sister's disappearance, but you've never shared with me what happened that afternoon."

Her hand shook as she took the bottle of water Tyler handed her and nodded her thanks. She'd met Tyler on a double date with Katie eighteen months after Sarah vanished. After weeks of immersing herself in every lead the police turned up, she'd learned to keep what she discovered to herself. Her parents, especially her mother, couldn't handle the emotional roller coaster. Most of it, she'd never even shared with Katie, let alone Tyler.

He leaned his shoulder against the stone wall beside her. "Tell me what happened the day Sarah disappeared, Nikki."

The minutes and hours clicked automatically through her mind, frame by frame. Detail by detail. As many times as she'd wanted to, she'd never been able to erase them. "I was supposed to pick her up after school. I'd promised to take her out for ice cream to celebrate a good grade on an algebra test. She hated math and was determined to do everything possible to avoid going to summer school.

"I'd just gotten off work. It was my first year teaching at Oak School Elementary. On my way to pick her up, I decided to stop at the mall to buy some shoes I'd had my eye on. The store was having a sale, and I figured I'd have plenty of time to grab them on my way and pick her up on time."

Days later, she'd found the shoes in the trunk of her car, still in the box with their tags and the receipt. She'd tossed them in the trash.

"I ended up getting to the school fifteen minutes late. I couldn't find her. I didn't think much about it at first. I thought she might have caught a ride home with a friend. But when I got to my parents' house, she wasn't there."

It was at that point she'd begun to realize something was wrong. Sarah would never have gone anywhere without telling someone.

"The police canvassed the neighborhoods, and we spoke to everyone at the school. Door-to-door in the surrounding neighborhoods, a grid search of the area. The police set up roadblocks, put out an AMBER Alert. The only clue we had was the Polaroid photo of Sarah found outside the school, left presumably by her abductor. No one we spoke to saw her get into a car. None of her friends or friends' parents. She'd just . . . vanished."

Tyler stood quietly beside her while she worked to settle her emotions. "We finally got an eyewitness statement from a student who remembered seeing her get into a car with a man. The description matched a serial killer the police and FBI had been looking for over the past few years."

"The Angel Abductor."

Nikki nodded. Even ten years later, the media's name for the man still managed to send chills through her. "After that day, I spent weeks poring over every phone call and lead the police received.

"I was the one who ended up working with law enforcement to make a long-term plan. My parents paid for a private investigator to look into the case, but I still went over Sarah's file dozens of times, memorizing every detail, looking for anything crucial that might have been overlooked. I kept meticulous notes, studied serial abductor and killer cases, and made sure the media was kept involved. I was completely focused on finding that one clue that would lead us to Sarah."

The missing persons file on Sarah had become extensive. Pages and pages of information containing medical information, personal descriptions, and coded dental characteristics, along with the initial entry report and categories and leads. She'd memorized them all, along with every fact they knew about the abductor.

"It didn't take long for me to realize that I—along with my entire family—had changed. My parents considered closing their restaurant, and at one point considered divorce. Thankfully, they had a lot of support in their church and eventually managed to slowly find their way out of the darkness. But I couldn't give up on the possibility that Sarah was still out there."

Alive.

Nikki paused while Tyler gave her the space she needed to continue.

"I finished up my first year of teaching, turned in my resignation, and applied to the police academy. I figured it would not only help me continue searching for my sister, but maybe I could help someone else who was going through what our family had suffered. Not knowing what happened to someone you love is like not being able to wake up from some horrid nightmare. I wanted—needed—answers, and decided that the best way for me to find them was to be on the inside."

"And all these years later you've continued to blame yourself for being late that day."

Nikki nodded. "I should have been there. I could have stopped what happened to her if I'd been on time."

Tyler's expression clouded. "Like I should have been there for Katie when she died?"

She stiffened at the question. "That's different."

"Different? Not to me. Three tours of duty in special ops, and I couldn't save my own wife."

Nikki looked up at him and caught the loss simmering in his eyes. Fifteen months ago, he'd returned from the Middle East with a bullet in his leg, a Purple Heart in his backpack, and six months of physical therapy ahead of him. Katie had begged him not to reenlist. What neither of them knew at the time was that three months later, she'd be the one lying in the morgue.

"Katie's death wasn't your fault," she argued.

"Just like what happened to Sarah wasn't your fault."

A stocky black starling landed on the pavement a few feet from them and grabbed the crust of a sandwich some tourist had dropped. She wanted to believe him, but after all these years, the numbing grief and guilt had yet to dissipate. She should have been there. Should have saved Sarah. But she hadn't. And that knowledge would haunt her until the day she died.

"And while you might not have been able to find Sarah, we can still find Bridget," he continued.

She wanted so badly to believe him. Just like she wanted to believe that saving others might begin to redeem herself, but today she was drowning in a familiar tidal wave of emotion. Because today had hit way too close to home.

She pressed her back against the wall. "What if I can't? It's been ten years since he surfaced. I have no idea how to find this guy."

"You can't do what? Save Bridget like you couldn't save Sarah?" Concern creased his forehead. "Isn't that what this is all about?"

"Yes . . . no . . . I don't know."

He took her hand, rubbed his thumb across the back of it. "What happened to your sister changed your life. Your entire family's lives. Just like losing Katie has changed mine."

"But you still feel guilty too."

Tyler's frown deepened. "Yes, and trust me, it's easier for me to dole out advice than take it myself."

"I think it's the not knowing that hurts the most. I don't know if she's alive or dead. Was she sold into sex trafficking? There's nothing I can do to help her. That moment when the unsolved case goes cold and is no longer active, your hope begins to strip away."

"It's called complicated grief," Tyler said. "Because added to the loss is the fact that there isn't any resolution to deal with when one goes through the grieving process."

Complicated grief.

No resolution.

The words fit. Her grief hadn't ended, because

the story hadn't ended. Nikki glanced back at the glass entrance to the visitor center. Officers were talking to tourists. Jack and Gwen would be here any moment, but all she could think about was Sarah and that photo. And the possibility that *he* was out there.

"I think it was hardest—and still is—on my mom." Her mind was lost in the past. "I know she thinks about Sarah every single day. I just want so badly to be able to find her and bring her home. To make everything right again."

"Except there's no turning back time when it comes to tragedy. I still wake up sometimes, convinced Katie's in the other room taking a shower or fixing me breakfast, and then reality hits and I remember that's not going to happen." He paused, still holding her hand. "Can I ask you a question?"

"Of course."

"Why didn't you ever share any of this with me before?"

"I don't know." Nikki searched for an explanation. "We lost Sarah before I met you, and afterward . . . you and Katie were in love, you got married, then you went off to war. It never was the right time."

And now all she could think of was that she had to be wrong. That the photo they'd brought to her was just some crazy coincidence. Or a copycat. Or maybe Jack was wrong about Sean

Logan, and he and Bridget were just having fun. Taking innocent photos . . .

But she'd seen the fear in Bridget's eyes as she stared into the camera. That wasn't a photo of a girl taking a selfie. Or of a friend snapping a photo for fun. She'd been terrified. Betrayed.

Tyler took a step forward and pulled her into his arms. "I'm sorry you and your family have had to go through this. As much as I miss Katie, and as difficult as the last year has been, at least I know what happened to her."

Nikki relaxed for a moment in his embrace, needing to feel safe, and allowed herself to feel the warmth of his breath against her neck and the pulsing of his heart against hers. But Bridget was out there somewhere, and every second counted.

She pulled back and caught Tyler's gaze. "I need to find her."

"That photo doesn't change anything, Nikki. You can't be responsible for every young girl that disappears. Your team can handle this one without you."

"But everything has changed. If this is him, I know every detail of the case, every file on this man. If my team has to stop to go over the files, how much time will be wasted that could be spent looking for her?"

"What about Matt and Jamie?"

"I can't be in both places, but the photo . . .

Tyler." She tried to blink back the tears. "If there is any chance at all that this is somehow connected to Sarah's abductor, I need to stay."

He ran his thumb across her cheek, wiping away a tear. "You're sure?"

"Yeah." Nikki nodded. "We've got a lot of work to do."

She had to do this—for Bridget and for Sarah —and for herself.

7

Five minutes later, Nikki headed to the visitor center's parking lot where Jack and Gwen had parked the team's twenty-foot mobile command post. She'd resolved to stay for now, at least until she could determine what was going on.

Jack stepped out of the passenger side of the newly purchased vehicle that had given them the ability to be at the location of an incident while providing them with state-of-the-art, on-site communications, a conference room, and a place to mobilize volunteers.

Jack sneezed as he walked toward her.

"You okay, Jack?" Nikki stopped short of the vehicle. "You look—"

"It's just hemlock." He tried to wave her concern away, eyes watering, nose as red as Rudolph's.

"Hemlock? You look awful." Nikki frowned. "Your eyes are bloodshot, your nose is red, and that . . . what's that on your neck?"

"I was hoping you wouldn't notice." Jack shot her one of his familiar goofy smiles. "This is the primary reason I try never to venture into the great outdoors."

Nikki's eyes widened. "No camping or hiking?"

"Summer camp when I was eleven." Jack sneezed again. "My mom dropped me off and promised me it would be a week I'd never forget. And believe me, I still haven't forgotten. Hay fever . . . poison ivy . . . swollen mosquito bites. The next year my mom listened to me and sent me to computer camp, where I finally found my calling."

"You're in the parking lot of the visitor center." Nikki laughed, shaking her head. "You're not exactly roughing it yet, Jack."

"He's just allergic to the great outdoors," Gwen said, coming around the front of the vehicle. "That, and he got stung by a yellow jacket at the last rest stop."

"There's nothing wrong with preferring a good sci-fi movie over a day in the pollen-filled, polluted air," Jack countered, pulling down the foldout steps beneath the side door of the command post. "Especially considering I'm like a magnet to anything that stings, bites, or hisses."

"Do you need to take some kind of allergy pill?" Nikki's amusement was quickly changing to concern.

"Nurse Gwen here has already doped me up with enough Benadryl and Tylenol for a dozen bee stings. And no, you don't have to worry about me going into anaphylactic shock." Jack sneezed. "You'll just have to listen to that all day."

"You're lucky," Gwen said. "My brother has

to carry an EpiPen with him everywhere he goes."

"Lucky? Yeah, I'm really feeling lucky today," he said as they started setting up the command center.

Ten minutes later, they were ready to brief everyone involved. Nikki made the introductions between the different agencies beneath the vehicle's rolled-out roof awning. For the moment, they were looking at a joint search between the local park rangers and the Gatlinburg Police Department, with their task force leading the investigation.

Nikki shoved aside the personal memories and held up the photo that had been bagged into evidence. "We've got a possible new lead on our abductor. This Polaroid is the same MO as that of the Angel Abductor, who terrorized East Tennessee in the early 2000s."

"Wait a minute. Your sister's case?" Gwen's gaze narrowed.

Nikki nodded.

"Couldn't it just be a coincidence?" Jack asked. "I thought he hadn't struck for at least a decade."

"He hasn't and, yes, it's possible that this is just a copycat. But if it's not . . ." Nikki ran her fingers across the photo. Part of her wanted to believe that this was simply a coincidence. That whoever had taken Bridget was simply playing the role of a copycat. But the other part of her longed for a chance to bring her sister's abductor to justice. Whatever that took.

"Care to fill the rest of us in?" Anderson clutched the brim of his ranger hat between his fingers.

"Of course." Nikki ignored the knot in her stomach as she attached the photo to the dry-erase cabinet front on the outside of the truck. "Ten years ago, my sister went missing after school in a Nashville suburb. The police tied her dis-appearance to a serial abductor in East Tennessee who took at least six girls between 2002 and 2005. The media named him the Angel Abductor."

"I remember reading about that case." Anderson stepped in front of the photo. "What do you know about him?"

"Pretty much anything you want to know." She drew in a short breath. "I've memorized case files and spent the past ten years trying to track this man down."

"Well then, it's a good thing the boss put you in as the lead in this case," Jack said.

Simpson, another park ranger, held up his pen. "Why did they call him the Angel Abductor?"

"His victims were all young girls with blond hair." Nikki spit out the details matter-of-factly. All she had to do was keep to the facts and leave her personal connection aside. "He left Polaroids of them—like this one—at the crime scenes. So while Jack might be right that we're only looking at a simple coincidence, or even a copycat, we can't ignore the similarities in the cases."

Jack nodded. "I agree. When is the last time he struck?"

"Almost ten years ago. The authorities never caught him."

"It wouldn't be the first time a serial killer showed up out of nowhere years later and decided to strike again," Gwen said. "He could have been sick, in prison, or simply lying low."

"If it *is* him, that typically means something had to have set him off," Tyler said. "Did they ever discover some kind of common stress trigger connecting the different victims? Something that set him off?"

Nikki thought through the question. "Nothing that specific. What I do know is that he was extremely meticulous and planned every abduction, presumably stalking his victims first. No DNA was ever found. Nothing that ever allowed police to make a positive ID. But as far as the man's personal life or habits . . . there's never been enough to make those kinds of conclusions."

"What about a description?" Anderson asked.

She didn't have to close her eyes to see the police sketch that had been circulated around the time of Sarah's disappearance. But even with the description, they'd never come up with a name beyond the one the media had circulated.

"Witnesses connected to each of the disappearances gave similar descriptions of a man, late twenties, reddish-blond beard, and small loop earring in his right ear, but no arrests were ever made and only four bodies were ever found. His MO was to stalk the girls and leave a Polaroid photo of each one at the crime scene. He took them from schools or deserted locations, killed them, then buried their bodies."

"So today, if this is our guy," Simpson said, "he'd be, what . . . in his late thirties? Maybe early forties now?"

"I've got the original sketch the police artist came up with right here." Jack stepped out of the truck where he'd just finished printing out the sketch, then added it to the whiteboard. "Given time, we can come up with a computerized sketch of what he might look like now."

Nikki stared at the familiar black-and-white sketch. He could have changed drastically, but at least it was a place to start.

"Here's something else that doesn't line up in my mind," Anderson said. "Technology has changed tremendously in the past ten years. I read the initial report that said Bridget's abductor used GPS technology to track her. That's a far cry from a camera even ten years ago, let alone a Polaroid camera that would have already been considered vintage by then."

"Yes, but there's no reason to believe he didn't keep up with technology."

"But the Polaroid photo?" Gwen asked.

"An added touch. A bit of nostalgia for him? That's what we need to find out." They could sit here all day asking questions, but every minute they spent discussing the whys was a minute they could be looking for Bridget. "All his victims were ages twelve to sixteen, white females."

"And where were they taken from?" Gwen asked.

"All six girls lived within a hundred-mile radius of Nashville. The four bodies that were found were discovered farther east. One as far as Morgan County." Nikki glanced at the map Gwen had hung on the whiteboard beside the sketch. "Many abductors don't run with their victims. Most are kept within fifty miles of the abduction location, often held in the home of the suspect. Those statistics didn't hold true in these cases."

"And he didn't stick to that pattern if he brought Bridget here."

"We need to get out there, now, and find her. Tyler, since you're here, we could use your input as well, especially with your psychological experience. A fresh pair of eyes always helps. Jack can ensure you have access to all case files currently available on the Angel Abductor. Look for anything that might give us a better picture of who this guy is."

Nikki turned to the rest of the officers. "Anderson, you and your rangers—along with those here from the Gatlinburg police—will be in charge of coordinating the search within the park. My team and I will continue handling the logistics of the investigation, as well as coordinating our efforts on the state level and with the FBI."

"What about the brother?" Jack asked.

"Kyle's driving in now and should be here within the hour. I've already had him establish himself as the link with the media, including coordinating with them all updates on the case after going through us. Gwen, I want a list of every outgoing and incoming call on Bridget's phone as well as a printout of all texts over the last two months. See if you can find anything that stands out. Jack, I want you to continue searching through her Facebook page, Twitter account, Instagram, and whatever else she was on. Go through her conversations to look for clues. They used social media to connect. Which means if this guy made a mistake and slipped up, that's where we're going to find it."

Nikki tried to ignore the wave of fatigue passing through her as the group split up. She moved in front of the whiteboard to tape up a recent photo of Bridget. "When Kyle gets here, I want him to help us reconstruct a detailed timeline of Bridget's last forty-eight hours. Someone had to have seen something."

She started to turn away, then stopped to study the sketch of the Angel Abductor. When the police had released the picture to the public, they'd admitted that not only was the description too vague but the sketch was also too generic. While she might not exactly know what he looked like, she did know the basic drive of the man they were looking for. Someone able to compartmentalize his feelings to the point where he felt no empathy. Someone with an abusive background. Someone wanting to be in control and call the shots.

Nikki felt the familiar wave of grief—mixed with a measure of panic—wash through her. She drew in a slow breath. She'd come to learn that she couldn't predict when or in what form grief might arrive. And that as much as she wanted it, she simply didn't have control over everything that happened around her.

"Nikki?" Jack's voice pulled her back to the present.

"Sorry." She followed him inside the command post, then sat down at the workstation beside him.

"I was actually going through some of this on my way here," he said. "Here's something you're going to want to see. Apparently Bridget had multiple Instagram accounts on her phone, and this one here shows a far different persona online than what her friends described."

"You're sure this is her?" Nikki asked.

"Yes." Jack scooted back to give her a closer look, then pointed to the screen. "Look at this one. Her screen name is Cat, but we're not talking about the furry kind."

"Then what are we talking about?"

"It's connected to cutting or self-harm, and look at these hashtags—#alone . . . #suicidal . . . #depression . . ."

Nikki scrolled slowly through the photos on the girl's account. Anorexic girls, protruding collarbones, and thigh gaps. Dark rooms and faces, and dozens of poems Bridget had written about death and loss.

"What do you think?" Jack asked, looking up at her.

"I think things are never as simple as they seem. Now we possibly know why she agreed to meet with him. She was struggling with who she was, and a guy showed up claiming to love her. She bought into the lie, making her an easy mark."

Jack tapped his fingers against the desktop. "Maybe I'm missing something, but I saw her other accounts. How does a popular girl get involved in this?"

Nikki pointed to a photo of Bridget. "That was Bridget on the outside. You just found the one on the inside. The one underneath the smile."

"So where . . . ?" Jack sneezed twice. "Sorry. Where does this lead us?"

"I don't know, but it's a clue into her life and what she was struggling with." Nikki glanced at her watch. "Do me a favor. Find out if Chloe and Mia have made it back to Nashville. I'd like to set up a Skype call with them as soon as possible and see if they knew about any of this."

Thirty minutes later, Nikki was staring at Mia's and Chloe's faces on the computer screen. Chloe's mom sat in the background, listening in.

"Mia . . . Chloe . . . I appreciate your taking the time to talk with me again," Nikki said.

Mia leaned forward. "Have you found Bridget?"

"Not yet, but I do have some more questions I'd like to ask you if that's okay."

The girls nodded.

"We found Bridget's phone. We've been looking through it, trying to see if we can find anything that might help us track her down. We found one of her accounts where she goes by Cat. And shares a lot about depression and anorexia."

Mia looked at Chloe, then shrugged. "It's nothing, really. She was just letting her feelings out. It's what we all do. Bridget spent a lot of time writing those poems."

"They're pretty dark. Was she depressed?"

Chloe glanced at Mia. "I don't think Bridget would like us talking about this stuff with anyone."

"Listen, girls, I have no desire to invade Bridget's privacy, but we need to find her. And it's possible what you can tell us will help us find a clue to where she is or even who might have her."

"Okay." Mia frowned, but she nodded in agreement. "We've been friends since we were in third grade. I guess things began to change after her dad died and her mom left. She never understood why her mom freaked out. Bridget's struggled ever since, but she really doesn't talk about any of that."

"So she never talks about her mom?"

Mia shook her head. "Not very often, though she did tell me a couple of weeks ago that her mother was planning to come and see her."

"When?" Nikki asked.

"She didn't say."

"Did Bridget seem excited?"

"Yeah, but I think she was nervous too. I mean, she missed her mom, but they hadn't seen each other for a long time."

So instead of talking to her mom or her brother, Bridget posted online, anonymously, to a group of strangers—people she'd never even met. It was a completely different world today than the one Nikki had grown up in. Social media had thrust kids into a world where it was far too easy to end up feeling completely alone in the middle of a crowd.

"What about cutting or suicide?" Nikki asked. "Did she ever talk about that?"

Chloe chewed at a fingernail. "Bridget cut a few times. Threatened suicide once or twice, but she never would have gone through with it."

"How do you know that?"

"Bridget could be a bit of a drama queen. We just thought . . ." Chloe hesitated. "We just thought she was looking for attention."

"Did you tell an adult? Try to get her to seek help?"

Mia dropped her gaze away from the computer's camera. "She made us promise not to tell anyone. And I guess we didn't think she was serious."

Nikki pressed her lips together, hoping they were right. "I know this has been hard, girls. But I appreciate your talking with me. If I come up with any more questions, I'll let you know."

Tyler, Jack, and Gwen were still sorting through Bridget's information when Nikki ended the call.

Tyler pushed back his chair. "I'm going to grab some water from the vending machine outside the visitor center. Anyone want something?"

"I'll come with you, actually," Nikki said, standing up. She needed a couple minutes of fresh air to think and clear her mind so she could begin to assemble the pieces of Bridget she'd been given. Whether she'd truly been suicidal or not, she'd clearly painted a persona of a vulnerable, hurting young girl. And *he'd* found her. A girl who was vulnerable and willing to respond to the attention of a stranger. Able to fall in love with the image of someone she'd never met.

They heard a scream from the visitor center's

lobby, which had been reopened to tourists, as she and Tyler walked by. Nikki bolted inside with Tyler, then froze.

A woman stood in the middle of the large room with a gun clutched between her unsteady hands. "Nobody move!"

Another scream rang through the room.

A ranger—Ford, according to his name tag—reached for his gun.

"Don't even think about it." The woman fired a blind shot, her hands still shaking. The bullet slammed into one of the displays of a black bear, shattering the glass six feet from where Nikki stood. The room went silent. "Nobody. Move."

A mother huddled beside the information kiosk, her toddler whimpering, while an older couple crouched next to them.

Nikki studied the woman. Late forties, slightly overweight. Hair unwashed and pulled back in a tight ponytail. But what bothered Nikki the most was the look in her eyes. She was clearly high on something.

"How did she get in here with a weapon?" someone shouted behind her.

"Don't move . . . none of you . . . I'm the one who'll be asking the questions." She pointed the gun at an old man clutching a map of the park to Nikki's left. It fluttered silently to the floor. "Because until I get the answers I'm looking for, the next person who moves, I'm going to shoot."

8

Time seemed to tick by in slow motion as Nikki absorbed the scene around her. The majority of the tourists who had been milling in the lobby of the visitor center had scattered at the sight of a gun. Those remaining now hid behind displays or the information counter. At least four were still potentially in the line of fire besides herself. Tyler—who'd managed to step between the shooter and a young girl and her mother—Ford, and a couple in their mid-forties crouched ten feet to her left.

Basic protocol made it a priority to isolate and contain a gunman, then secure the perimeter in order to keep the gunman and any civilians separated. But in this situation, they weren't going to have the luxury of setting up tactical and negotiating teams. Neither was there time to get information on who the woman was or why she was here.

Jack and Gwen were still back at the command post. Once someone discovered what was going on, they'd bring in backup. But for now, it was up to her, Tyler, and Ford to handle the situation themselves.

We need a way out of this, God. A way out where no one gets hurt.

Nikki took a step toward the woman. She needed to find a way to connect, and that began by hearing her out. "My name's Nikki Boyd. I work with the Tennessee Bureau of Investigation, and I'd like to try to help. You said you had questions?"

The woman shifted the weapon in front of her, aiming it this time at Nikki. "I said don't come any closer."

"Okay." Nikki held up her hands and took a step backward to give the woman some space. "I'm moving back now."

"I know who you are. You're with them, and they . . . refused to help me."

"I want to help you."

"No . . . no, I don't believe you." She held the gun out in front of her, clearly panicked. "I want everyone over here, standing in front of the information counter where I can see you."

"Okay." Nikki nodded at the other hostages. "You heard her. Everyone move slowly toward the counter."

Something moved in Nikki's peripheral vision. She shifted her gaze to the right where the ranger stood. Ford had turned toward the counter and was slowly drawing his weapon from the holster on his hip.

But he wasn't fast enough.

The woman's weapon went off again. This time the ranger dropped to the floor. The little girl to her left screamed.

"You should have listened to me," the woman shouted.

Nikki glanced back at the ranger. Blood had already begun to pool around the midsection of his tan shirt.

Nikki held up her hands. "I'm going to help him."

"I didn't mean to shoot him, but I'm not going to let them win this time." The woman's hands were shaking, her finger still against the trigger. She was breathing hard and fast. They had to find a way to de-escalate the situation and get the gun away from her. Because if they didn't, this could quickly turn into a bloodbath.

"Nikki . . ."

Ignoring Tyler and the risk, Nikki hurried to the ranger's side, pulled off her fleece jacket, and pressed the fabric against his side in an attempt to stop the bleeding. She looked up at Tyler, caught his gaze, then nodded for him to take over. They were going to have to use whatever resources they had. And at the moment, her one trump card was Tyler.

She could sense a brief moment of hesitation in his eyes before she turned to concentrate on the ranger. But years of special ops training had given him the negotiating skills needed for a situation like this.

Tyler held his hands up. "My name's Tyler Grant."

"Are you with them too?" she asked.

"With the police?"

She nodded, her jaw tense, gun still held up in front of her. Finger resting on the trigger.

"No." Tyler kept his voice calm and even. Only Nikki could sense the battle raging inside him. "I don't work with the police, but my job is to help people. And I'd like to help you. The first thing we need to do, though, is take care of this man. If you let him go, we can make sure he gets the medical treatment he needs—"

"No. I don't trust them. They took my husband."

"Who? The police?"

Nikki caught the panic in the ranger's eyes. "Ford . . . Ford! I need you to stay with me. Come on. You're going to be fine."

She quickly evaluated the situation while Tyler continued to talk. He needed to convince the woman to let Ford go. His breathing was steady but rapid, his pulse weak. Any gunshot wound— no matter where on the body—could be life threatening. In this case, there was the high probability of massive internal injuries.

Nikki continued pressing on the wound. "He's got to get medical help, Tyler."

"I'm sorry about your husband," Tyler said, "but she's right. The ranger needs medical help."

Nikki looked up. Sweat beaded on the woman's forehead. Her hands shook. Her rapid speech probably meant she'd taken an "upper" drug like cocaine rather than drinking alcohol. But people were capable of doing all kinds of crazy things with adrenaline rushing through them.

"No . . . no one is leaving. Not until someone answers my questions."

Tyler took a step forward. "What are your questions, ma'am?"

"Ma'am . . ." She let out a nervous laugh. "It's been a long time since someone called me ma'am."

Nikki watched the woman's eyes shift to the right to the couple at the far end of the information desk, then jump back to Tyler.

Tyler took another step forward. "What would you like me to call you, then?"

"Wait . . . Don't come closer." She gripped the gun tighter and pointed it at Tyler, her hands still shaking.

"Okay." Tyler raised his hands in defeat, then took a step back, but his gaze never left the woman's face. "Can you tell me your name?"

She hesitated again, as if sizing him up. "Loretta. My name's Loretta."

"Loretta." Tyler smiled. "My grandmother's name was Loretta. She used to make me lemonade and peach cobbler in the summertime."

"I like peach cobbler."

"I do too. You said you had a question, Loretta. Can you tell me what it is?"

Nikki felt her heartbeat accelerate. Ford's skin had paled to a chalky white. Blood had already soaked through a double layer of her fleece jacket. They were running out of time.

"You're going to be okay, Ford. Stay with me . . ."

"I'm looking for someone," Loretta said. "Her name is Bridget Ellison."

"Do you know Bridget?" Tyler asked. "Because we're also looking for her."

"Yes. I know Bridget."

"Do you know where she is?"

Loretta pressed her lips together. "The last time I saw her she was eating an ice cream cone. Chocolate mint with sprinkles. She loves sprinkles. Has loved them for as long as I can remember."

Nikki watched as Tyler took another step forward. "You're her mother, aren't you?"

Caution flickered in Loretta's eyes. "How'd you know?"

"I've seen her picture. She looks like you. She has your brown eyes. And the same color hair."

"Except the blond highlights in her hair are natural. I color mine." She pulled a folded piece of paper out of her pocket and held it up. "They gave me this flyer when I got here. She looks so . . . grown-up."

"We're trying to help find her, and we could

106

use your help as well. But first, I need you to let the ranger go. Would you do that for me?"

She was still holding the gun in front of her, her attention on the flyer they'd been handing out. Nikki saw that Jack and Anderson were just outside the other exit doors behind her, ready to react if given the opportunity. "I don't know. I need to find Bridget."

Sirens sounded in the distance.

"Someone called the police?" Panic laced Loretta's voice.

"It's an ambulance," Tyler said. "The ranger needs a doctor. Let us take him outside."

"I don't know . . ."

"Please, Loretta." Nikki shifted her weight beside Ford, careful to keep continual pressure on the wound. "He's going to die without medical help, and I know you don't want that."

Nikki could see the flashing lights of the ambulance as it drove into the parking lot. Police backup would be there as well, ready to take over the situation.

"I promise I won't go anywhere," Tyler said, "and I'll try to answer your questions."

Loretta glanced out the window. "I'll let two paramedics with a stretcher in."

"You made a good choice, Loretta. Thank you," Tyler said. "I'm going to call someone and let them know it's safe to come inside and get the ranger."

"Tell them not to try anything heroic," Loretta said. "And no one else leaves. This isn't over."

Nikki turned back to Ford. He was still conscious, but his pupils had dilated and his pulse was weakening. He was going into shock. "We're going to get you out of here, Ford. The paramedics are coming for you right now."

A minute later, two uniformed medics rolled Ford out on a stretcher. Nikki rubbed her blood-stained hands against her pant legs as the glass door to the center shut behind them.

God, don't let him die . . . please.

Tyler motioned for Nikki to move beside him. "Nikki works on the state's missing persons task force. She's working with the park rangers and the local police to find your daughter."

"I said I don't believe you." Loretta's voice cracked. "The police took my husband. Promised . . . they promised he would be back, but he never came back."

"I'm sorry for whatever happened to your husband," Nikki said, "but my job is to find people, Loretta. People like Bridget. Which is what I'm trying to do, but I need you to trust me so I can help you."

Nikki caught the conflict in Loretta's eyes.

"I saw her picture on TV. She was such a beautiful baby. She never cried. I could put her on a blanket on the floor, and she would play, content for hours." Loretta stared at Bridget's photo on the flyer, then looked up at Nikki. "Why didn't somebody call me and tell me she was in trouble?"

"Your son tried to call you."

"Kyle?" Loretta's frown deepened. "Where is he?"

"On his way here right now. He's been doing everything he can to help us."

"I thought . . . I thought they were going to hurt her. Like they hurt my husband."

"No one wants to hurt Bridget," Nikki said. "We want to find her."

Loretta's hands were trembling harder now. Nikki glanced down the row of hostages. Until the gun was out of the woman's hands, none of them were safe.

"Loretta, have you had any contact with your daughter?"

"Of course. I'm her mother. She sent me a card for my birthday last month." Loretta smiled. "It had a flower on the front. A red rose."

"Does she call you?" Nikki asked.

"She emails me sometimes."

"What do the two of you talk about?"

"School. Boys," Loretta said. "Do you think you can find her?"

"Yes, I do, but not as long as I'm in here. I need to be out there. Talking to people who might have seen her. Making sure everyone sees her picture. Can you let me do my job so I can find your daughter?"

Loretta looked down at her weapon, shoulders slumping. "I shouldn't have brought the gun."

Nikki took another step forward. "No, you shouldn't have."

"I didn't think . . . I didn't think anyone would listen to me."

"I'm listening. Let me have the gun, Loretta. And I'll do everything I can to help you find your daughter."

Loretta hesitated, then slowly handed Nikki the gun.

"They're going to arrest me, aren't they?" Loretta said.

Nikki made the call. Local police moved in to handcuff Loretta and read her her rights. Nikki handed the gun to one of the officers as Kyle arrived at the front door.

"Clear the room and make sure everyone is okay," she said to Jack and Gwen, before turning to Tyler. "Thank you."

"You okay?"

"Yeah." Nikki glanced down at her clothes, not missing the worry in his gaze. She needed to wash her hands and change, but first there was something else she needed to do. "Just glad it's over. I need to speak with Kyle. He needs to know what's going on."

Tyler nodded. "Go."

Nikki hurried outside the building behind the officers and Loretta. "We need to talk, Kyle."

"Wait a minute." He hesitated as they led his mother past him toward one of the squad cars. "What's going on?"

His mother looked back and caught his gaze. "I'm sorry, Kyle."

Nikki pulled him aside. "They're arresting your mother. You'll get a chance to talk with her later, but for now you need to stay out of the way."

He watched his mother walk away, then turned back to Nikki. "They told me she came in with a gun and took hostages. That she shot someone."

"I'm sorry." She hesitated, knowing it was going to take time for everything that had happened to sink in. "But right now we need to talk about your sister."

"Did you find out something?"

Nikki jumped straight to the point. "Did you know Bridget was struggling with depression and cutting?"

"Yeah, I tried to get her to go to counseling, but she hated it. Said they didn't understand her, so I didn't make her keep going."

"She was also communicating with your mother."

"What?" Kyle shook his head. "She never told me that. And me . . . I was always so busy. This is all my fault."

"Why?"

"If I'd been around more, paid more attention to what she was doing—"

"Don't go there, Kyle. All you can do is focus on what's happening right now."

"I need to talk to my mother."

"Not now, Kyle."

But Kyle was already headed for the squad car. He made it to the vehicle just as they were about to put his mother inside. "You walk out of our lives and we don't see you for months on end, and then you think you can just show up and try to fix things?"

"Kyle—" Nikki started.

"I'm sorry." Loretta turned around to face her son. "I know I wasn't a good mom, but after your father died . . . I didn't know how to take care of you, and Bridget, and myself."

"You know how to drink. And party."

"I wanted to help." Loretta's voice had dropped to almost a whisper.

"With a gun?"

"I just wanted to protect her. When they took your father, I couldn't stop them. I thought . . . I thought they took Bridget away as well."

"The police aren't the enemy here." Kyle's voice rose. "Don't you see that?"

The flyer that Loretta had stuck in her pocket fell out and fluttered to the pavement. "I've missed so much. When did her hair get so long? Last time I saw her she had it cut short."

Kyle picked up the flyer. "She decided to grow it out. About a year and a half ago. You'd have known if you'd been around."

One of the officers motioned at Kyle. "Sir, I'm going to have to ask you to step away now—"

"I was trying to protect her." A tear slid down Loretta's face. "I know I'm not perfect, but I never stopped loving the two of you, no matter what has happened between us."

"What's happened between us? Well, let's see. You're a drunk. You deserted your family. Shall I go on?"

"He took her, and you were too busy to notice what was going on."

"Who, Loretta?" Nikki felt her heart pound in her ears as she took a step forward. There was something about the way she'd phrased her sentence. Was it possible the woman knew something? "Do you know who took Bridget?"

"Maybe. There was a man who'd been following her. She told me she was scared."

"You knew she was being followed and didn't tell me?" Kyle said. "You—"

"Enough. Both of you." Nikki motioned for them to stop. "At this moment, I don't care who failed who. I think we can agree on one thing. We all want to find Bridget." She turned to the officer. "I need to know what she's talking about."

The officer shook his head. "And I need to take her down to the station and have her booked. She just shot a ranger."

"I realize that." Nikki rushed on. "But I've got a girl missing and a woman who might know something. Please."

"Meet me down at the station in thirty minutes, and I'll give you first dibs."

9

Thirty-five minutes later, Nikki and Jack stepped inside the small interrogation room at the station back in town where Loretta Ellison sat rocking in her chair. Nikki slipped into a chair, wearing a pair of jeans, navy jacket, and white blouse she'd picked up on the way, replacing the bloodstained outfit she'd been wearing when Ford had been shot. The latest word from the hospital was that he was still in surgery but was expected to make it. She hoped so. Both for Ford and his family's sake and for Loretta.

"We'd like to talk with you for a few minutes about Bridget," Nikki said.

"Did you find her yet?"

"I'm sorry, but no."

"And the man I shot. They haven't told me if he's still alive."

"The last update we received, he's in surgery. The doctors are expecting him to pull through."

Loretta pressed her fingers against her temples. "I've disappointed my son again. I need to see him again. To try and explain."

Nikki studied the woman's face, aged, she was sure, beyond her years. It wasn't hard to feel sorry for her, despite what she'd done. Nikki would never forget the moment everything in her own life had spiraled out of control. Or the fact that she could have easily become the person sitting across from her.

"I'll make sure you get a chance to speak with Kyle," Jack said, still standing, "but we'd like to ask you a few more questions about your daughter."

Loretta looked up at him, eyes bloodshot, hands shaking. Assuming the woman had been high when she came into the visitor center with a gun, she was crashing now. "I didn't mean to shoot him, but it was his fault. He . . . took my husband. And now Bridget . . ."

Nikki had gone over Daniel Ellison's file when she arrived at the police station. According to the autopsy, he had died of a heart attack while in police custody after being arrested for stealing a car found with narcotics.

Nikki leaned forward and rested her arms against the table. "I'm very sorry for the loss of your husband, but the police arrested him, Loretta."

"I still can't trust them." Loretta traced an imaginary line on the table with her finger. "Said he was in trouble for stealing some car, but all I know is that he never came home."

"It's hard to lose someone you love." Nikki swallowed the emotion threatening to surface. She needed answers, and in order to get them she needed to connect with the woman. Needed to earn her trust. "My sister was abducted when she was sixteen."

Loretta looked up at her, frowning. "Did you ever find her?"

"No. That's why I want to help you. I know how hard it is to lose someone you love. And even harder not to know where they are. I want to find your daughter, Loretta. And I think you might be able to help me."

"But I don't know where she is." The woman started coughing.

"Would you like some water?" Jack asked.

Her fingertips gripped the edge of the table. "No . . . I'll be okay."

"Back at the visitor center you said 'he' took her," Nikki said. "Like you knew who might have taken her? I need to know who you were talking about. Did someone threaten to take Bridget?"

Loretta was losing focus. Rocking in her chair again. "Maybe."

"Loretta?" Nikki leaned forward. "I need your help to find Bridget. Remember? Just tell me what you know. You must have had a reason for saying that."

"She . . . she sent me a message a week or so ago. She seemed scared of something."

"Did she tell you what she was scared of?" Jack asked.

Loretta shook her head. "I think she didn't want me to worry, though I couldn't help it. I always worry about her."

"Think, Loretta. Did she ever mention someone specific? Perhaps someone she believed was watching her or stalking her?"

"She thought someone—an older man—had been following her."

"Did she know who he was?" Nikki prodded. Gwen was going through Loretta's phone records and text messages, but she had to make sure they didn't miss anything. "Who had been watching Bridget?"

"Don't know. She never gave me any details. Told me later it was nothing. Just a creepy feeling like you have when someone walks over your grave. When I heard she'd gone missing, I remembered she'd told me that."

"I need you to tell me everything Bridget told you, Loretta. When did the man follow her? Where was she?"

Loretta clasped her hands together. "Once . . . once while she was jogging, maybe. A second time I think she was . . . leaving school."

"And she was afraid?" Jack asked.

Loretta nodded. "She wouldn't tell me she was afraid, but I could tell. The first time she thought someone was following her, she sent me a message and told me she ran into a store until she was sure she'd lost them. I told her to tell

Kyle. Later she told me to forget the whole thing. That she'd watched some horror movie with her friends and it had creeped her out. Set her imagination on overdrive."

"And these conversations you had with Bridget. Did you call her or simply text each other?"

"We texted," Loretta said. "She likes to communicate that way."

Nikki quickly sent Gwen a message, telling her to look specifically through the conversations between Bridget and her mother.

"Tell me more about Bridget," Nikki said.

A slight smile appeared on Loretta's face for the first time. "She was always happy. Hardly ever cried. And so beautiful. I thought about putting her in one of those pageants you see on TV, but she loved sports and playing outside. She was always a tomboy. Never wanted me to dress her up in frilly clothes."

"When's the last time you saw her?" Nikki asked.

"Christmas, a year and a half ago. Kyle invited me over for dinner. I was surprised. We don't much get along. Not since Daniel died. He blames me for not being able to take care of Bridget."

"And since then?"

"I . . . I've had some problems with drugs. Drinking. Messed me up after Daniel died. They told me I couldn't take care of Bridget anymore."

119

Yet another reason Loretta didn't trust the authorities.

"How often do you talk with her?"

"Every few weeks. Emails and texts, mostly."

"What else do you and Bridget talk about?"

"She tells me about school and her volleyball games. I promised her I'd come to one of them someday. About her friends. Boys she likes. Classes she likes. She's smart, but I don't think she tries hard enough."

"Did she ever talk about a boy named Sean Logan?"

"Sean . . ." Loretta shrugged. "Don't remember the names. I tease her sometimes. She seems to like a different boy every week. She's such a sweet girl. A little sad and lonely. I don't understand young people today. They talk all day on their phones but still seem lonely. It wasn't like that when I was her age. I had my first job when I was fourteen, washing dishes for the pizza place in town. But Kyle was right. I don't know how to take care of myself, let alone a teenager."

Nikki leaned forward. "And is there anything else you know that might help?"

"No . . ." Loretta's hands shook as she moved them to her lap. "I don't care what happens to me, but please . . . please find my girl."

Back at the visitor center, Nikki grabbed a Coke from the vending machine. She took a sip, hoping the early afternoon sunshine would improve her mood. Loretta clearly believed Bridget had been afraid. Sometimes an abduction was simply a window of opportunity, but abductors often stalked their victims before they took them—like the Angel Abductor. The victim might not know their abductor personally, but it wasn't uncommon to discover there had been contact prior to the crime. And if Loretta was right, Bridget had this connection with her abductor as well.

A couple with three energetic kids in tow strolled past her as she headed back inside. The man held Bridget's flyer, turned and said something to the woman, then crumpled up the paper and dropped it into the trash. Nikki drew in a breath of fresh air and let it help calm the adrenaline still pumping through her. Maybe they hadn't seen Bridget, but someone had to have seen something.

She headed back toward the command post vehicle. Manpower was essential if they were going to find Bridget. The local police department had assigned one of their officers to be the liaison between local police and the volunteers who had come forward. This would guarantee not only that their help was effective, but that any evidence encountered was safeguarded. Each volunteer was signed in, then assigned a specific task, including fielding calls. Most of them, though, were spending the day passing out flyers with Bridget's photo and talking to hikers who were emerging from or entering the trailheads.

Inside the vehicle, Nikki walked over to where Gwen was working, leaned over, and braced her arms against the table where Gwen was still going through Bridget's phone. "Please tell me you've come up with something we can use."

Gwen slipped a strand of dark hair behind her ear. "From what you told me on the phone, Loretta was telling the truth. There were dozens of emails between her and Bridget, as well as some text messages."

"And . . . ?"

"Two weeks ago, she wrote 'Hey Mom, there's this old, creepy guy I've seen twice now, following me. Not sure what's up with that.' Three days later she says, 'I shouldn't have worried you. I'm sure it's nothing. Never watching another horror movie!' "

"And her mom's response?" Nikki asked.

" 'I'm supposed to worry. I'm your mother.' " Gwen pushed her chair away from the table and leaned back. "She never mentioned it again. I'm assuming because she didn't want her mother to worry."

"Any description?"

"Nothing that helps."

Kyle knocked on the door of the vehicle, holding a stack of flyers, then handed them to

Nikki. "I had a bunch more flyers made up. I'm heading out now to make an appeal to the public."

"Kyle, wait," Nikki said, stepping outside. "I just returned from speaking to your mother. I know your relationship is strained, but she'd like to see you."

He glanced at his watch. "Maybe later. I'm getting ready to meet a reporter for an interview they've promised to broadcast."

She wanted to tell him how important it was, but that wasn't her place. Tragedy tended to either bring people together or rip them apart. She'd seen it firsthand with her own family. The only thing that had saved them was the support of family and friends, and prayers. She could only pray that he and Loretta someday found healing, because she had a feeling nothing she could say or do was going to change his mind right now.

Tyler stepped out of the truck, a printout in his hand. "I'm not finished, but I went ahead and printed out my initial observations. I don't think any of it's going to be new, though."

"Thanks. I really appreciate it. This will help." She took the list he'd made and read through it quickly before turning to watch Kyle disappear across the parking lot. "Loretta never should have come. She's going to go to jail for what she did this morning, and all she wanted to do was find her daughter. I know what that feels like."

"Yes, but you didn't bring a gun inside a public place, hold a bunch of hostages, and shoot an officer," Tyler said. "Just like you, she's made choices along the way."

"I just hope she can get some help." Nikki folded her arms across her chest. "Was your grandmother's name really Loretta, or were you just trying to connect with her?"

"Loretta Caroline Hall Grant." Tyler smiled. "She was my father's mother. Married when she was fourteen, had twelve children over the next decade and a half. Eight of them lived."

"Wow. She must have had a hard life with all that loss."

"She did, but you wouldn't have known it from talking to her. She never grew past five feet, but she had more fire than anyone I know. She died when I was nine, but I remember her so clearly. She smelled like roses and made the best peach cobbler in the county."

"You must take after her."

"Smelling like roses?" Tyler nudged her with his shoulder.

"No. I was talking about the fire part." Nikki laughed, but her expression quickly sobered. "I know that wasn't easy in there for you today, but you did good."

"Instinct kicked in."

"Still . . . Thank you." She stared down at an oil

spot next to her. "I know I put you in a difficult situation."

"You didn't have a lot of options."

"No, I didn't." The seriousness of the situation enveloped her, bringing with it a degree of vulnerability. "But you did well in there, though I'm not surprised. We make a good team."

"Yes, we do." He grabbed her hand and laced their fingers together. "And you did well in there because you understand what she was going through."

"Still, I can't help but think she just needs someone to believe in her. A second chance with her daughter . . . and her son. And now it might be too late." Nikki glanced across the landscaped yard. Kyle had gone down to the police station after their interview had ended. Now he had to worry about both his sister and his mother. "Do you think he will be able to give her what she needs?"

"I don't know. There's a lot of hurt and rejection in their relationship that isn't going to be easy to overcome."

"Nikki?" Gwen stepped out of the truck. "We just got a call from someone you're going to want to speak with. His name is Brandon Knight, and he's been staying in a cabin about a mile away from where Bridget vanished. Says he saw her leave this morning with a man driving a silver Ford Focus."

10

Nikki felt a seed of hope begin to sprout. For the first time in seven hours, they finally had a possible eyewitness. The bottom line was that they could analyze every crime scene—what happened and what the motives were, and ask all the right questions. But in the end, witnesses were their best way to identify suspects.

Nikki headed back to the truck behind Gwen. "Is he still on the line?"

"He was calling from his car on his cell and is on his way here right now," she said.

"Here?" Nikki stopped short of the door. "Wartburg's two hours away from here. Didn't he talk with the local police?"

"He called and gave the dispatcher the information he had. Says he must have been taking a shower when the police stopped by the first time when canvassing the area."

"Still, why come all the way here?" While an enthusiastic witness was always welcome, this seemed like more than simply the act of a Good Samaritan.

"Said he already had an interview in Gatlinburg scheduled for this afternoon," Gwen said, "so when he saw the update on the news, he decided to come straight here. I'll go make sure the conference room in the truck is set up."

Nikki turned back to Tyler.

"I'll be fine," he said, answering her unasked question. "I'm still going through the files you asked me to look at."

"Thanks." She shot him a smile, thankful he was here. Hopeful they were about to take a leap closer to finding Bridget. "Let me know if anything pops up you think might fit with this case."

A moment later, she stepped into the eight-by-eight conference room in the back of the truck that boasted a table and five chairs. It wasn't an interrogation room, but maybe the informal setting would work in their favor.

"Brandon Knight?" Nikki asked, as Jack and another man walked into the room a few minutes later.

"That's me." Knight smiled at her.

Nikki shook his hand, then sat down across from him, next to Jack. "I appreciate your taking the time to come in and talk with us. I understand you drove all the way from Wartburg. That's a pretty far drive."

Knight leaned back and fiddled with the bottom of his leather bomber jacket. "I told the other officer that I'm a writer and have been staying out there for the past few days."

"And how did you find out about the abduction?" Nikki asked.

"I'm a bit of a news junkie. I was watching this morning and saw that a girl had gone missing. When I saw her photo, I realized I'd met her last night."

Nikki handed him a picture of Bridget. "And is this the girl you saw get into the car?"

"Yeah . . . she's the girl on the news. Bridget, right?"

"Yes."

"And you have a job interview here in town?" Nikki asked, curious as to who would show up at an interview in jeans and a bomber jacket.

"A job interview? No." Knight chuckled. "I had an interview scheduled—for the book I'm working on—for later this afternoon in Pigeon Forge. It wasn't much farther to come all the way into Gatlinburg."

"You're quite the Good Samaritan," Nikki said, still not completely buying the man's story. "What kind of writer are you?"

"Murder mysteries." He rested his hands in his lap. "I needed some time away to meet a deadline. My parents own the cabin where I've been staying, and I usually end up coming here two or three times a year."

Nikki pulled out her phone and quickly typed a message to Gwen.

Mystery author? Check out.

She looked back at him. "You said you saw Bridget leave this morning?"

"Yes."

"What time?"

"Early. Around five. Five fifteen at the latest."

"And you'd seen her once before."

"Yes, I met the girls and her brother . . . Kyle, I think his name was, just briefly when they first arrived. I'd been out walking my dog, and they were unloading their car."

"Last night?" Jack asked.

"Yeah."

"How long have you been staying in the area?"

"Got here last Wednesday and plan on staying through the rest of this week."

"And this morning?" Nikki asked.

"I woke up early, somewhere around three thirty or four. My mind was spinning. I'd been dreaming, actually, about a twist to my plot. I woke up and wrote it down, then couldn't go back to sleep. At about five I decided to get outside and take a walk."

"And you walked past the house where they were staying?" Nikki asked.

"Yeah. There's a trail that runs through the area. Leads from my parents' house past theirs, toward the park."

"And this morning? What exactly did you observe?" Nikki asked.

"There was a car in the driveway when the girl came out of the house."

"Could you see the driver's face?"

"Not clearly. Because of where the trail is, I wasn't that close. She came out of the house. He was waiting for her in his car."

"What kind of car?"

"A silver Ford Focus. At least . . . I don't know . . . ten years old. I didn't get a license plate number, because I didn't think anything of it at the time, but I do know they were Tennessee plates."

Bingo. The same car found deserted with Bridget's hat.

"You're good with details, Mr. Knight," Nikki said.

"I'm a writer. I enjoy observing people. Imagining what they're doing. Where they're going."

"Did she look scared?" Nikki asked.

"I couldn't see her face, but I do know she didn't get right into the car. She stood there for a few minutes, talking to him."

"Like she was trying to decide if she was going to get in the car or not?" Nikki asked, verbalizing her own thoughts.

"Maybe, but honestly I have no idea what they were talking about. I was too far away for that."

"What was she wearing?"

"It was dark, but it looked like a track suit and some kind of . . . beanie."

Her phone beeped and Nikki glanced at the message.

Seems legit. No priors.

Keep checking. Nikki responded to Gwen, then looked up from her phone. "Did anything else seem odd?"

"Just that it was early. After they drove away, I didn't think anything about it—at least, not until I watched the news this morning. To be honest, I was focused on my story line and wasn't paying too much attention. There weren't any signs that anything was wrong that I saw, and trust me, I would have picked it up if there had been."

"Meaning?" Nikki asked.

Knight laughed. "I'm a mystery writer. I see villains around every corner. And I know it sounds crazy, but every person I see is a potential story. Every suspicious action possible runs through my mind. Hazards of the trade."

"And with Bridget?" Jack asked.

"I don't know. At the time it seemed more like an old friend picking her up."

"So the bottom line is that she didn't look as if she was being taken against her will."

"No. Not at all."

Nikki frowned, surprised at his answer, while she tried to connect the dots. As far as they knew, Bridget had been expecting Sean to pick her up. The boy she'd fallen in love with. They knew now that there really was no *Sean Logan,* but Bridget presumably hadn't known this. So why would she have willingly gotten into the car with someone else? Had she known the man she'd left the cabin with?

"What about the driver? Can you tell me anything else about him?"

"Like I said I never got a close look at him, though he did switch on the overhead light briefly at one point. I think he was handing her something. My guess would be late forties, early fifties, Caucasian. I think he was wearing some kind of hat. I don't think I can give you much more than that."

"So he wasn't Bridget's age."

"Definitely not."

Then why had Bridget willingly gotten in the car with him? It didn't make sense. "Okay. I'd like you to work with the sketch artist to see if you can come up with a composite of our suspect."

"It'll be pretty basic, but I can try."

Whatever they came up with would be better than nothing. They'd put out a BOLO with the sketch and hope someone would recognize him. But once again—from what Knight had told them so far—the description was more than likely going to be too vague.

"You think he's involved?" Jack asked while Gwen set up Knight with a sketch artist at the precinct in town.

"I don't know. You have to admit there's something strange about his story. He drove two hours to give us a description."

"He did have an interview, Nikki. Gwen checked it out. Maybe he's just trying to be a hero. Get his name in the paper. You know, mystery writer solves case for police. I'd assume that would be great publicity."

Nikki laughed, but only to cover her growing frustration. "You're right. I just wanted answers so badly. Instead Knight claims she just got in the car with him. Why would she do that? Tell me, why would she get in a car with a man three times her age when she was expecting Sean Logan?"

An hour later, Nikki stuck the finished sketch of the man Knight saw onto the crime board next to the original composite police had come up with of the Angel Abductor. Generic enough it could be him. Or a hundred other men within a ten-mile radius.

She took a sip of the fresh cup of coffee she'd just poured while the others worked quietly at the workstations. She'd probably already ingested enough caffeine and sugar to keep her awake another twenty-four hours.

Why'd you get in that car with him, Bridget? And where are you now?

So many questions, and they were still no closer to finding her.

"Gwen, we need this sketch sent out to every law enforcement agency across the state."

"Already done." Gwen stepped up beside Nikki, hands on her hips. "I know that look on your face."

Nikki ignored the comment. Because that *look* conveyed that she was sick and tired of going in circles and still not having a substantial lead. "Can you see any similarities between the two sketches?"

"It's hard to tell. Same build, age is about right, but it's been a long time. Build and height are similar, but he could have had plastic surgery, his hair dyed, lost or gained weight . . ."

She was right. Ten years was a long time. They needed more.

"I don't want to keep grasping at straws that keep us running in the wrong direction, but there's clearly a connection between the cases. The stalking, the Polaroid . . ."

"How much of this information was given out to the public?" Gwen asked.

"Young girls. Blond. Buried them in shallow graves. The police left out the specifics of the Polaroid at the time, though I suppose it's not impossible to think it's public knowledge after all these years."

Sarah's abductor had been meticulous. This guy had left behind the Polaroid picture, which matched the MO. But finding Bridget's hat and phone just didn't fit.

"We have an eyewitness of Bridget's abductor,

but no real leads. She couldn't have just vanished without any trace."

And yet Nikki knew it was possible. Most criminals got caught because they were either too cocky, they talked to the wrong person, or they simply did something stupid.

But not this one. Not yet, anyway.

"This guy's smart," Nikki said.

"He seems smart because we haven't figured out who he is," Gwen said. "Most serial killers and serial abductors aren't brilliant. If they were, they wouldn't have low-level jobs and make such poor decisions."

Like murdering young girls.

"We've got the sketch out to the public," Gwen said. "Someone's going to see it and turn him in."

Before or after he kills her?

"Here's my question," Tyler said, looking up from the computer he was working on. "Why haven't we heard anything from this guy for the past ten years? If anything, from the information I've been reading about him, he was becoming more confident. Bolder with his abductions."

"I can think of half a dozen reasons why," Gwen said. "Maybe he's been in jail or sick or even dead. For all we know, whoever took Bridget is just a copycat."

"So all we really know is that person Bridget fell for, Sean Logan, doesn't exist," Tyler said, "but she still got into that car willingly."

"She didn't look so willing in that Polaroid shot," Nikki said. One thing no one could argue with was the fear in her eyes. "Which leaves us with another question. What happened between the time she got in that car and he took that photo? She might be young and impulsive, but from everything we know about Bridget, she's not stupid."

"Stupid, no, but you saw the stuff Jack came up with," Gwen said. "She was hurting and looking for love."

"Maybe our witness missed something," Gwen said.

"Or he was lying." Nikki knew she was going out on a limb, and a flimsy one at that, going back to Knight, but she didn't care. It was her job to examine every angle. Every potential suspect. "Maybe Jack was right when he said he was only after publicity, but what if Knight *is* the one who took her?"

"Then why would he come to us?"

"Maybe he thinks he can get information. Or maybe simply to satisfy the need to believe he's won."

Gwen didn't look convinced. "It wouldn't be the first time a perpetrator has posed as a witness, I'll give you that much. But Jack's been putting together a full background check on the man right now, and so far his story checks out."

"That doesn't mean he's innocent."

"You're talking about Brandon Knight?" Jack asked. He took off his earphones, then scooted his chair back.

"Yes. Why?" Nikki asked.

"I might have a few answers for you. Brandon Knight was telling the truth . . . just not all of the truth."

Nikki frowned. "What do you mean?"

"I called his agent a little bit ago. He's been fairly successful as a midlist mystery writer. And according to his agent, he really does have a deadline next week. He's received a few small awards here and there, but she said his book numbers have been dropping over the past few years. His one bestseller was a true-crime novel based on the murder of that A-list actress Riley Holmes."

"That was a bizarre case," Nikki said. Riley Holmes had been murdered fifteen years ago in a ritualistic killing the night before her long-awaited movie premiere, causing a huge stir in Hollywood and across the nation at the time.

"After that, he switched to writing mystery novels, thinking he'd ride the wave of the success of his breakthrough novel."

"But switching genres didn't work for him?" Nikki asked.

"Nope. He never gained the audience he'd hoped for and has only had moderate success ever since."

"Why didn't he go back to writing true crimes?" Gwen asked.

"Apparently he has. Or at least, he's trying to. His appointment was with a woman by the name of Shirley Roberts. Her husband, some Wall Street genius, was murdered two years ago, and it became another high-profile case. But after a bit of digging, I discovered she changed her mind about helping him with the book and canceled on him. Apparently he was going there to try to convince her to change her mind."

"Because without her, he doesn't have much of a story," Nikki said.

"Exactly."

"I don't get it, though," Gwen said. "What does all of that have to do with our Angel Abductor?"

"Maybe he thinks his luck just changed," Jack said. "He meets a girl and her family, then sees the man who abducted her."

"He's planning to play the hero and get a story," Nikki said.

"But that isn't all the news I have," Jack continued, clearly pleased with himself. "I've also been going through the text messages from the last twenty-four hours on Bridget's phone and found one from Sean."

"And . . . ," Nikki prodded.

"He told her he had a flat tire but was sending his older brother to pick her up. He was going to meet them as soon as he got his tire fixed."

Nikki's stomach clenched as a piece of the puzzle fell into place. "Now we know why she got into that car with him without a fight."

"Can you trace the number he used?" Nikki asked.

"I tried, but it's a dead end. Another burner phone, and it's been turned off."

Nikki felt her frustration grow. "I suppose I get the whole 'she was just looking for someone to love her' scenario, but there had to have been red flags along the way. Something in her gut that was telling her things were off."

"Love can be blind," Jack said. "How many women have you known who fall for the wrong guy and choose not to see it? That's why we have domestic abuse cases of women who never leave."

"He's going to kill her if we don't find her," Nikki said. "You both realize that, don't you? And because of what? Because she trusted some guy she met over the internet. Believed he wouldn't lie to her, and then got in the car with a stranger because he said it was all right?"

"After the Angel Abductor took his victims, what did he do with them?" Jack asked.

"And how much time do you think we're looking at?" Gwen added.

"Three out of the four were killed and buried within forty-eight hours."

"So he could be here looking for a place to bury her," Gwen said.

The thought set off a familiar wave of panic in Nikki's gut. Because everything she knew about their presumed killer pointed to the fact that if they didn't find her—now—Bridget Ellison was as good as dead.

11

What were they missing? Nikki tapped her fingers against the conference room table in the back of their mobile command post while thunder rumbled in the distance. The dark clouds she'd seen this morning were supposed to bring with them a storm by tomorrow morning. She'd spent the last hour going over all of the notes Gwen had made, trying to dig deeper. But he'd hidden his tracks well. And even with Brandon Knight's information, they still didn't have enough to identify the man who had Bridget.

She drew in a breath, then slowly let it out, trying to let go of the tension that had settled in her muscles. A plate of forgotten pizza one of the volunteers had brought earlier lay shoved aside next to her. She should eat. Should take a break. But fear for Bridget had been compounded by worry over her sister-in-law and the baby and the memories of Sarah she couldn't seem to shake today.

Like that last family dinner they'd eaten together at her parents' restaurant.

For twenty-seven years her mom and dad had worked tirelessly to keep Boyds' BBQ in business. It had been a family effort. Nikki had learned the value of hard work by washing dishes on weekends in high school, then later waitressing all the way through college.

Despite the hard work and long nights, she'd never come to resent her parents. Somehow, family had always managed to come first. Like Sunday nights. They'd grab their favorite corner booth, stuff themselves on her dad's barbeque, and spend an hour catching up on what had happened during the week while live music played in the background of the packed joint.

"I understand someone's birthday is just around the corner," her dad had said, digging into his plate of barbeque, coleslaw, fried okra, and Mama's homemade jalapeño corn bread.

"I sent out my invitations yesterday," Sarah said.

"I heard there's a certain boy on the invite list." Luke, older than Sarah by two years, was constantly teasing her.

Sarah shrugged like it was nothing, but the gleam behind her blue eyes said otherwise.

"Give her a break, Luke." Matt was always the first to jump in and rescue Sarah.

"Come on," Luke said. "I'm just curious. Does this boy like you?"

Sarah frowned at the question. "He . . . I don't know . . . He always acts goofy around me."

"That means he likes you, Sarah," Nikki said, popping a piece of fried okra into her mouth.

Sarah nudged Nikki with her elbow. "You're saying that because you're my sister. I'm not sure he even knows I exist."

"I'm saying that because it's true," Nikki said. "Boys have weird ways of showing girls they like them. Like acting goofy."

"I confess, it's true," Matt said, holding up his hands in defeat. "And it worked with Jamie. I've decided to ask her to marry me."

Matt and Jamie had married eight months later, and from day one, Jamie had wanted half a dozen kids. But a string of miscarriages and months of doctor appointments and tests had set them on a path they hadn't signed up for. Everything had finally changed with this baby. At least, that was what they'd believed.

Nikki quickly checked the messages on her cell phone, hoping she'd just missed hearing from her mom while she'd been busy working. But there was nothing. She let out a sharp sigh, wondering if she should interpret that as good or bad.

She dialed her mom's number, deciding that doing something was better than worrying. The call went straight to voice mail.

"Mom . . . hey, it's Nikki. I haven't heard from you for a while, so I thought I'd check in. Just give me a call with an update when you get a chance."

She ended the call, still trying not to worry.

Her mom was probably just in a part of the hospital that had bad cell phone reception. Which was normal. It didn't signal that there was necessarily a problem.

"Nikki?" Gwen called her over from the other room, pulling her away from her thoughts and back to where she needed to be at the moment. Her being distracted wasn't going to help them find Bridget. "We've got another call that just came in that's worth checking out."

"What have you got?" Nikki asked, heading into where Gwen and Anderson were sitting at the workstation.

"I was just patched in on a call from someone who says he saw a man fitting the description of the man in the sketch."

"The sketch our mystery writer gave?"

Gwen nodded.

"Where did the call come from?" Nikki asked.

"Right here in the park. They were on the Little River Road when they saw him. Man said his name was . . ." Gwen glanced down at her notes. "Robert Hayes. His wife's name is Dorothy. He said that he and his wife were driving this direction from Cades Cove and had planned to spend half a day driving through the park. They had stopped at one of the trails and saw him heading to his car. They had the flyer and called right away. I've got the exact location written down."

"You think it's legit?" Nikki asked.

"They gave me a license plate number and a description of a car. It was a black, four-door Chevy Impala. Said by the time they were able to get back to their car, he was pulling out, headed in the direction of Cades Cove."

"Got a name on the car?" Nikki asked, hovering over Gwen and her computer.

"One second . . . Yeah. Here it is. It's registered to a Justin Miller. He's got an address about five miles outside Gatlinburg on a couple acres of land and, it looks like, a pretty extensive record."

Nikki went and stood in front of the park map they'd added to the whiteboard. "How far up the road would that put him?" she asked Anderson.

"Fairly close," Anderson said. "There have been several bear sightings the past hour as well, which means traffic is moving slow. If he has her, he'll want to blend in and keep to the speed limit."

"What if he dumped her body?" Gwen asked the question Nikki had wanted to ignore. "I'm sorry—"

"No." Nikki shook her head. "We have to look at all the possibilities. Get a team out to his property and see if they can find anything."

"And I'll get a group of rangers and a tracking dog to the location now to do a quick search of the trail and nearby riverbank where they saw him," Anderson said.

"Good." Nikki tapped on the map. "Where do you think he's going?"

"Definitely looks like he's headed west in the direction of Cades Cove, but there are a couple other ways out of the park along that road. Here . . . and here," he said, pointing to the map.

Which meant if they didn't find him soon, the chances of losing him grew with every minute that passed.

"Gwen, let's get Gatlinburg police to set up roadblocks on these spots." Nikki grabbed her jacket off the back of a chair. "Can you get me out there as well, Anderson?"

"I've got my vehicle here in the parking lot and can take you myself," Anderson said, grabbing his keys.

"Great." Nikki nodded at the officer, then turned to Tyler, who was still working. "Want to come with us, Tyler? After what happened this morning, who knows . . . we might need you."

"If you need me, I'm there," Tyler said.

She nodded her thanks, then headed out the door with the men behind her. She did need him. More than she'd realized.

A minute later Nikki slid into the passenger seat of the ranger's car, her adrenaline pumping with expectation. She'd been in this situation a hundred times. A hopeful lead—like the phone call—was what kept them moving. All she could do now was pray it was enough.

She tried to relax as Anderson followed the winding road away from the visitor center, intent on finding their suspect. The view from the road was stunning, which meant traffic was heavy with tourists enjoying an afternoon drive. Below them, the Little River ran parallel to the road with its rapids, small waterfalls, and ferns. Along the road were overlooks, trailheads, picnic areas, and paved hikes. All places where their abductor could potentially hide out.

This wasn't the first time Nikki had taken this route, but today, she barely saw the picturesque view millions of visitors flocked to each year. Instead, Bridget's photo was seared across the front of her mind.

"I keep going back to the same question," Nikki said, still needing to work through the facts they had. "If this is him, why head into the park that's packed with tourists?"

"It would make sense that he's running scared," Anderson said.

"Maybe, but like I've said before, everything he's done has seemed clear and calculated. Stalking her. Arranging to meet her. Leaving us the photo. He's got a plan."

He'd stalked her for months, while gaining her confidence, and got her to trust him enough to pick her up from where she was staying despite the fact that he wasn't Sean Logan. Running scared just didn't fit.

"Which means he knows the park," Tyler said.

Anderson pressed through the tourist traffic, flashing his lights when needed, in order to get through.

"I think you're right, Tyler, but why the park? No matter how I look at it, it still seems like a foolish move."

"If you ask me," Anderson said, "it's the perfect place to get lost. There are plenty of stories of people who simply vanish in crowds."

Nikki glanced at the officer. "Simply vanishing seems so . . . final?"

But she knew it was possible. Someone had taken her sister, and after ten years and thousands of man-hours logged, Sarah had vanished without a trace.

"We look for twenty, maybe thirty missing people a year," Anderson continued. "Most of them we find within twelve to twenty-four hours. Only a small handful of cases take months. But then there are those who've never been found. A year ago, a six-year-old was playing hide-and-seek, hid behind a bush, and completely vanished, despite efforts of law enforcement, the National Guard, and thousands of volunteers. A girl vanished in 1976 while on a school field trip. Again, thousands of volunteers spent months looking for the teen but never found a trace of her. Five years later a woman was hiking with friends and went missing. All of them seemingly vanished into thin air. If you don't want to be found, this park is as good as it gets."

Nikki had studied the cases he'd mentioned. Some hinted at the possibility of a serial killer or an opportunistic predator. Others were convinced Bigfoot was involved, or that the victims had encountered a natural phenomenon like a mine shaft or some kind of sharp drop-off. Just the dense undergrowth of the park made searching in some areas impossible.

But the risk of bringing Bridget here still outweighed the advantage, in Nikki's mind.

"What's your personal explanation of people who have vanished in the park?" Nikki asked.

Anderson made his way around another car whose occupants had stopped to watch a white-tailed deer. "It's hard to say, but there are as many explanations as there are people who have opinions. In each of these cases, none of the victims were ever found. They just . . . vanished. No bodies, no clues, no suspects, nothing. I know I've never encountered Bigfoot. Which pretty much leaves two possibilities. Either they died from natural causes, or they were abducted."

Anderson's radio buzzed with a call from dispatch. Another ranger had just spotted the suspect's car.

"Suspect's vehicle has just passed the Elkmont turnoff, but he's refusing to pull over," the dispatcher relayed.

"How far ahead are they?" Nikki asked.

"A quarter of a mile at the most," Anderson responded, still trying to maneuver through the traffic.

Red brake lights flashed in front of them. Nikki strained to see what was going on. A dozen cars were stopped in the middle of the road, blocking the way.

Nikki's fingers tapped against the armrest. "We've got to get around them."

The ranger eased his vehicle through the line of cars. A man had climbed out of his car, camera in hand. A group of kids hung out the window, next to an SUV with its back hatch open.

"There's a bear up ahead causing the holdup," Anderson said, pointing to the right.

Nikki spotted the bear close to the side of the road, digging for bugs in a tree. Anderson flashed his lights, not wanting to scare the animal as he weaved carefully through the line of cars until they were finally out of the bottleneck and could speed forward.

A minute later, Nikki spotted the second ranger vehicle.

"The suspect's car's in front of him," Tyler said.

Anderson flipped on his lights, then sped to catch up with the two vehicles.

"He's still not stopping," Nikki said.

God, please let her be here. Let her be alive . . . Please.

Nikki felt her heart race as the suspect's vehicle sped up. He'd been meticulous up to this point, but everyone had a weak point. It was too easy to believe you had everything under control. To miss a crucial detail that in the end would become your downfall. This situation was no different.

The car ahead of them picked up speed down the narrow, tree-lined road.

"This is what I was hoping to avoid," Anderson said, gripping the wheel as he pressed on the accelerator.

The vehicle swerved ahead of them, barely avoiding hitting another car head-on. Over-compensating, it fishtailed, then veered off the road to the left, slid down the steep embankment, and plunged into the river below.

12

Nikki watched, horrified, as the car slammed into the riverbed. The current swept over the hood. The vehicle bobbed for a moment, then settled against the rocks.

If Bridget was in there . . .

She banged on the dashboard. "Stop the car. I'm getting out."

Anderson pulled over and slammed on his brakes. The other rangers were already heading down the embankment.

"Go. Both of you," Tyler shouted. "I'll contact park dispatch to report the emergency, then direct traffic before some rubbernecker causes another accident."

"Make sure the search and rescue team responds along with the rescue vehicle. With that storm coming in, the river's already started to rise."

Nikki was already out of the car, crossing the road. She skidded down the steep embankment, glad she still had her sturdy boots on. Two rangers had already made it to the suspect's car. Anderson followed behind her. The river wasn't deep enough to completely swallow the vehicle, but the impact of the crash could have been enough to seriously injure the passengers inside.

God, don't let it end this way. Not when we might have just found her . . . Please, God . . . Please . . .

Water swirled around her legs as she stepped into Little River, the coldness sucking her breath away. She pushed against the current, making her way to the car behind the other officers, who were opening the driver's door. Water gushed into the car and lapped against the man who sat clutching the wheel. A trickle of blood ran down his temple.

The similarities between the man and the sketch were uncanny. And add to that the fact he'd tried to run . . .

One of the rangers held up his hand to stop her from approaching the car. "Ma'am, I'm going to have to ask you to—"

"I'm Special Agent Boyd with the Tennessee Bureau of Investigation."

"She's with us, Bruce," Anderson said, coming around the vehicle behind her.

Nikki looked through the windows of the backseat and the front passenger side. Except for the driver, the car was empty.

Where was Bridget?

The rangers pulled the driver from the car, pinning down his arms when he started to pull away.

"Justin Miller?" She walked up to the man,

shouting above the roar of the water. What if it was too late? What if he'd already killed her? Buried her? "Tell me. Where is she?"

He struggled to keep his balance between the officers as the water rushed past their legs. "Who?"

"Bridget Ellison. Is she in the car?"

"I don't know what you're talking about." His gaze pierced through her like a steel blade.

"Tell me where she is!"

Anger coursed through her when he didn't answer. She slid into the driver's seat. The front windshield was cracked but not broken. Water lapped at her calves. She was looking for something . . . anything that might give a clue that Bridget had been here. A couple of beer cans floated in the water next to a cell phone, a charger, and a ball cap. But no obvious sign Bridget had ever been here.

Grabbing the cell phone before it floated away, Nikki shoved it into her pocket, popped the trunk, then trudged through the rushing water toward the back of the car. It was the only other place to look. Hiding Bridget in the trunk made sense. He wouldn't have wanted anyone to see her.

The trunk opened. Spare tire, jumper cables, a flashlight, a couple of empty water bottles, a tactical rifle case, a small ice chest, and some hunting gear.

But Bridget wasn't in the car.

Nikki slammed the trunk shut, then sloshed back through the water toward the embankment and the officers.

"Find anything?" Anderson asked.

"She's not here, but there's a rifle case and hunting supplies." Nikki's stomach twisted, the disappointment palatable. "Found a cell phone we might get something out of."

"I've already got a crew coming to get the car pulled out, but you need to get out of the water. You're going to freeze."

Miller looked at her again with his icy gaze. He had to be lying. It had to be him. The Angel Abductor. The man who took Bridget. Late forties. About the right height. She stood near enough that she could smell the liquor on his breath and clenched her hands at her sides, straining with everything she had not to belt him.

"Wait," Nikki said.

The officer holding Miller paused.

"Tell me, where is she?"

"Who?"

"The girl you abducted this morning."

"Abducted? Are you crazy?" The man laughed. "I thought you were after me for DUI. So I had one too many. Arrest me."

"We're planning to. But I also have a witness who can put you at the scene of the abduction. And there are weapons in the back of your car."

"I haven't broken any laws by having a weapon in my vehicle, and I didn't abduct anyone."

"We'll give you time to question him back at the ranger station, Agent Boyd," Anderson said, starting up the embankment. "For now, we all need to get out of this river."

Miller shot her a twisted smile as he looked back at her. He was lying. Hiding something. She had to be on the right track. Maybe he was working with someone. Maybe he had already killed her. But he knew who Bridget was.

He brushed past her as he and the officers made their way toward the embankment. The moment she moved in behind them, he jerked away from the officers, knocking one over. Before anyone could react, he grabbed her and dragged her away from the car in the thigh-deep water.

Nikki felt his icy grip on one arm, the other around her neck. She felt the blade of a knife pressed against her throat as Miller stumbled away from the ranger back into the water, dragging her with him.

Immediately the officers drew their weapons.

"Don't do this," Anderson said, weapon raised, a half-dozen feet away from them.

Nikki fought to control her panic. If he'd taken Bridget—if he was the Angel Abductor—he was capable of murder.

"There's nowhere to escape," Anderson shouted above the rush of the water. "Let her go."

Miller pulled Nikki back a step from the car, the icy water swirling around them. "I swear I'll kill her."

Nikki glanced around her. Heavy rains in the past month had made the water level higher than normal. She looked up at the embankment. A crowd was growing at the top. Tyler and another officer were making their way toward them. She could see the fear in Tyler's eyes. But the officer was right. Miller might think he could get away with this, but there was nowhere for him to go.

Despite that, he pulled her back another step, dragging her deeper into the strong current. After absorbing a number of smaller streams, the river had gained considerable strength at this point, causing her to have to struggle to keep her balance. Miller took another step back across the uneven bottom of the river, while the blade of the knife pressed harder against her neck.

"He's right. There is no way out of this." Nikki fought to keep her voice even. "This is only going to make things harder for you."

"You're accusing me of kidnapping someone. Another strike and they'll put me away for life."

"If you're innocent, adding the abduction of a government agent isn't going to help you. Just tell me where she is."

"Help me? Right. You already believe I'm guilty."

He took another step backward, pulling her with him. He clearly wasn't thinking rationally. The water was getting deeper. Nikki fought against the cold. Teeth chattering uncontrollably, she waited for an opportunity to slip away from his grip. He took another step and stumbled. A second later, he was under the water. Nikki's knees buckled as he dragged her with him. Water swept over her, pulling her downstream, farther away from the officers.

He was still hanging on to her, dragging her with him as the current pulled them away from the car and the officers. Nikki gasped for air as she went under, trying not to panic. She'd read of drownings in this river. While parts of the river were a lazy oasis for tourists, there were other sections with strong currents and hidden sinkholes. Fighting against his grip, she tried to find her footing, but the water was too fast at this point. Her limbs too numb.

She managed to surface and grab another deep breath of air before Miller pulled her under again. But they were going too fast.

His fingers dug into her arm. She sank into the darkness. Nikki fought for air. Her head smashed against a rock. Stars exploded. But she had to stay conscious. Had to get away from him, or both of them were going to drown.

Images flashed through her mind as she fought for the surface. Sarah . . . Bridget . . . Jamie . . . Tyler . . .

Struggling to keep her head above the water, Nikki drew in another deep breath. With every ounce of energy she could muster, she dove down into the water, breaking away from Miller's grasp. He tried to grab her, but she swam deeper until she was finally free.

Seconds later, with her lungs burning, she made it to the surface and drew in a breath, but she was still unable to get her footing as the current dragged her farther downstream. She could see Miller's red shirt as he bobbed a few feet away. Struggling to stay above the surface of the water.

They were shouting for her. Tyler, Anderson, and the rangers. Somewhere nearby, but she couldn't see them. Her arms ached; her head throbbed from where she'd hit it. She knew the rangers trained for swift-water rescues, learning to use the current to actually assist in the rescue. But most of the time there was no way to overcome the power of the water.

Her legs hit something and she stumbled to her feet as she felt the bottom of the river.

"Nikki?"

Something slapped the water beside her. She grabbed for the rope connected to a flotation device. With the water churning around her, there was no way to put the vest on properly. Sliding her hands through the armholes, she pulled it as tight as she could against her chest.

The rope went taut. They were pulling her toward them. Carrying her up the embankment. Tyler was suddenly there, wrapping his arms around her. Telling her to be still. Telling her that everything was going to be okay. But she couldn't stop shaking. Couldn't feel her hands.

"It's cold . . . so cold."

"I know, baby. I know. But you're okay now. I've got you."

Someone handed Tyler a blanket. He wrapped it around her, still holding her tight. She could feel his breath against her face. His arm around her shoulders. Warm. Secure. Safe.

"Where is he?" she asked, worried about Miller. If they lost him, they'd lose the only lead they had to Bridget.

"They're pulling him out now. This part of the river is shallow."

"I can walk," she said, then questioned her statement. Her legs felt like jelly.

"Are you sure?"

She nodded, but was thankful he didn't let go of her. She had to keep pushing herself if they were going to find out what he'd done with Bridget. Her legs burned as she made her way back up the embankment, her head spinning as she tried to walk.

Tyler was still holding on to her when they

made it to the road. "We're almost there, Nikki."

At the top, Tyler took another blanket and wrapped it around her shoulders.

"Did they get him?" She searched the river.

"Yeah, Anderson and another guy just pulled him out."

"I want to question him as soon as we get back."

"You're not doing anything until we get you warm and checked out."

"That was him, Tyler, but she wasn't there. She was supposed to be in that car."

"We're going to find her, Nikki."

"I don't know anymore. What if we're too late?"

Tyler sat her down in the back of a squad car that had just pulled up and wrapped his arm around her waist. "We'll wait here for the ambulance."

"I'm fine, Tyler. I need to talk to Miller—"

"You can talk to Miller, but for now, I'm going to make sure you're okay."

She nodded, too tired to argue. Her teeth were still chattering. Her head still throbbed. She needed to focus. But she'd hoped with this lead that all of this would be over. That she could go back to Nashville with Tyler. See her family. But Bridget was still out there somewhere.

Nikki watched as Anderson and another officer topped the embankment with Miller, hand-cuffed him, and led him toward the other vehicle.

"Why wasn't she there?" she asked.

"I don't know, Nikki. Maybe it's not him. You know as well as I do that the description was vague. Someone knows a girl is missing. They see a man who fits the description and they call it in. Maybe it was nothing more than that. A coincidence."

"Then why did he run? She's here, Tyler. I can feel it. He never took his victims far, but he always had a plan. We have to figure out what that plan is before it's too late."

Nikki leaned her head against Tyler's shoulder, his arms tight around her, as she closed her eyes and started praying.

13

Gwen handed Nikki a stack of clothes she'd managed to come up with. Her third set for the day. "Compliments of Anderson's wife."

"I need to meet her. She's a lifesaver."

"She's about your size. Even the shoes should fit," Gwen said, shooting her a sympathetic gaze. "Which is good because yours are going to take awhile to dry out. Do you need anything else?"

"Another mug of hot coffee?" Nikki asked. Medics had checked her out and deemed her fit to go back to work despite Tyler's clear, yet unspoken, objections. "Never imagined the water would be so cold this time of year."

"You got it." Gwen walked with her down the short hallway. "You can change here in the staff bathroom. That will give you a bit more privacy. As soon as you're ready, we'll head to the station to meet with Miller. Jack has already left."

"Thanks."

Nikki locked the bathroom door behind her, then started peeling off her wet clothes. She pulled on the gray T-shirt and jeans that looked to be about her size. The coral zippered fleece might not be classified under professional attire, but it would help warm her up. At this point she wasn't sure she was ever going to thaw out again.

She studied her pale reflection in the mirror, knowing that what she was feeling wasn't simply about what had happened out there in the river. She'd been scared, but she'd get over being held at knifepoint. It was the possibility she'd looked into the eyes of her sister's abductor that had chilled her more than the icy waters.

Which was why she was second-guessing her ability to control her emotions. What if she *had* made a mistake in taking this job? Her first time to take the lead on a case and she was falling apart. That couldn't happen. She'd allowed everything about this case to become personal, which in turn had left her struggling to function. Memories swept through her like she was back in the river. Pulling her under, out of control, and she didn't know how to fight back. Wasn't sure she knew how to come up for air.

Nikki took in a deep breath, tugged down the bottom of her shirt, then glanced back into the mirror. She ignored her bloodshot eyes as she tried to do something with her damp hair. Not that it mattered.

She needed answers from Miller, but that wasn't all she needed. She needed to talk to her mom. To hear that everything was okay. Everything was going to be okay. That Jamie and the baby were fine. That they'd find Bridget. And in the process, they'd find Sarah's abductor.

She pulled out her cell phone and speed-dialed her mom's number, about to leave another message when she finally answered.

"Mom?"

"Nikki. Are you okay?"

She hesitated. "Yeah. I just . . . I just wanted to check in." *And hear your voice.* "I hadn't heard from you for a while. I left a voice message earlier."

"The cell phone use is limited where I am. But what about you? I've been worried about the girl you're looking for. Have you found her yet?"

The question hovered between them like a heavy weight. Nikki had taken on a job she couldn't afford to fail, because if she did . . . Bridget would become yet another statistic.

"No. Not yet." Nikki pressed her back against the bathroom wall and stared at the white tiles. She could hear the worry in her mother's voice. She didn't have to talk about her cases to know that her mother followed every news update on missing children. Always a reminder of what she'd lost.

"We think she was abducted and taken into the park. I'm going to interview a suspect right now, but I wanted to find out about Jamie and the baby. I've been worried."

There was a long pause, on her mother's end this time. Nikki's stomach churned.

"I was waiting for some news before I called

you," her mother finally said. "We still don't know anything."

Oh, God, please . . . please . . . don't let anything happen to either of them.

"I'm scared, Nikki," her mom continued. "This baby means so much to both of them. And Matt. For him to lose them both . . ."

"She's going to make it, Mom." She had to. "Jamie's strong, and this baby . . ."

This baby was a gift. God wouldn't take their baby away from them. They'd waited so long . . . Except sometimes God didn't save those they loved. Sometimes he allowed horrible things to happen.

"They're going to be okay, Mom. Just promise you'll call me with an update as soon as you know something. Please."

"I will, sweetie. I promise."

Nikki hung up, still trying to press in emotions that refused to stay locked up. All the potential problems she'd been warned about when she took this job. Fear that the emotional impact of the cases would get under her skin. That there was no way she'd be able to separate the past from what she had to do. That she'd end up running on feelings and not just the facts.

Had she already gotten to that point? The point where she was so desperate to find Bridget and her abductor that she was grasping at straws and seeing things that weren't really there?

A knock on the door pulled her back to the present.

"Nikki? You okay?"

Nikki wiped away the tears under her eyes, drew in a deep breath, and opened the door. Tyler stood outside.

"I just wanted to check on you," he said.

"I'm fine." She sucked in another deep breath of air. "All I need is the coffee Gwen promised, and I'll be ready to go."

She smiled, hoping to convince him she was telling the truth. Because she wasn't going to tell him that while her hands might not be shaking anymore, her insides still felt like Jell-O. Didn't want him to know that all she really wanted to do was run.

He leaned against the wall beside her. "You know, we could leave for Nashville now and be there in a few hours. Your family needs you. And even with that photo of Bridget, your team can handle this."

She shook her head. "No, I have to do this. I have to find her."

"Why? Because of guilt over Sarah?"

"No, because . . ." She stopped and turned to face him, reminding herself that Tyler had nothing to do with the anger simmering in her gut. "I have to do this because this is my job."

She started back toward the parking lot. Maybe her job *had* become an unconscious act of trying to redeem herself. So that every time she saved someone, it managed to chip away at the mountain of guilt she carried in her heart.

Except even she knew that saving Bridget wouldn't bring back Sarah. Or erase the layer of guilt she carried with her.

"Nikki . . ." Tyler reached out and grabbed her hand, stopping her in the middle of the hall-way. "I thought I was going to lose you."

She looked up at him, her eyes rimmed with tears, and caught the pain in his expression. "You didn't lose me. You're not going to lose me."

"I know." He ran his thumb across the back of her hand and pulled it against his chest. "It's just that seeing you in the water . . . It reminded me of the day I lost Katie. I watched Miller grab you—"

"It's okay," she said, wrapping her arms around his neck and feeling him pull her against him. "I'm okay."

Or at least she would be.

He held her tightly as memories swirled around both of them. He made her feel safe. Made her feel certain that nothing bad could happen to her as long as he held her. And made her wish he'd never let go.

"I need to talk to Miller," she said, finally pulling back.

"I know."

He walked with her down the hall, holding her

hand as he matched her strides. "Do you think he's the Angel Abductor?"

"It's possible. He fits the description."

"I just want you to be careful. Please. I know too well how emotions can tangle up your ability to see straight."

She stepped out into the fading afternoon sunshine, knowing he was right. And at the same time, hating that he was right. Her emotions *were* affecting her ability to look completely objectively at the situation. But she also couldn't forget that she was good at what she did. And while she trusted Jack and Gwen completely, they needed what she knew in this situation.

A minute later, Anderson drove her and Gwen to the Gatlinburg police station, where they'd booked Miller for driving under the influence as well as kidnapping and threatening the life of an officer. Nikki hoped to add kidnapping of Bridget to the charges.

Jack met her outside the interrogation room. "So far, he's refusing to cooperate."

"Has he asked for a lawyer?"

"No. He just keeps insisting he knows nothing about an abduction."

"He knows something. We just have to figure out what."

She'd seen his eyes. He was hiding something.

She stepped into the small interrogation room and studied his profile as he sat at the rectangular table. The cockiness she'd seen earlier had gone, replaced by a hint of fear in his eyes. So much for not believing he had anything to lose.

"I'm Special Agent Boyd. I'm part of the Tennessee Missing Persons Task Force." She sat down across from him. "What were you doing in the park?"

"What do you think I was doing?" He sat across from her, arms folded against his chest, jaw stuck out defiantly. "I was there like everyone else. I needed some time away. Normally, it's quiet and peaceful up here . . . until my brakes go out and a bunch of cops wrestle me out of my car."

"Your blood alcohol level was above the legal limit, which by itself could mean up to a year in jail and the loss of your license," Nikki said.

"So I had a couple of drinks."

"Did you see the flyer about the missing girl when you entered the park?"

"Yeah, along with every other person. And I saw the sketch of the man who took her, but that isn't me."

"Really?" Nikki held the sketch in front of her. "If you ask me, it looks a lot like you."

"I already told you I drank a few too many, but I didn't abduct the girl."

Nikki shoved a photo of Bridget in front of him. "So you're telling me you've never seen this girl."

"No. If I had seen her, I would have called it in."

"Here's the problem. We have a witness who saw someone matching your description this morning outside of Wartburg, where Bridget Ellison got in a car with you."

"Wartburg? That's two hours away. I spent the night in the park last night." Miller steepled his hands in front of him. "And I'll say this one more time. I don't know anything about the girl."

"If you weren't guilty, then why didn't you stop? And why did you grab me?"

Miller's gaze dropped. "I panicked, but I didn't take some girl."

Nikki slapped her hands against the table, then scooted her chair back before signaling Jack to join her outside the room.

"We're not getting anywhere," she said, closing the door behind them.

"You think he's telling the truth?" Jack asked.

"About Bridget? I don't know. Maybe, but I still think he's hiding something."

"Listen, Nikki," Jack said. "I know you want to find Bridget's abductor, and trust me, so do I, but the evidence we've got is still too vague. What if he's telling the truth? What if we have the wrong person?"

"Then what do we do next?"

"We keep looking."

Gwen made her way down the hallway toward them. "I think I might have something. I've been going through Miller's file. Besides his other run-ins with the law, he was arrested three years ago as a part of an illegal poaching ring."

Nikki frowned. "That doesn't prove he didn't have something to do with Bridget's abduction."

"Not in itself, but there's more. Officers at the scene of the crash not only found the hunting supplies you saw in the trunk but an illegal cache of bear parts in the ice chest, and bear bait."

"You've got to be kidding me," Nikki said. "He almost drowned me over bear parts."

"I know you wanted it to be him, but so far they haven't found any evidence that Bridget was in his car."

Nikki frowned, realizing her best lead had more than likely just evaporated. Poaching explained the gun and hunting supplies. He'd go down for DUI, illegal hunting, and the attempted kidnapping of an officer.

But not for kidnapping Bridget.

"It doesn't surprise me," Jack said. "I had a buddy involved in an undercover job. They infiltrated the poachers' social circles and illegal hunting parties and took down dozens of them. Hunters will pay up to a thousand dollars for guaranteed kills."

"I've heard of this, but how do they get away with it?"

"They're good at evading the rangers and game wardens. They're not out there hunting in front of people. It's done on the side, at night."

"If you're right about Miller, that means we're back to square one. Again." Nikki reached up and touched the tender spot on her head where she'd hit it against the rock, and frowned. "I want to go in there one more time. We can use this new information as leverage to make sure he wasn't involved with Bridget's disappearance."

Jack nodded. "Okay."

Back inside the interrogation room, Nikki sat down across from Miller. "We have some updated information on you, Mr. Miller, starting with the fact that you lied to us."

"I wasn't lying. I said I didn't kidnap that girl."

"Maybe not, but there's something else."

"What are you talking about?" Miller slammed his hands against the table. "I was in the park—"

"Doing what? Poaching? Because we have evidence suggesting you weren't exactly in the park on an afternoon drive. I suggest you tell us the truth unless you want to be charged with kidnapping."

His gaze shifted as he weighed his answer. "I was hunting."

"Where?"

"On the border of the park."

"Were you with anyone?" Jack asked.

"I was by myself."

"Mr. Miller, I suggest you stop and think before you tell me another lie."

"I was with a client last night. I bait the bears

with food, luring them to return repeatedly to the same spot, then when they come back, I can guarantee a kill for my client. Their behavior is pretty easy to predict."

"And then you sell the bear parts?" Jack asked.

Miller avoided their gaze. "I've got a few buyers."

"The money must be pretty tempting. Money from your clients for every kill. Additional money to sell the parts your clients don't care about." Jack leaned forward, bracing his arms against the table. "I want names. You can either go down for hunting violations, or we'll press on with the kidnapping charges."

"No way. I know what the fine is. I'll go with the hunting violations. I was poaching."

"That's a smart choice, I suppose. Most violations are classified as criminal misdemeanor and come with a two-thousand-dollar fine and a two-year hunting license revocation." Jack leaned forward again, smiling. "But here's the thing. You were caught on federal land with bear parts in the back of your car, which means we can see that your charge is elevated to a federal crime. That, along with what you did to my partner here, will get you a whole lot more prison time."

Miller's face paled, but the victory was hollow. The man might be going to prison for a long time, but that meant they were back to square one with Bridget.

174

14

Nikki stood in front of the whiteboard, staring at the sketch of their suspect while trying to connect the dots in her mind. Missing persons cases meant continual revising of their plan of action as the investigation developed. Coordinating with other agencies—including now the FBI, notifying all of the missing persons registries, utilizing the media, investigating family and witnesses, and monitoring volunteers. And at the same time continually praying they weren't missing some-thing.

Gwen handed her the updated media report. "You look tired."

"It's been a long day, but I'm fine."

"Have you eaten yet? If you wait too long, that Chinese takeout someone just brought in is going to be gone, and let me tell you, it's good."

Nikki tapped the file against her palm and laughed. "Hungry or not, I have a feeling Tyler's going to make sure I eat something."

Gwen glanced across the small space to where Tyler was working while listening to music with a pair of earphones, then leaned forward, her voice lowered. "I know I'm being nosy, but are the two of you dating? I noticed he doesn't wear a ring, and if he happens to be single . . ."

"We're just friends." Nikki pressed her lips together, wondering what Tyler would think about the question. As far as she knew, dating wasn't even a blip on his radar. "He lost his wife a year ago in an accident. We planned to spend the day together remembering her. Katie was my best friend."

"Oh. Wow. I'm so sorry." Gwen took a step back and shook her head. "That was completely out of line of me. I know they're out there, but sometimes decent men are so hard to find. He seems like a really great guy."

"He is a great guy. Don't worry about it. There was no way for you to know."

"Still . . . I know you're handling a lot. To have to deal with a friend's death on top of every-thing else today. We all know this is personal for you." Gwen's smile faded. "You've met my sister, Raine."

Nikki leaned back against the desk. "Yeah, she's what . . . fourteen?"

"Thirteen going on twenty-one." Gwen laughed. "But I keep thinking about how I'd feel if that were my sister out there. Even with our job, I honestly can't imagine what it would really be like to not know where she was."

"It's hard not to worry, isn't it?" Nikki said.

"I worry about her all the time. If something happened to her like what happened to Bridget

. . . and to your sister. Because of this job I know the statistics. I see the families' reactions and what they have to cope with, but I know that doesn't make it the same as being in your shoes as someone who's been there." Gwen hesitated. "I'm just not sure how you do it. How you do *this* every day."

"Sometimes, I'm not sure either." Three months of working together had taught Nikki to not only respect Gwen's skills as an agent but trust her as a friend as well. "But I always appreciate it when people don't assume they know how I feel. Though to be honest, most of the time I'm not sure how I'm supposed to feel. Like in this case, I'm not the victim, and yet things are hitting way too close to home. When I took this job, I thought I could handle the emotional part. I thought that helping families would somehow make up for the loss, but then on days like today . . ."

"It doesn't make up for it, does it?" Gwen said.

"No. Not completely anyway."

Nothing would ever be able to completely make up for losing Sarah.

Jack walked into the room from outside, his eyes still looking bloodshot from his allergies, and sneezed. "Sorry. Kyle's doing another interview with someone in the local media in about ten minutes. He asked if he could speak to us about a couple of ideas when he's done."

"Of course," Nikki said. "Has he spoken to his mother yet?"

"As far as I know, he hasn't."

In the end, it was Kyle's decision, but it was going to take a considerable amount of effort on both sides, especially with the added strain of Bridget's abduction, to mend their relationship.

"We've just received an initial report from the forensic team who went through Bridget's house. It should be available for you now. They're still evaluating the contents of her room and computer and will let us know if they come up with anything new. So far there's nothing much there."

Nikki's phone rang. She glanced at the caller ID. Ryan. "I'll be back in a minute."

She headed outside, hesitating before answering Mr. Perfect's call. She'd meant what she'd said to Tyler while hanging off the side of that cliff. Three dates, and she still wasn't sure what she thought about Ryan. Not that there was anything so far *not* to like. Her parents liked him. Her brothers even approved. And as far as she could tell, they were all right.

Maybe that was the problem. Tyler was always calling him Mr. Perfect. But no one was perfect.

"Ryan . . . hey."

"You sound tired. Bad timing?"

"No . . . well . . . yes, honestly. I'm working a case."

"A case? I thought this was your day off."

"It is. Or rather, it was." Nikki couldn't help but chuckle. Some day off. Twelve hours ago she'd been hanging off the side of a mountain wondering if her rope would hold her. Add to that all that had happened while searching for Bridget, and even for someone who was an adrenaline junkie, she'd had enough excitement for one day. "I got called in. A young girl went missing near the Smoky Mountains."

She hadn't told Ryan where she was going or that she'd planned to spend the day with Tyler. Not that he expected her to tell him everything. It was one of the things she disliked about the awkward first stages of dating, when they were still getting to know each other. Explaining her relationship with Tyler would just . . . complicate things.

"I saw it on the news this morning," Ryan said. "Any good leads?"

"A few, but nothing substantial yet, unfortunately."

"I won't keep you then. I just wanted to tell you that I had a really good time last night."

She smiled. He'd taken her to dinner, then to the Nashville symphony, something she hadn't been to in years. The night had been romantic, even magical. But finding a way to balance her personal life with her professional life had never been easy. Somehow both sides had a way of tangling themselves together at the most inopportune times. She found that out with the last guy she'd gone out with. Ryan, though, was . . . different. He'd somehow managed to get her to actually consider the possibility of a relationship with him.

She gnawed at the inside of her lip and felt the flutter of butterflies in her stomach. "I had a good time too."

"I'm glad to hear that, because I'd like to do it again. Soon."

She paused again. Yes, she enjoyed spending time with him and even knew he was someone she wanted to get to know better. Then why the hesitation? She was being silly. It wasn't as if she were leading him on. There was nothing wrong with getting to know the man better. They were simply two people with similar interests who enjoyed spending time together.

Then why did she feel as if something was missing? That certain unexplainable spark she'd seen in her parents' marriage. The same spark she was looking for in her relationships. She rubbed the back of her neck. Today was not the day to make any significant decisions. Once this case was behind her she knew she'd regret not giving him another chance.

"Nikki?"

"Sorry . . . I'd like that too. What did you have in mind?"

"I thought we could do something different this time. You mentioned how much you liked climbing. I've got a friend who owns an indoor rock climbing gym, if you're up for it."

She started walking across the parking lot—empty except for a scattering of law enforcement vehicles—needing to stretch her muscles. The visitor center was already closed, and all the volunteers had gone home for the day. Normally, she'd jump at the chance at hanging on the side of a cliff, man-made or not. After today's accident, though, she wasn't exactly clamoring to get up there again. But neither did she want to put him off.

"I do love climbing, but listen, can I get back to you about it when I get back to Nashville? I'm not sure when I'll finish up this case, or even when I'll be back in town, for that matter."

She wasn't ready to tell him that this case had become personal. That she was staying because she was going to find this guy.

"Not a problem," Ryan said. "Just give me a call when you're back and are free, and we'll make a plan."

No pressure? No trying to persuade her? Maybe he *was* perfect.

"Thanks, Ryan. I'll do that."

"Before I let you go, though, I did want to say that I . . . I hope you feel what I'm feeling. Like there's this connection between us. And no, you don't have to answer."

Nikki pressed her cell phone against her ear. Maybe she'd spoken too soon.

"Especially not over the phone," he continued. "It's just that I haven't met a woman like you in a long time. Too many of the women I meet seem to be on this fast track to becoming—I don't know—some sort of trophy wife, but you . . . you're different. I've seen the compassion you put into your work and your determination to ensure justice wins. I guess the bottom line is that I want you to know that I'm enjoying getting to know you."

Nikki felt the emotions of the day tug on her. Juggling her past with current responsibilities and family and then somehow trying to find a way to add someone like Ryan to the mix . . . Sometimes she simply didn't know how to do it.

"Nikki? You still there?"

"Yeah. I'm still here." Nikki smiled. "Thanks, Ryan. I appreciate the compliment. I'll be in touch once I'm back in Nashville."

Nikki hung up the call and stared out across the darkened parking lot, wondering if she'd made the right decision. Or if she was simply leading Ryan on. Marriage and family were definitely something she wanted. Someday. Not that Ryan was probing for a commitment. Not yet. But she'd seen how he looked at her, and read between the lines of some of the things he'd said. He wasn't just looking for a casual relationship. He was thirty-six and ready to settle down with the right woman. And at the moment, it was beginning to look like he believed that woman was her.

Tyler walked up to her carrying two containers of Chinese takeout, pulling her away from her thoughts. "I wondered where you'd gone. Gwen told me you hadn't eaten yet, so I decided to grab some before it was gone."

"Why does that not surprise me?" Nikki laughed, dropping her phone into her back pocket. "I told her you'd make sure I ate."

"Someone's got to keep you in line." He led her over to an empty wooden bench in front of the entrance of the visitor center. "Chicken cashew or crispy beef?"

"Switch halfway?" she asked, reaching for the chicken cashew and a pair of chopsticks.

"You bet."

Chinese takeout was Tyler and Liam's Friday night dinner of choice. Nikki couldn't remember how many times she'd brought their favorites from the Chinese Garden, then ended up staying to watch a movie or play Wii with Liam.

"You're smiling," Tyler said, digging into his beef. "Good news?"

"No news." Nikki bit the inside of her lip and

searched for a piece of chicken with her chopsticks. "Just a phone call, then Kyle wants to speak with us. He has some ideas on working with the media."

"Then that's not why you're smiling." Tyler sat back and looked at her. "I know. Mr. Perfect called."

Nikki stared down at the patch of stones beneath the bench and felt a blush creeping up her cheeks. "Why would you say that?"

"You bite the inside of your lip when you're nervous. Couple that with the grin on your face, I put two and two together. Am I right?"

Nikki stabbed at a piece of chicken. "You're impossible. I'm not nervous talking with him. Especially considering the fact that at this point, he's just a . . . friend."

Tyler took another bite. "If you say so."

"I do say so."

"But you're telling me you don't like him."

"Fine." She looked up at him. "Maybe just a little."

"Why?"

"Why do I like him? He's . . ."

"Perfect?"

"Stop. No." Nikki set the box in her lap. "He's not perfect. Sort of, but I don't know. Maybe that's the problem."

"I don't see why it's a problem. He makes you smile."

Nikki let out an exasperated breath. Why did Tyler—why did anyone—care about her dating life? "It's just been awhile since I've received compliments . . . besides you, of course."

"Then tell me how Mr. Perfect is a problem."

"His name is Ryan, and no one is perfect." Was that really the core of the issue? Fear she was going to find out he wasn't perfect? "He has to have at least one bad habit. One annoying characteristic that drives me crazy. But he doesn't. Or at least I haven't found it yet. I like being with him. He makes me laugh. He compliments me enough, but not too much for it to seem fake. I like him."

"And that's a problem, why?"

"It's not a problem, though it does up the chances that he's . . . I don't know . . . a serial killer or a bank robber or something."

"A serial killer." Tyler chuckled. "Yeah, that makes sense, because that describes most serial killers and bank robbers."

"You're making fun of me."

"Never."

She shook her head but couldn't help but laugh. "I'm serious. Dating is just . . . complicated."

"Why is it complicated? Why can't a guy just be nice? Why can't he have good manners, open the car door for you, pay for your dinner, and tell you how beautiful you are without worrying you're going to take it wrong?"

"Because every guy I've dated for the past couple of years has ended up having some annoying habit that I couldn't overlook. At first they seem perfect, or at least almost perfect. You know, during those first moments when they want to impress me. And then after a couple of dates—if it even lasts that long—they forget and start talking too much about themselves or their ex-girlfriends, or they agree with everything I say, which is annoying."

"And so when you do find Mr. Perfect, it what? Scares you off. You're just waiting for Dr. Jekyll to turn into Mr. Hyde."

Nikki took another bite, trying to figure out how to answer his question. "I'm sure you're probably right, but I think I'm waiting for the ball to drop. Waiting for that bad habit to appear. The one I decide I can't live with. Because, let's face it, I don't have a great track record when it comes to dating."

"Maybe not, but maybe you're looking for something that isn't there." He nudged her with his shoulder. "Take our relationship for example. I'm not a serial killer, or a bank robber for that matter. We know how to be ourselves with each other. And I come in pretty handy when you're hanging on for dear life off the side of a cliff."

"Maybe that's what I'm looking for," she said.

Someone just like Tyler. Nikki shook off the

thought before it had a chance to take root, and she grabbed a cashew with her fingers. "Anyway. You make me sound . . . I don't know. Indecisive."

"I've never known you to be indecisive. Except perhaps with Mr. Per—Ryan."

"Thank you. And I know I'm not making any sense. Katie would have understood."

"I'm sure she would have, though she never accused me of being perfect."

"Your and Katie's relationship did seem perfect. At least from the outside. You adored her, and she thought you hung the moon."

"Then you've forgotten. Because you, more than anyone else, knew we struggled just like any married couple. I'm messy, and she could be stubborn when she wanted to. Switch?" He held out his carton.

Nikki nodded and handed him her chicken cashew.

"We had plenty of fights, you know that," he said. "I can think of a couple of times when she went to see you after some argument we got into."

"But you never let any of that ruin your relationship."

"Because after a rough beginning, we decided we had to take our marriage seriously. Divorce was never an option."

"But that's just it." Nikki turned to Tyler, catching his gaze. "I don't need perfect. I just want someone who looks at me and sees my imperfections and decides to take a chance with me anyway. Someone who will tell me how he feels, love me despite my flaws, and maybe take out the trash while he's at it."

The realness of two people being together, sharing who they were, the good and the bad.

"Somehow I have a feeling that one of these days Mr. Perfect—or someone close to it—will sweep you off your feet, and at that moment you'll know he's the one."

"Maybe."

Tyler finished up his last bite of food, then dropped his chopsticks into the box. "Your smile's gone."

"I'm just frustrated. And I'm not talking about Mr. Perfect. I need to get back to work, but all we keep hitting are dead ends in this case. I don't know what else to do."

"You once told me if you don't have a good lead, utilize logic until you're on the right track again. Can I throw out my two cents?"

"Of course."

"Try looking at things from a different angle. Because it's like someone is leading this investigation, but it's not you."

"What do you mean?"

"Think Hansel and Gretel and a trail of bread crumbs. It's like everything so far has been too . . . too convenient."

She shook her head, not following him. "It's called following the evidence."

"Yes, but things just don't seem to be adding up. You don't take a girl after implementing some detailed plan, then leave a trail of crumbs behind you for the police to follow. It doesn't make sense. And you don't bring someone you've just abducted into the Smoky Mountains Park unless you have a surefire plan of escape. What if you're following the wrong trail?"

Nikki grasped the edge of the bench. "What do you mean? You think he's purposely trying to throw us off?"

"Think about it. You have her hat in an abandoned car, the phone, and a photograph. But she could be halfway to Alaska by now for all we know."

If he hadn't already killed her.

"You mentioned earlier whoever brought her here needed to be someone who knows the park," he said.

"That's logical."

"So let's keep looking at it logically. In the park, there are paid rangers, volunteers, tourists, and thru-hikers."

Nikki laughed. "That narrows down our search."

"I think we can assume that whoever took her, assuming he did bring her here, knows the park. Because I don't see him making a plan without having an exit strategy."

"You heard what Anderson said, though. He wouldn't necessarily need an exit strategy."

"True," Tyler said. "The park covers over five hundred thousand acres. Bridget wouldn't be the first person who vanished without a trace inside the park. And if you think about it, his chances of not getting caught are high."

Nikki shuddered and zipped up her jacket. "So in other words, instead of being some sort of stupid mistake, the park becomes the perfect place to disappear."

"Exactly." Tyler took her empty takeout box and tossed it in the trash can. "I think this is some sort of game."

"Okay." Nikki looked up at him. "Then I know who might be able to help us."

15

Nikki leaned back against the passenger seat of the car the local PD had loaned them and closed her eyes as Tyler turned left onto a two-lane road just outside of Gatlinburg. She'd managed to finish her dinner under Tyler's watchful eyes, but only because she knew she needed the energy to combat the heavy fatigue—both physical and emotional—she was fighting. Sleep would come later, but for now she had to keep going. And try not to let memories of Sarah's abduction completely overwhelm her . . .

That morning she'd dropped Sarah off at school early. Sarah had worn her favorite *I Love New York* sweatshirt with jeans and a pair of red sneakers, her long blond hair pulled up in a ponytail. She had been her usual bubbly self as they'd talked about Brice Mitchell on the way.

"Camy told me that Brice is planning to come to my birthday party."

"Didn't I tell you he liked you?"

"Yes, but that was only because you're my sister."

"Say what you want," Nikki said, stopping beside the curb in front of the school, "but I was right."

"I'll see you after school, Nikki." Sarah paused before shutting the door. "Oh, but before I forget, I need you to convince Dad to buy me that new dress we found last week. He doesn't think I need another one."

Nikki laughed, then promised Sarah she'd do her best. And that she'd be back at three.

At three fifteen that afternoon, Nikki's entire world had begun to crumble.

She fought back the tears. Missing Sarah as much today as the moment she'd realized she was gone.

Even Ryan's call had managed to push her in a direction she didn't want to go. As if adding one more card to the house of cards would bring everything crashing down. She tried to brush aside the new layer of guilt that had begun to form. Ryan hadn't deserved her curt response, but neither could he begin to understand what she was going through. He seemed to thrive on numbers, end-of-the-month financial reports, and business meetings. In contrast, her work forced her to delve into the world's darkness. And sometimes, on days like today, that darkness spilled over into her world, threatening to pull her under.

Which was why she couldn't allow herself to give in to the fear that would only paralyze her. Not now. Not knowing that Bridget was out there somewhere.

"You're awfully quiet," Tyler said, dragging her from her thoughts.

She opened her eyes and glanced at him. "I'm just . . . thinking."

"About?" Tyler prodded.

"About Sarah and Bridget, mainly. And hoping Sam can help."

"Tell me more about Sam before we get there."

Nikki shifted in her seat, her fingers clutching the armrest. "Sam retired from the force about a year after Sarah disappeared, but during his last year, he was the lead investigator working on her case."

"And your connection with him?"

"He realized how determined I was to stay as involved as I could in the investigation. He never tried to put me off. Always managed to find time to answer all my questions. We've kept in contact all these years. He became both a friend and a mentor."

"Sounds like a good man."

"He is a good man. After his retirement, he formed a private investigation agency with a couple of his buddies. They've actually solved a number of cold homicide and missing persons cases. And he's never stopped looking for Sarah."

Tyler glanced at the GPS, then pulled into the driveway of a modest, two-story residence just outside the city limits. "Are you sure you're up to this? You look tired."

"I am, but this is important."

"We could meet him in the morning after you've gotten some sleep."

"I'm fine, Tyler."

Tyler turned off the engine, apparently realizing there was no use arguing with her. She could see the same fatigue reflected in his eyes as well. Peeling back the layers of an abduction was never easy.

Sam met them at the door with a huge grin on his face, not looking a day older than he'd been on the force all those years ago when she first met him.

"Nikki. It's about time you came to see me. If I remember correctly, you owe me a visit."

"It has been a long time . . . too long." Nikki gave the man a big hug, then turned to Tyler. "Tyler, I'd like you to meet Sam Bradford. Sam, Tyler's a longtime friend of mine who's been volunteering with the case we're working on."

Sam shook Tyler's hand, then motioned them both into the entryway. "This girl was destined to become a detective. Even a decade ago, she knew more about the details in every missing persons case across the state than I did. She was smart, determined—"

"But none of that was enough." Nikki tried to shake the growing frustration seeping through her.

"You're right," Sam said. "Those cases were the toughest part of the job for me."

"Sam?" Irene, Sam's wife, bustled into the entryway. "Are you planning to invite them in, or catch up in the middle of the entryway?"

"Sorry. Please come in."

Even this late, Irene looked like she'd just stepped out of the hair salon with her perfectly styled short hair and a smart navy-blue pant-suit.

"It's great to see you, Nikki, though I would have enjoyed seeing you under different circumstances. You don't make it out this direction near enough." Irene gave Nikki a hug, then linked arms with her. "Come in. Both of you. Give me your jackets, then I'll get some coffee going. Weatherman said at eleven that the cold front's about to hit, and I think he's right. The temperature's dropping like an anchor."

"And I know how late it is—"

"Don't give it another thought." Irene smiled. "Sam's work has always come first in our marriage, and after forty years, I finally stopped resenting that fact. You're both welcome, so make yourselves at home. I'll go get that pot of coffee going."

Nikki stepped into the cozy living room that clearly had Irene's decorative touch. Sam nodded toward the long tan couch with orange accent pillows, then sat down across from them on a matching recliner.

Nikki glanced up at the mountain scene

hanging above the couch. "Is that one of Irene's paintings? I remember how much she loved to paint."

Sam nodded. "She's good, isn't she? That one's of the Blue Ridge Parkway."

"She is good. And what about you? Still working on cold cases?" Nikki asked.

"Yep. It keeps me out of trouble—or so Irene says." Sam rested his arms against his thighs. "Let me tell you, though, if you ever decide to retire from the force, I'd hire you in a heart-beat."

Nikki laughed. "Who knows? I might just take you up on that offer one day."

Sam leaned back. "I've always regretted not being able to find your sister. Finding her body would at least bring closure to your family, but I couldn't even do that."

"Neither of us could," she said.

Nikki picked at a chipped fingernail. She'd known that seeing Sam would resurrect old memories forever linked to Sarah. He'd been the one who'd sat in the living room with her family on that first day, asking question after question. Then, when the weeks had turned into months, he'd still call every once in a while to update them on the investigation. He'd sat with Nikki for hours, teaching her procedure, sharing with her any new leads they were following, and listening to her ideas.

"But we still haven't given up hope," she said finally. "At least, I haven't."

"You never can. I've learned that. And your family? How are they?"

"My mom still has nightmares occasionally, but she volunteers with a missing persons organization, and that really seems to have given her a sense of purpose. It's a bit . . . therapeutic, I guess. She still struggles, though, especially at Christmas and Thanksgiving, but all in all they've managed to move forward as much as they can. My father pours himself into his restaurant and still enters his sauces every year in the local barbeque festivals and competitions."

"What about your brothers?"

"Luke's twenty-eight now and still wants to be a professional musician. He works at my dad's restaurant and entertains the customers a few nights a week. Matt's married to Jamie and they're expecting a baby. She's in the hospital right now, actually, after some complications with her pregnancy."

"I'm sorry. I know this is hard on you."

"My father warned me when I took this job that it was going to be difficult to separate my emotional self from my professional self. He was right."

"You wouldn't be human if you could separate the two, Nikki. I can't tell you how many times I've sat in someone's living room during some of the worst moments in their lives. And while I've lost track of many of them over the years, I'll never forget their faces or their names."

"I guess I thought if I could help, it might bring some sort of meaning out of what happened to Sarah."

"And this case. You really think I can help?"

"That's what I'm hoping," Nikki said.

"I have to say, your call intrigued me," Sam said. "I've seen the reports on the news about the missing girl, but you said you believe it's connected with your sister's abduction?"

Nikki glanced at Tyler, then nodded. "How much have you seen on Bridget Ellison's abduction?"

"Just what's been on the local news. I'm guessing by your being here that you haven't found her yet?"

"No. And all we've got so far is a bunch of dead ends."

"I'm still not sure how I can help."

Nikki decided to jump straight to the point. "We found a Polaroid photo of Bridget—just like the other girls connected to Sarah's case."

"Whoa . . ." Sam stared at her. "Are you telling me that whoever took this girl is using the same MO as our Angel Abductor?"

"The Angel Abductor?" Irene walked into the living room and set the tray on the coffee table.

"I thought the man behind those abductions died years ago."

"That was one conclusion," Sam said, "but no one knows for sure. For all we know he could still be out there."

"I've been reading through the files," Tyler said. "There were specific things that the police kept from the public. The Polaroid, for example, was never released."

"That's true, but after all these years, it's always possible for something like that to have leaked out."

Nikki leaned forward and took the mug of coffee Irene offered her. "Thanks, Irene. We need to determine if this is just a copycat or if our abductor really is back. And we need to find him."

"Wow . . . It's been so long, but I think all of us who worked that case believed he was dead. The authorities have always given us a tremendous amount of cooperation over the years digging up cold cases, but I've never stumbled across anything that pointed to him. Of course, we never had more than a rough sketch of what the man looked like.

"And you know as well as I do that his trail went completely cold after your sister went missing. I'm honestly not sure how I can help. It's been so many years, I have no doubt that you know more about those cases than even I do."

"Maybe, but that doesn't mean there isn't something we've both missed. Do you have all of your notes on my sister's case?"

"He has case files on every investigation he worked in one of the extra rooms." Irene laughed. "I don't even go in there. It's his private domain."

"I need your help to determine who this guy is."

"And if he really is the Angel Abductor?" Sam asked.

"Then it's up to us to ensure he never strikes again."

Two hours later, they were set up at the dining room table, still going through the dozens of files, police reports, lists of evidence, and notes Sam had. Thanks to adrenaline and unlimited refills of coffee, exhaustion had been shoved to the back burner for the moment.

"We always thought there might be a connection between all the girls," Nikki told Tyler, as they continued through the files. "But we never found it."

"I cross-checked every connection I could think of, but you're right," Sam said. "There was never anything."

"After all these years, I'm wondering if it's even possible to find anything new," Irene said, topping off her husband's half-empty mug. "I can't tell you how many late nights Sam has pored over these files, and I know you've done the same thing, Nikki. If there was something to find, don't you think you would have already found it?"

"Probably, but we have to be missing something. We never found him."

"I know it's believed he stalked his victims, but is there any evidence that they knew him?" Tyler asked, drumming his fingers against the table.

"Not that we know of," Sam said. "But like Nikki said, we never found a common denominator between all the girls."

Nikki leaned back in her chair and tried to stretch out the tight muscles in her neck. "Bridget's abductor contacted her via social media, and she developed an emotional attachment. But we still don't know if she was just a random victim or if he chose her specifically. If it is the same abductor, he's changed along with the advances in technology."

"How long did he keep the girls alive?" Tyler asked, opening up another file.

"The longest was . . ." Sam looked to Nikki. "Two days?"

"Except for Jessica Wright," Nikki said, wishing sometimes that the details weren't so readily available. "She went missing after school on June 15 and was found dead five days later. But the autopsy revealed she'd been killed two days before."

"In their investigation, the authorities came to the conclusion that the abductor had chosen his victims ahead of time. The problem was that we don't know what kind of contact—if any—he'd had with the girls ahead of time, because he killed them all."

Nikki tapped her fingers against the table. Something niggled in the back of her mind. Cases lined up over the years tried to blur, but she'd kept meticulous notes and files and read every line of every report. She'd also made detailed profiles of abductors and serial killers. Some were able to hide in plain sight with jobs, homes, and sometimes even families. Some fit the profiles; others, not so much. But they weren't all white males, just like most of them weren't the insane, evil geniuses Hollywood often portrayed.

"What if that isn't true? What if he didn't kill them all?" she asked finally.

"What do you mean?" Tyler asked.

"There was a girl who was kidnapped about six months before Sarah vanished." Nikki looked up at Sam. "You led the investigation. She managed to escape from her captor."

"I remember that case. Her name was Amanda Love. She didn't speak for days but was finally able to give us a description. It was close to the general description of the Angel Abductor, but we eventually dismissed that theory."

"Why?"

Sam shrugged. "Nothing else about the case fit."

Nikki paused as a memory of a conversation came to the surface. "Do you have a copy of Amanda's file?"

"Yes." Sam stood up. "What do you need?"

"The transcript of her conversation with the police. In it she said that she spoke to her abductor before he took her."

Like Bridget.

Two minutes later, Sam handed her a file.

Nikki flipped it open and started scanning through the transcript. "Here . . . She told the officer who interviewed her that she was leaving the library after checking out a pile of books for a research paper. She dropped them on the way down the front stairs. A man stopped to help her pick them up. Said he was a teacher who was going to start teaching math at the local middle school. Asked her if she had any advice for a new teacher. Then he left.

"At the time, Amanda told us she never thought anything about the conversation. But when we followed up on that conversation, there wasn't a new math teacher starting that year." She tapped her finger against the paper. "He ended up being her abductor."

But Amanda had managed to survive.

Nikki had followed Amanda's story during the media storm surrounding her disappearance and more recently when Amanda did an interview with CNN on the ten-year anniversary of the day she'd escaped. She was twenty-six now. A constant reminder to Nikki of what might have been if Sarah had escaped. But while Amanda might have managed to elude her captor, she hadn't been left without emotional scars. During the interview, she'd talked about her ongoing nightmares. Her fear of strangers and dark places . . .

"My partner and I followed that lead," Sam said, "but we never could conclude 100 percent certain he had been the Angel Abductor. And Amanda was blindfolded during her abduction, so we were never able to get a good description beyond the vague sketch of the man who talked with her at the school. She was able to confirm that the voices matched, though. The man at the school and the man who abducted her. But that's all we were ever able to get."

The conversation around Nikki faded . . .

She and Sarah had been sitting in a booth in the back of their parents' restaurant a few months before her abduction, eating barbeque sandwiches and French fries and catching up. The room was quiet after the lunchtime rush. Above them the walls were covered with retro signs and vintage guitars.

Sarah stuck a fry into her mouth. "We're getting a new biology teacher. I met him after school today. He was lost and looking for the lab."

"What about Mr. Philips?" Nikki reached for her chocolate milk shake. "I have a hard time imagining him ever leaving. He's been around forever."

Sarah shrugged. "I don't know. Maybe he's retiring. He's got to be close to seventy."

"Seventy?" Nikki laughed. "I don't think he's that old, but he does have to be close to retirement age. Can you believe he was my biology teacher?"

"I told you he was old."

"Thanks." Nikki rolled her eyes. "So this new teacher . . . Did he seem nice?"

"I guess. He didn't say much. I pointed him in the right direction, and he said thank you."

"Now for the next question you know I have to ask," Nikki said, dipping a French fry into a pile of ketchup. "What about boys? Anyone you like at the moment?"

Sarah took a sip of her Coke and blushed. "Okay, there is this new guy, though I'm sure he doesn't even know I exist."

"Why not?"

"He's popular and runs track. But he's so cute."

"You're popular and run track, so what's the problem? Have you ever talked to him?"

"Once or twice."

"What's his name?"

Sarah's smile had widened as a dreamy look settled in her eyes. "Brice."

"Nikki?" Tyler's hand brushed her arm, pulling her back to the present. "You okay?"

She glanced up at him. "Yeah, I'm just tired."

Emotionally . . . physically. She was fighting an inward battle. Knowing she had to stay focused if they were going to find Bridget. Knowing also that there was no way to avoid those emotions.

She stared down at the file in front of her, the memory of the conversation still strong. How had she forgotten that conversation? Three years later they'd celebrated Mr. Philips's retirement in that very restaurant.

"I just remembered a conversation I had with Sarah a few months before she was abducted." Nikki stared across the piles of files. "She mentioned speaking briefly to a man at her school who needed directions to the biology lab. Said he was a new teacher."

"What if that was a part of his MO?" Sam asked. "What if that's how he first found his girls?"

Nikki nodded. "We're going to have to search the video footage at the school."

"You know that the chances of us finding footage of him, while possible, are slim," Tyler said. "It could have been months ago."

"I know, but it's worth a shot. All we need is a photo of this guy . . ."

But he was right. More than likely any footage that had been captured had already been erased.

"It's worth looking into, but you can't do that until tomorrow. Which means if you ask me, you all need to stop for the night. It's after midnight." Irene laid her hand on her husband's arm. "Not getting any sleep and not being able to function won't help Bridget."

"I know, but we're still not any closer to finding her." The yellow walls of the dining room began to close in on her. Nikki pushed her chair back. "I'm sorry. I . . . I just need some fresh air."

16

Nikki sat down on the top of Sam's front porch steps. How was it that between the four of them, they'd spent hours going through every file Sam had collected and still come up with nothing concrete? Because looking for Bridget's abductor among hours of footage could easily end up being another dead end. He'd know to avoid getting caught on camera. Because whoever this guy was, he knew how to play them. Knew how to get under her skin.

Like Hansel and Gretel. A trail of bread crumbs. Was that really what this was? A part of some game he was playing?

She rubbed the back of her neck, trying to untangle some of the knots that had settled in over the past few hours. They needed to catch this guy in a mistake. Which surely was inevitable. Most criminals ended up being caught because of their own carelessness, inexperience, or even arrogance. Other times it was an escaped witness or a fluke, like finding a dead body at a routine traffic stop. Hollywood tended to make their serial killers brilliant, but the reality was they were all fallible.

She shifted on the step and stared out across

the dark clouds covering the night sky. Temperatures had dropped. A light mist had begun to fall. But she didn't care. Maybe the cold would help numb her heart.

The front door opened and closed behind her. Tyler handed her a fleece jacket and sat down beside her. "Irene insisted."

Nikki couldn't help but smile as he squeezed her shoulder. "She's a sweetie."

"Yes, she is. And you're as tight as a board."

"I know, and I'm sorry I just walked out, but I needed to clear my head."

"We all needed a break. Why don't you wait a minute before you put on the jacket?"

He nudged her down to the next step, slid in behind her, and started working out the knots in her neck and shoulders. He moved slowly across the muscles and pressure points until she finally felt herself relaxing.

"Why haven't you ever offered to do this before?" she teased, letting out a soft groan. "My knots have knots, my head feels like it has a bomb about to explode inside it. But after this, I just might be able to function again."

"Good." Tyler laughed. "Katie used to beg me for back rubs, especially when she was pregnant."

Nikki lowered her head and felt her muscles continue to loosen as he concentrated on her neck, then moved to her shoulders and down her spine. She breathed in slowly, trying not to worry about what their next step should be, but instead focusing on the comfortable silence between them and the calm reassurance of his touch.

"Better?" he said after a few minutes.

"Oh, yeah. More than you can imagine." She slipped into the jacket and shifted around in order to rest her forearms on his knees, and looked up at him. "But except for the long shot that they can find footage of this guy at Bridget's school, I feel like tonight has been a waste of time. I'm wondering now if we should have been out there looking for her."

He pulled the jacket tighter across her shoulders, then brushed a strand of her hair behind her ear. "Where would you look?"

"I don't know. That's the problem." She caught his gaze again, but this time, the intimacy of the moment shot through her.

"I don't remember you always second-guessing yourself like this."

She swallowed hard, then turned away, not ready to examine what had just passed between them. Or why her heart was thudding at his nearness.

"This time the stakes have risen," she said. "This is not only about finding Bridget but about finding the person who took Sarah."

The rain was starting to get heavier and splashed against her feet. She scooted up the steps until she was completely under the covering.

"And on top of that," she continued, "every lead ends up being a dead end. Every time I turn around, I feel as if I'm back at square one."

"You're going to figure this out."

"And if I don't?" she whispered.

He wrapped his arm around her and she allowed herself to nuzzle her head against the warmth of his shoulder. "Somehow, I just know you are."

"I hope so."

Moments of silence passed between them. Comfortable, and yet holding an edge of newness she didn't understand. She sat back up, wanting to ignore the new layer of confused emotions triggered, she knew, by his nearness.

"Did you ever get through to Liam?" she asked finally.

"Just before Mom put him to bed. He had a great day with her and is doing fine. Which reminds me of the other thing Irene said."

"What's that?" Nikki asked.

"She's insisting you crash on their couch for a couple of hours until you need to relieve Jack and Gwen. And I think she's right."

"There are still more files to go through." Nikki rubbed her temples, staving off the headache that was threatening to return. "We're no closer to finding anything since we got here, but I can't help but think we're just missing something."

"Maybe so, but you need to rest. No one expects you to work all night, and you'll feel better if you sleep."

She rested her chin on her knees. "I don't think I can sleep. I just keep thinking of Bridget out there. I know what this guy did to the other girls, and it's cold tonight with the temperatures dropping. What if he dumped her somewhere, what if—?"

"We don't know any of that."

"Which is the worst part. The not knowing." Nikki shook her head. "You should have gone home, Tyler—"

"When I agreed to stay and help, I wasn't expecting this to be a simple nine-to-five job. And besides that, I wanted to be with you. But you won't be able to help Bridget if you don't take care of yourself."

"You sound like my mother," she said, nudging him with her shoulder. "She's always worrying that I'm not eating enough or not getting enough rest." The memories were there at the forefront again—this time of all the nights she'd come home to a takeaway bag of barbeque on her kitchen counter and a handwritten note from her mother. "I remember the weeks after Sarah went missing. I was teaching full-time. I'd come home at night, grade papers and tests, then spend the next few hours corresponding with media contacts and poring through the case information I had. I didn't hang out with friends. I was convinced I couldn't stop looking, because if I did, I might miss something that would lead us to her."

"Like you're doing tonight?" he asked.

"Daddy would bring me food from the restaurant, convinced I wasn't eating enough."

"You probably weren't."

"No, but I didn't care. I just wanted to find her and bring her home. I never gave up hope, but now . . . after all these years . . . I don't know. I thought if I took this job I'd be able to find girls like Bridget, but I'm afraid that part of me isn't able to handle this emotionally."

He took her hand, pulled it against his chest, waiting for her to continue.

"Before I joined the task force, I kept the bigger goal in the back of my mind and was able to keep my personal stuff separate. But lately, when I'm assigned to a new case, it dredges up all the old emotions. I'm supposed to be the professional. The one who can put her feelings aside and just do my job. But it's hard. And this time . . . knowing that it could be him . . . the man who abducted Sarah . . . out there." She looked up at him, her eyes wide with questions, and shook her head. "I don't know if I'm cut out for this."

"I can't answer that for you, but what I do know is that you're making a difference."

"And where is God in all this? It just seems so . . . wrong."

"You're questioning your faith?" he asked.

"Don't you? I want to scream at God. Ask him why we never found Sarah. Beg him for answers, but the answers are never there. And that's changed me. It's changed my entire family and how I see God. And I think that scares me the most."

She and Tyler had talked about their losses over the last year. About how those losses had changed them, but she'd always felt as if she were skirting around the reality that sometimes her faith threatened to crumble beneath her.

"Did you ever just want to throw in the towel?" he asked.

"On God?" She caught his expression in the porch light and realized this wasn't about her anymore. It was about him and losing Katie. She couldn't forget she wasn't the only person who'd loved and lost. Today had magnified that fact over and over.

"I have. More often than I want to admit," he said.

The rain had slowed to a gentle patter. She realized their questions might never be answered. Questions of how and why. The longing for justice in a world where sometimes there simply wasn't any.

Tyler rubbed his thumb across the back of her

hand. "I can't help but wonder what Katie would think if she could see how I'm handling things. Or rather how I'm not handling things."

"In what way?"

He drew in a deep breath and let it out slowly as if contemplating his answer. "I used to think my faith was unshakable. But in the time I spent on the ground in Iraq, I saw things that horrified me. That changed me. Things I never spoke of, even to Katie. And yet somehow, through it all, I never lost my faith. It was as if I knew I was on the winning side, and God had sent me to stamp out evil. Which meant as hard as it was, I was the good guy. The hero who came home with the Purple Heart."

These were things they never talked about. Even his Purple Heart was stuck in a drawer and never mentioned.

"And after Katie died?" Nikki asked, not wanting to push him to a place he didn't want to go but wanting desperately to understand him better.

"Everything changed. And now . . . I don't know, Nikki, I can't find my way back. I'm like one of the missing girls you're searching for. Lost, with no idea how to find my way back home."

She waited silently for him to continue, hearing the vulnerability in his voice. A car drove by, its light picking up the splatter of rain in the narrow beam of headlights. The same way he was giving her insight into how he felt.

"There are things about my relationship with Katie that you don't know about. I know you think we had the perfect marriage, and it *was* good, but there were problems between us when she died." He hesitated for a few moments. "When I came home from the Middle East that last time, it really messed Katie up. I'd been shot, and she was scared. She threatened to leave me if I signed up for another tour."

"To leave you?" Nikki tried to digest the information. "I can't see Katie ever leaving you. She told me she was worried. Afraid even that if you went back again you'd come home in a body bag. But she never hinted she didn't support you."

"I didn't think at the time she would have actually followed through. I think she just wanted to scare me. And it did. I left the military and changed my career because of her."

Nikki looked up at him, catching the trace of resentment in his voice. "I thought going back to school was your idea."

"It was the obvious next step, and I knew I couldn't blame her. Shoot, I'd been almost killed. She was pregnant and facing being a single mom. And she was tired of waiting for me to come home after each tour. And when I did, not knowing if I'd be coming home injured or in a body bag." He drew in a deep breath. "We both knew plenty of guys who came home missing limbs or dealing with PTSD, and on one level she accepted that could happen to me, because when she married me, she signed up for more than just a husband. But after I was shot . . . she told me she couldn't take it anymore."

"So you left the military."

He nodded. "For her."

"Did you resent her?" In all the time they'd spent together, especially over the past year, he'd never mentioned that it hadn't been his idea to leave his military career. Never said a bad word against Katie.

"For a while, yes. I resented it. Resented her for pressuring me to leave, because I loved my job and my country. Not being there to defend it has been a tough transition. I was used to being out on the field, not sitting in a classroom hour after hour."

"What about now?" she asked.

"I don't know. Today reminded me that I still want to be out there saving lives and making a difference. I thought I was doing the right thing for my family when I went back to school, but now with Katie gone . . . I don't know. I have to think of Liam and what he needs." He shook his head. "What really bothers me is that I know all the right answers—about God, about life and death, but it doesn't help. I *know* Katie is in a better place. I know she's in the presence of God. But none of that makes me miss her any less."

She'd watched him over the past few months, knowing he was struggling. She figured when he was ready he'd come to her and talk. Not that she had the answers. She still couldn't understand why God allowed someone to take Sarah. Or why God would allow a young mother to be ripped from this world in an instant.

But he had allowed it.

She'd thought the same questions as well. Most of the time she simply accepted she wasn't going to come up with another answer. God made the world. Sin entered the world and God had given man a choice. Free will. It was as simple as that.

Except it wasn't simple at all.

Because even with those explanations, she still wrestled with layers of deep-seated emotions and the constant trying to figure out how to let go.

Tyler leaned forward, resting his elbows on his knees. "I go to church, listen to the pastor, and end up wanting to run out of that building by the end of the sermon because I can't justify what God did. And then I feel like a hypocrite for being mad at God and blaming it all on him. Instead, I smile and keep going to church for Liam. And because I know Katie would want me to be there, and her parents expect me to be there, but that's it. I don't feel the way I used to, and to be honest, I'm not sure I want to at this point. I don't have anything left to give."

Nikki stared out at the terraced yard, now soaked with rain, and contemplated her answer. "Maybe that's okay."

"Yeah, I'm sure God is happy I show up at church with the attitude of wanting to be anywhere else but there. I'm sure he's okay with the fact that I blame him for what happened to Katie."

"I'm serious," she said. "If he knows what you've been through, then he knows that you have to work through your grief. Isn't blaming him a stage of the healing process?"

"I know plenty of people who have suffered loss and react completely opposite to the way I have. They tell stories of how tragedies have strengthened their faith, but I'm not like that, Nikki."

How many times had she felt the same way? Instead of tragedy strengthening her faith, she felt instead that she was holding on for dear life like she had been yesterday morning on the side of the mountain. Like she was hanging on a tattered rope—one false move and it would all be over.

But surely God understood their pain as well as their reactions.

"I want to blame God," Tyler continued,

"because I know he could have stopped my losing Katie and Liam losing a mother. I get the fact that bad things happen to good people, and we will all experience pain, but that doesn't make it any easier."

"I know, because not only have I felt the same thing myself, I've watched my mother struggle to move forward. She's never completely healed from losing Sarah, and I'm not sure she ever will."

"But she didn't lose her faith," Tyler said.

"No, but her faith—or maybe just the way she looks at life and God—has changed."

"I don't know. I accept the fact that Katie's gone, because I have no choice, but that doesn't stop me from questioning. Or feeling guilty in the process." Tyler clasped his hands together, not even trying to mask the defeat in his voice. "It's ironic. I'm supposed to be going to school to learn how to counsel people to deal with loss, but when it comes to myself . . . I'm completely lost, Nikki."

She looked up at him, not knowing how to respond. Wishing desperately she could take his pain away.

"But I'm also ready to find a way out," he said. "So I can start living again. I need to for Liam, and I know Katie would want me to. I just don't know how."

He was close enough that she could read the

pain in his eyes. Anything she'd thought had passed between them earlier had been clearly imagined on her part. He was still in love with Katie.

"Thanks for listening to me," he said.

"Always."

He glanced at his watch. "You need to sleep."

She might feel like arguing, but as usual, he was right. The case had drained her both physically and emotionally.

He pulled her up from the porch step and they walked into the house. Sam and Irene were sitting at the kitchen table drinking mugs of tea, still going through Sam's files.

"So did he finally convince you to get some sleep?" Irene asked.

Nikki forced a smile. "Just for a couple hours. I'd like to head back to the command post by three and get a jump on things. But thank you. Both of you."

"Anything to bring that girl home," Sam said. "Just lock the door on your way out when you leave. I'll come by in the morning to see you."

A minute later she was settled on the couch.

"What about you?" she asked Tyler.

"This recliner's probably more comfortable than the bed I sleep on at home." He pulled a light blue afghan from the back of the couch, pulled it over her, then bent down and kissed her on the forehead. "Good night, Nikki."

"Good night, Tyler."

"As soon as we find her, I'll buy you that breakfast," he promised.

"I'm counting on it."

She watched him walk away, then closed her eyes, her thoughts still on Katie, Sarah, Bridget . . . and Tyler . . . and willed herself to sleep.

"Nikki?"

Nikki sat up at the sound of Tyler's voice and tried to reach through the fog that had settled on her brain. She glanced at her phone—2:45. "My alarm didn't go off."

"I turned it off. You were sleeping so peacefully. I thought I'd give you another ten minutes."

A dimmed light still glowed over the large dining room table where they'd been working. Boxes and files lay among an empty bag of Oreos and the bag of microwave popcorn Irene had fixed for them.

Nikki rubbed her eyes as the frustration of the past twenty-four hours rushed over her. If they didn't stop him now, Bridget wasn't going to be his last victim.

She glanced up at Tyler. "What about you? You've got to be exhausted as well."

"I closed my eyes for a few minutes on the recliner. I'm used to not sleeping more than four or five hours a night."

Another result of Katie's death. "That doesn't mean it's good for you."

"I'm fine. Can I get you some coffee? Irene left a pot in the kitchen we can heat up."

Nikki sat up, forcing herself to wake up. "That would be great. Thanks." Her phone vibrated on the coffee table beside her. "That's got to be either Jack or my mom this late."

"I'll be back in a minute."

Nikki stood up, stretching her back as she picked up the phone, her brain still seared by a heavy fog of fatigue. "Hello?"

"Nikki?"

"Yeah . . ." She tried to place the voice, but came up blank. "I'm sorry. Who is this?"

There was a short pause on the line. "Did you find the photo I left you?"

17

Did you find the photo I left you?

The words shot through Nikki like a hard punch to the gut, sucking the air from her lungs. The room spun. It couldn't be him. She'd wanted to believe they were just dealing with a copycat, because he'd dropped out of the game years ago. She'd always imagined him turning up dead after a drunken brawl in some deserted back ally, or locked away in some high-security prison, caught for another crime he'd committed. Because the alternative meant he was still out there. Silently snuffing out the lives of other young girls one by one.

Like Sarah.

Like Bridget.

"I'm disappointed, Nikki," he said. "I expected more of a response from you."

She started to hang up, then hesitated. She had to be right. This couldn't be *him*. Just some bad imitator wanting some attention. But if she hung up and it was him, or if he really did have Bridget . . .

"Who is this?" she asked.

"Do you really need to ask that? Sometimes I think you know me better than anyone, Nikki, after all these years of searching for me." He laughed. "By the way, I've been wanting to congratulate you on your recent promotion. I'm sure you've become a huge asset to the governor's latest special task force after you've studied every case of missing girls you could get your hands on. Memorized abductors' MOs and profiles—mine included. It's funny, though, how you're their poster girl, and once again, you haven't been able to find the girl you're looking for."

Nikki sat back down on the couch, her legs shaking. "If you're who you say you are, tell me where Bridget is."

"I might. In time. But not now. She's not who I want to talk about."

She looked up as Tyler walked into the room with two mugs of coffee in his hands. Nikki mouthed *Angel Abductor,* then switched to speakerphone.

Tyler's eyes went wide. He set the mugs down on the coffee table, pulled out his phone, then started recording the call.

"If you don't want to talk about Bridget, then why are you calling me?" she asked.

"I thought we could talk. I've always enjoyed getting to know the girls. Getting them to trust me before I took them. You wouldn't believe how easy it is. Throw a bit of charm their way, a few compliments . . ."

225

Nikki fought the nausea spreading through her. Tyler squeezed her hand and motioned for her to keep him talking.

She gnawed on her lower lip and nodded. "Tell me where Bridget is."

"Once again you surprise me, Nikki. I thought you might be more interested in talking about the day Sarah vanished. You can't imagine how disappointed I was when the authorities didn't find her, considering the clues I left."

"Is she alive?" Nikki couldn't fight the growing emotion pressing against her chest. Ten years of searching, hoping, praying . . . She was realistic enough to know that the chances of Sarah being alive were slim, but even if there was only a chance of finally finding out the truth . . . Even that would help fill in the holes of grief left behind by her sister's disappearance. "Please . . . please tell me where she is."

His hollow laugh mocked her. "Begging doesn't suit you well, Nikki. It makes me feel you're not a worthy opponent, and I'd hoped that you were more worthy than Sam Bradford and the rest of his team."

"Sam?"

"He was more focused on his retirement than closing another case. He missed things he shouldn't have, but you . . . you should have found them, Nikki."

"What did I miss?" She caught Tyler's gaze.

She'd gone over and over every transcript, witness report, and piece of evidence available. Just like last night, everything appeared to be nothing more than dead ends, and nothing had managed to lead her any closer to Sarah. "If you wanted me to find her, tell me what I missed. Surely it can't make any difference if I know now."

"She was wearing an *I Love New York* sweatshirt that day and looked so pretty with the sunlight streaming behind her. It made her hair look almost white," he said, ignoring her question. "Just like an angel."

Nikki squeezed her eyes shut, trying to fight back the tears as he continued speaking. The summer before Sarah disappeared they'd taken a family trip to New York and seen the Empire State Building, the Statue of Liberty, and walked through Central Park. Sarah told her she would have been happy to have spent the entire week at the Metropolitan Museum of Art.

"She told me you'd promised to pick her up," he continued. "Figured you must have gotten caught up in traffic. She was worried about a test she had the next day. Spanish, if I remember right. She was worried she wasn't going to have enough time to study if she didn't get home soon, so I offered her a ride. It was so easy."

"No." Nikki's voice cracked. "Sarah never would have gotten into the car with a stranger—"

"Who said I was a stranger? Who said any of them were strangers?"

"So you did meet them in person before you took them."

"It wasn't that hard."

The tension in her neck was back. Pulsing across her head to her temples as she tried to absorb what he was telling her. That *was* the connection they'd missed. Each girl had known or at least had been familiar with him before he'd even attempted to take her.

They'd missed that connection. Even after she'd looked, cross-referencing everyone from gardeners to school personnel, people at church and after-school dance classes. She'd looked at each one meticulously, and like the police, she'd eventually made the assumption that the abductions had been random. But he'd planned each one. Possibly even weeks in advance.

"You're there with Sam now, aren't you?" he said, breaking into her thoughts. "Desperately trying to figure out what the two of you might have overlooked. Hoping that you'll be able to find a connection in Bridget's abduction that will in turn end up leading you to your sister."

She felt the warmth of Tyler's hand and drew in a slow breath. She wasn't going to engage in an argument. She needed information. Needed him to keep talking.

"Sam's not working this case anymore, but

you're right," she said, "we never found a connection. But you must be calling me for some reason. You must want me to know what that connection is."

In all the profile studies she'd read on him, she'd never felt as if he'd wanted recognition. But maybe she'd been wrong. Or maybe he'd changed over the years. Maybe he'd continued quietly killing young girls, using a different MO.

"Are you still there?" she asked.

"I'm here," he said finally. "But I've already given you enough. Now you're going to have to find the connection. And find out why I'm back."

Nikki's heart raced. She'd managed to fool herself into believing the Angel Abductor was gone, even though it wasn't uncommon for years to pass between crimes committed by serial killers. Some simply stopped, never getting caught. Others quietly took their secrets to the grave.

She pulled the afghan tighter around her shoulders, still shaking. She wasn't done yet. She needed to keep him talking. "You haven't really told me anything. What do you want from me now?"

"I've said enough. I'm sure we'll speak again soon."

"No, wait . . ."

The call went dead.

Nikki dropped the phone onto the coffee table

as if it were poison and watched it skitter across the surface. Her heart raced. Her stomach felt as if she was about to heave.

"Nikki?"

She stood up abruptly, pulling away from Tyler's grasp. Turning too quickly, she jammed her elbow into the lamp on the side table. It tumbled onto the hardwood floor, shattering the glass base.

The sound of breaking glass echoed through the quiet house. Tears burning her eyes, she knelt down and grabbed one of the large shards of glass, stabbing herself in the process. Blood pooled at the end of her finger. She automatically stuck the injured spot in her mouth.

"Nikki, stop." Tyler grabbed her wrists and eased her back onto the couch. He grabbed a tissue from a box on the floor beside the couch and started wrapping her finger. "Forget about the lamp. I'll clean this up. Call Jack and have him trace the number."

"It won't matter. It'll be another dead end."

She felt completely frozen inside. As if a part of her had died—again—from hearing his voice. And that wasn't all. Accusations and guilt flooded through her. If they'd caught him a decade ago, they wouldn't be looking for Bridget today. And Sarah might still be with them.

"Nikki." He knelt in front of her, tilting back her chin with his thumb so she had to look at him.

"None of this is your fault, but I need you to focus. Maybe he's simply getting scared, I don't know, but you need to call Jack. He might not be able to trace who bought the phone, but he might be able to get us a location."

She nodded, took the phone he handed her, then punched in Jack's number. He had to be nearby. Watching her. He knew she was here with Sam. She didn't expect Jack to be able to give her a name. He was too smart to have not used a burner phone. He'd simply called because he knew how hearing his voice—and not knowing who he was or where he was—would destroy her.

"Everything okay?" Sam flipped on the switch near the doorway as she hung up the call with Jack, flooding the living room with light. "I thought I heard a crash."

Nikki still sat on the couch, phone in her hand, her forearms resting on her legs, trying not to shake. Trying not to relive every moment of panic she'd allowed herself to succumb to since her sister's abduction. Or the fact that she'd just spoken with the man who ripped her family apart forever.

"I'm sorry, Sam . . ."

Tyler looked up from where he was carefully picking up the shards from the lamp she'd broken. "The lamp fell over."

"Forget about the lamp. I'll be right back."

He returned a moment later with a dustpan

and broom. "Why do I get the feeling this isn't really about the lamp?"

"He called me," Nikki said, still unable to move. "The man who kidnapped Sarah."

"Whoa . . . the Angel Abductor called you?"

Nikki still shivered despite the warmth of the room. She could feel herself shutting down like she had the afternoon Sarah had gone missing.

Sam grabbed a plastic trash can from beside the desk and held it while Tyler dumped in the glass. "What did he say?"

"That we missed clues. That he was disappointed we hadn't been able to find Sarah."

"I recorded the call," Tyler said.

"I want to hear it."

Tyler sat down on the couch across from Nikki and replayed the conversation. Sam leaned against the armrest as he listened to the conversation, the lines on his forehead marked with worry.

Tyler stopped the recording at the end, then set down his phone.

"What do you think, Sam?" Nikki said. "Do you think this guy's for real?"

Sam shrugged. "I don't know."

"And why now?" Nikki asked. "Why surface after all these years, and why involve me?"

"Because it's personal?" Sam said, throwing out ideas. "Because he wants something. Maybe a reaction from you?"

Nikki tucked her feet underneath her and pulled the afghan tighter across her shoulders. She didn't know how to put the pieces together. Didn't understand what he wanted from her. All she knew was that he'd left her feeling vulnerable, and they still weren't any closer to finding Bridget.

"What about tracing the call?" Sam asked, running his hand across his graying beard.

"Jack's trying to get a location on the phone right now."

"You're still exhausted," Tyler said.

"It's part of the job—"

"He's right, Nikki," Sam said. "This isn't just a lack of sleep we're talking about. You're emotionally exhausted."

She glanced at her watch. "I need to go relieve Jack and Gwen."

"Your boss can get a couple of officers to man the command post tonight in case any more leads come in," Sam suggested. "I'm going to make the call now. I've still got contacts within the local police department."

Nikki frowned at the two men. She couldn't fight them both. And she wasn't sure she was going to be able to function without a couple more hours of sleep.

Her phone rang again. This time it was Jack. "What did you find?"

"Traced the phone to the other side of town."

"But he knew I was with Sam."

"It was either a lucky guess," Jack said, "or more than likely, he could be tracking your phone like he did with Bridget. I could send some uniforms your way if you're worried—"

"No." Nikki brushed away the concern. "I'm probably just overreacting."

"Get some rest then. We'll see you in the morning."

"Fine. Give me two more hours."

"Three," Sam countered. "And this time, Nikki, you sleep in the guest room. Tyler—"

"This recliner's perfect for me."

"You always were a bully," she said to Sam, not trying to hide her relief.

"We'll all do better in the morning, Nikki, and you know it," Tyler said.

"Six o'clock, and not a minute later."

18

Nikki glanced at her watch. Something had woken her up. The faint smell of cigarette smoke lingered in the air. She searched her mind. Bridget had gone missing. They'd come to talk to Sam. And *he'd* called.

She shivered in the darkness, her eyes finally adjusting to the light, and wondered why the room felt so chilly. She didn't remember the room being so cold when she went to bed.

She looked toward the window. Lacy white curtains fluttered in the breeze. She scurried out from under the comforter into the icy room and checked the window. It was open. Her fingers gripped the sill. No wonder she was freezing. She reached for the thick robe lying across the end of the bed, wondering why she hadn't noticed the open window before. Irene must have aired out the house and forgotten to close it.

Nikki started to shut the window, then paused as movement outside caught her attention. A figure stood silhouetted at the end of the drive, staring at the house. The hairs on her arms stood up. She grabbed her service weapon she'd left on the bedside table. She couldn't find her shoes in the dark, but if she didn't hurry, he'd be gone.

Tyler snored softly on the recliner in the living room. She knew he'd bark at her for going outside without any backup, but she didn't wake him.

She slipped through the front door and looked toward the end of the driveway.

Whoever she'd thought she'd seen standing there in the darkness was gone.

She tugged the robe tighter around her waist, then started slowly down the drive, careful to stay hidden in the deep shadows of the tree-lined drive. Her bare feet pressed against the sharp gravel in the driveway, but she ignored the discomfort. Surely she was letting her imagination run away with her. Just because she hadn't noticed the window was open when she'd gone to sleep didn't mean someone had opened it while she'd slept. Fatigue had a way of playing with one's mind.

She eased down the drive, shivering with the drop in temperature. The brief weather report she'd caught had predicted lower than normal temperatures over the next forty-eight hours due to a spring storm moving in across the mountains. She held her weapon in front of her, every one of her senses alert for signs of movement along the driveway and street. Just because he'd called her on the phone didn't mean he was nearby. But that window had been closed. She was sure of it. And he knew she'd been with Sam. Which meant he was here. Watching her. Waiting for her. Taunting her.

Something clattered ten feet ahead of her. A cat screeched, then ran out from behind a trash can on the curb, vanished a moment later into a hedge.

I'm starting to lose it here, God. I need some direction. A way to put an end to this . . .

Nikki shook her head, heart pounding, still trying to sweep away the cobwebs that had formed from not enough sleep. She'd been running on empty both physically and emotionally. And she knew what happened when fatigue settled in.

You started seeing things that weren't there. Plots. Conspiracies . . . Maybe the figure had been nothing more than a figment of her imagination. She looked down the quiet road for any signs of movement. Streetlights cast yellow beams across perfectly manicured lawns. Porch lights reflected off cars in the neighbors' driveways. A dog barked in the distance. The wind rustled in the trees. But beyond that, the night was quiet.

She kept walking toward the road, fully awake now.

Where are you?

She was ready to put an end to the games. He'd had the upper hand for the last twenty-four hours. She needed to find a way to turn the tables. To put him on the defensive.

"Nikki?"

She spun around and pointed her weapon at the figure in front of her. "Tyler?" She dropped her gun to her side. "What in the world are you doing out here?"

"I could ask you the same question. Something woke me up, so I went to check on you. When I realized you weren't in your room—and noticed that the front door wasn't locked—it didn't take much detective work to deduce you'd gone out of the house. What I don't know is what you're doing out here by yourself."

She took a step deeper into the shadows. "I . . . I thought he was here."

"Where?"

"I don't know, but I woke up and the window in my room was open. When I looked outside, I thought I saw a man standing at the end of the driveway."

"You probably just had a bad dream, Nikki—"

"No. He was standing right there"—she pointed to the end of the driveway—"looking at the house. He wanted me to see him. Wants me to know that he's out here watching me."

"If you're right—if he is here—that means he's playing with you again. And you shouldn't be going anywhere alone."

Her phone beeped as a text message came in.

She unlocked her phone and read the message.

Eeny, meeny, miny, moe
Catch a killer by his toe.

Any doubts that her imagination had been working overtime vanished.

"What does it say, Nikki?"

She handed him the phone so he could read it.

Tyler grabbed her arm and started toward the house. "I want you back inside. Now."

Nikki followed him to the house. Once inside, he locked the door behind them.

"I'm going to send him a text," she said, pressing reply on the message.

"And accomplish what?"

She hesitated. "I don't know."

"You need to report this to the local authorities and your team. I don't want you handling this alone anymore."

Nikki made the call, then sat down on the couch, her fingers tight around her heart necklace. What if she'd put Sam and his wife in danger by coming here? And Bridget . . . she was still out there somewhere. Scared. Alone . . . If she was still alive. Twenty-four hours had passed. She knew how he worked. He would toy with her, kill her, then vanish. Just like he'd done with the others.

"We're going to find her," Tyler said, reading her mind.

She shook her head. "You can't promise me that, just like you can't promise me I'll ever find the answers to Sarah's abduction."

"I know. I just . . ." He sat down on the couch beside her and took her hands. "I want to fix this for you so badly."

"I know, but no one can fix this. Just like Katie, no one can bring back Sarah or those other girls. Even if we find him, there are still no guarantees we'll find Bridget alive. You were right. I don't know why, but he's been playing with us all along. It's as if killing the girls isn't enough. He wants to prove to me—to all of us—that he's better. That he's in control."

She'd worked through the situation over and over in her head, but all she'd managed to realize was that once again, he was winning.

She stared at a dark spot on the floor. "I can't do this anymore, Tyler."

"Can't do what?"

She hadn't consciously thought of quitting. Not yet. But now that she'd spoken the words out loud, it suddenly seemed like the right thing to do. Her mom and dad had cautioned her from the beginning about taking the position. Friends had warned her that she was too close emotionally. Even her pastor had questioned her decision. And they'd all been right. She was too emotionally close to the situation to be able to handle this kind of work. She'd thought she'd be able to separate the past from current cases, but so far all she'd managed to do over the past twenty-four hours was unravel.

She pulled her hands away from him. "I'm going to turn in my resignation."

"What are you talking about? If you quit, you let him win, Nikki."

"He's already won."

Justice had never been served with Sarah and the others, and now, another girl was more than likely dead. And he was free to go out and do it all again.

"No. He hasn't won." Tyler tipped up her chin with his thumb, forcing her to look at him. "He only wins if you stop trying to save them. Which is why you can't quit. This isn't over."

"You don't understand." She wadded up the afghan between her fingers. "I've searched for him for ten years. Ten years, Tyler, and in the end, he's still free and there's nothing I can do about it. I can't bring Sarah back or the other girls. I can't erase the guilt. And when I think about what he might have done to her, I can hardly breathe. When I think about what he could be doing to Bridget right now . . ."

"You're wrong, Nikki. I do understand."

Her breath caught in her throat. The living room clock ticked off the seconds in the background. Loss had marked both of them. Taken away pieces that could never be replaced. And pulled them into that place of darkness she fought every day to escape.

He dropped his hand into his lap. "Every morning when I wake up, a part of me begs God for a chance to redo the past. I would do anything to be able to have traded places with Katie. Because I should have been the one who died, not Katie. And now . . . now I have to face every day without her. I have to be both mommy and daddy to Liam, when I don't know how. And in losing her . . . her death was my fault."

Nikki's eyes widened at the confession. "Your fault?"

The three of them had gone boating that day, Tyler, Katie, and Liam, on the forty-foot sailboat Tyler had inherited from his father. No one had expected only two of them to return alive.

"Katie had been feeling off that week," he said. "She was so tired of being pregnant and bloated. I thought a day on the water would make her feel better."

Nikki shook her head. "I still don't understand how anything that happened that day was your fault."

"She hadn't told me she was having dizzy spells, but the water got rough that afternoon. I should never have taken her out there. It was my job to protect her, and I wasn't there. I couldn't stop her from dying."

Katie had slipped, hit her head, and fallen into the water. By the time Tyler managed to pull her out, she was gone.

He sat beside her, jaw tense, his gaze lost in the heartaches of the past. "I served in the Middle East for three tours and somehow managed to cheat death while good men died around me. They gave me a Purple Heart for being wounded in the line of duty to my country, and yet I let Katie and our baby die. And after all those arguments we had over my leaving the military . . . suddenly none of that mattered anymore."

"You didn't let them die." Nikki couldn't fight the emotions anymore. Her eyes burned with tears, but her heart hurt even worse.

It had been an accident. No one—not even the police—had blamed him after the initial investigation had been completed. It had simply been one of those freak accidents no one had control over.

Like Sarah.

Nikki pushed away the thought.

"Her death was an accident . . . Not your fault."

"I know. Deep down I know that, but sometimes . . . I just can't stop thinking, if I could go back and change that day. If I'd been with her at that moment instead of below deck . . ."

But neither of them could go back and change

the past. She looked up at him and caught the deep sadness in his gaze. Just like with her, he was going to carry this guilt with him the rest of his life if he didn't learn to let it go.

"Tell me how we can let go of the past."

"I don't know." He wrapped his arms around her, pulled her against him. "I don't know. But what I do know is that I've seen you with Bridget's brother and mom, and you have a source of empathy that most can only pretend to have. You've been there. You understand, and they respond to you. And that matters. Because it matters to them."

Nikki closed her eyes for a moment, still not convinced. "But it brings the loss of Sarah rushing back every time. I'm tired of living through those moments again and again. The moment we realized Sarah was gone. The panic and worry and frustration of not being able to find her. I thought helping others would help me let go, but if anything it makes her loss even more real."

Like a knife reopening wounds that had never completely healed.

"Which is why no one—especially me—would fault you if you walked away from this," he said. "But I truly believe if anyone can find this guy, it's going to be you."

A light flipped on in the hallway. Nikki looked up as Sam walked into the living room.

"Morning," he said with a yawn. "I was hoping you'd sleep in a bit more, Nikki. It's not even six yet."

"I woke up a little while ago . . ." She hesitated, not wanting to say why or what she'd seen.

"He was out in the driveway," Tyler said, speaking her fears out loud. "And he sent her a text. He's playing with her. With all of us."

"This has to stop," Sam said. "While you go back to town, I'm going to keep going through these files. See if I can find something we missed. Call in a few favors and see if I can find something that matches up to what's going on today."

"You've already done so much, Sam—"

"You don't think I'm involved in this?" Sam's frown deepened. "I want this guy as much as you do. He killed at least six girls, and I couldn't bring him in. That alone keeps me up at night, and I'm sure I could say the same for you, because the emotional drain is starting to show in your eyes."

Nikki let out a breath of relief. "Thank you."

"Irene is planning to make some of her famous banana pancakes before the two of you head off, but then I'm going to send her to her sister's for the next couple of days until all of this blows over. Just in case this guy decides to come back."

"I think that's a good idea. And, Sam—"

Nikki's phone rang and she pulled it out of her pocket. "Thank you again. For everything."

Sam folded his arms across his chest. "We're going to find this guy. And once we do, we're going to find a way to put him away for the rest of his life."

Nikki answered the call.

"Nikki? This is Ranger Anderson."

"Morning, is everything all right?"

"Looks like we might have a new lead on your girl. I just got a call from one of our regular volunteers who works here at the park. He made a run up to one of the campsites to do some routine maintenance. While he was there, he found a ring. Said he didn't think anything about it until he was watching the news this morning." Anderson hesitated. "It matches the description of the ring Bridget was wearing."

19

Nikki met up with Jack and Gwen at the mobile command center just after six thirty with a large coffee in hand, still trying to pump enough caffeine into her body to override the lack of sleep. She'd already shared with them the details of what had happened earlier that morning, keeping her thoughts of quitting to herself. Tyler had convinced her not to make any hasty life-altering decisions, but that didn't mean she was done considering it.

Low clouds gathered above them, leaving a light mist in the air as the predicted storm continued to roll in. Weather between March and May was always unpredictable. And while April was typically mild, severe storms during this time of year weren't uncommon, including tornadoes, strong winds, and even snow flurries given the right conditions—easily destroying any evidence potentially left behind by their abductor.

For now, though, all she could do was follow their latest lead and pray it was the break they needed. She could still hear his voice replaying in the back of her mind and wished she could understand what game he was playing. Maybe he'd really had Bridget's ring, but as far as she was concerned, he could just as easily be using the ring to throw them off.

Kyle arrived right behind them, wearing the same long-sleeved shirt he'd had on yesterday. Someone had apparently convinced him to sleep a few hours at one of the local hotels, but she couldn't help but wonder if he'd slept at all.

"Did you get any sleep?" she asked him.

"Not really." Kyle's eyes were puffy, his frown pronounced. "I was just told you might have a new lead."

Nikki glanced at her teammates, not wanting to get his hopes up on a lead that may or may not go anywhere. "One of the volunteers who works in the park found a ring yesterday at one of the campsites. We believe it's Bridget's."

Kyle's face paled. "Our mother gave it to her for her birthday when she turned fourteen. She never takes off that ring. If he killed her, then—"

"We don't have enough information yet to know what happened at this point, Kyle."

"But if it *is* hers . . . It's been over twenty-four hours, and we don't have any proof she's still alive except for this ring? If she's dead—"

"You can't start thinking that way, Kyle." Nikki shook her head. "Not now. Not ever. All you can do is take one day at a time and keep praying for that miracle."

"What do you want me to do in the meantime?" he asked.

"Exactly what you've been doing. Keep answering the phones. Send out approved updates on Facebook and to the media. Make sure the volunteers that will be arriving soon have plenty of flyers. What you're doing is making a difference. The more people who see her face, the better our chances are of finding her."

"You'll tell me if you find out anything, won't you?" Kyle asked.

She nodded. "You know we will."

But Nikki caught the doubt in his eyes. The realization that you were stepping deeper and deeper into a nightmare with every day that passed. And there was no way to know when you'd be able to wake up. It took all of your energy. All of your rational thoughts. And sometimes, your very sanity.

"Anderson should be here any minute with Randall Cooper, the man who found the ring," Nikki said after Kyle left. "We can interview him as soon as they get here."

Gwen shook her head. "We'll keep going through Bridget's online profiles. I'm still convinced he had to have slipped up somewhere."

All they needed was one mistake.

Nikki glanced at her watch as she walked into the conference room. "Gwen, get an update from the local authorities who were watching the phones last night, then go ahead and get the volunteers up to speed."

"You got it."

Statistics played through her mind like a funeral dirge. Seventy-five percent of abducted kids were dead within the first three hours. And they were way past that timeframe.

Anderson showed up at the door to the conference room, carrying the ring in an evidence bag and wearing his uniform and "Smokey the Bear" hat.

"Morning." He set the evidence bag in front of her on the table. "Cooper's on his way here now."

"Morning. That's great." Nikki smiled up at him. "Before we get started . . . I know I thanked you yesterday, but please make sure your wife knows how much I appreciate the clothes."

Irene had washed and dried Nikki's clothes, but she'd opted to wear the warmer fleece with today's drop in the temperature.

Anderson chuckled. "It's not the first time she's come to someone's rescue, but I'll be sure to let her know."

"Thank you." Nikki set down her coffee, then picked up the photo of the ring they'd gotten from Bridget's Facebook account and compared it to the ring itself. Anderson had been right. The sterling silver floral band was a perfect match.

She held up the ring to the light and read the inscription.

To my Bridget with love.

There was no doubt it belonged to Bridget.

She glanced up as Jack walked into the room, his eyes still red, his face blotchy. "It's definitely a match."

He picked up the bag and read the inscription out loud, then sat down. "Wow, I guess there's no question there."

"Mr. Cooper . . . ," Nikki said. "What exactly does he do here in the park?"

"A bit of everything." Anderson folded his arms across his chest. "He's been volunteering for five . . . maybe six years and has been involved in everything from assisting in the visitor center to maintenance to litter control. Yesterday we sent him up to fix a cable that had snapped on one of our food storage systems that keeps away the bears. He's pretty willing to do whatever we need."

"So you would classify him as a reliable witness?"

Anderson nodded. "Don't know why not. I've never had any reason to doubt his character before."

"Good. Anything else you can think of before he gets here?"

Anderson set his hat on the table and shrugged. "He's a hard worker who keeps to himself mostly. A bit eccentric, I suppose, but he's friendly and the tourists love him. He spends his off time searching for planes that have gone down in the park and has his own share of ghost stories to tell, but for the most part, he's just another volunteer with a love for the outdoors."

"Is that common?" Jack asked. "Hunting for downed planes?"

"You'd be surprised. It's a bit like geocaching, but they call it wreck-chasing. In this park alone, there's been over fifty recorded crashes over the past few decades. And like missing people, a handful of them have never been found. Which means you've got treasure hunters, conspiracy theorists, and even proponents of alien abductions searching on any given day."

"But you don't think he's capable of kidnapping."

"Kidnapping?" Anderson shook his head. "I didn't think Cooper was a suspect."

Nikki leaned forward, realizing she was the one sounding like a conspiracy theorist. But if Tyler was right—if this guy *was* playing games with them—they couldn't assume anything. "He's not at this point, but after last night, I'd put the pope on my suspect list if he gave me a reason."

Anderson frowned. "I understand that, but Cooper's an older man who volunteers."

"He also has time on his hands *and* knows the park. I'm just making sure I don't miss anything."

"I'm sorry. You're right to not cut any corners." A call came in on Anderson's radio. "He's just arrived at the visitor center. I'll go get him."

Jack leaned against the table while they waited for Anderson to return. "You really think this guy's involved?"

"I have no idea, but the hat, the phone, and now the ring . . . This guy isn't sloppy. And we know now that he's playing with us."

"Any theories as to why?"

Nikki turned to Jack and caught his gaze. "Why does anyone abduct a sixteen-year-old girl and murder her in cold blood? He's killed a minimum of six girls. Made them disappear without a trace. That's careful and calculated. Not sloppy, like leaving a hat or a ring in plain sight. He might think this is a game . . . but it's one we're going to win."

A couple of minutes later, Anderson stepped back into the room with Randall Cooper. He offered him an empty chair and made quick introductions. Nikki shook his hand, then took another sip of her coffee as she studied the older man. Like all the volunteers, he wore UPS-colored brown pants and a khaki button-down shirt with a name tag. Late fifties, five foot ten, and clean-shaven with a light, jagged scar on his right cheek, he was clearly in good shape physically for his age.

"Mr. Cooper." Nikki sat back down in her chair next to Jack. "I appreciate your coming to talk with us so early. I understand you have possible information for our missing persons case."

"I hope so. It was pretty upsetting to hear about that girl this morning. We see it here in the park from time to time, but it's usually because they take a wrong turn or run into a bit of bad weather. Not an abduction. That's frightening."

"Yes, it is," she said, certain the tourists must like the man, with his warm smile and friendly disposition. "How long have you been working in the park?"

"Six years in August as a volunteer. I retired early, so I'm here pretty much full-time. Don't live near any family, and it beats sitting around doing nothing."

"What kind of work are you involved in, here in the park?"

"I've done it all, but right now I'm what they call a Cultural Resource Interpreter. Most days, though, I'm called into other jobs, depending on what is needed for the day."

"What exactly is a Cultural Resource Interpreter?"

"Basically, I share the cultural history of the area with the visitors. That and a few ghost stories thrown in for free."

"I've always wondered why there were so many ghost stories around these mountains," Jack said.

Cooper chuckled. "It's been said that the Smoky Mountains have more ghost stories per square mile than any other spot in the country. My father grew up around here and used to tell them all the time. The explanation's simple, really. You've got Cherokee history, tales left behind by frontiersmen, two wars, and two peoples with a knack for storytelling—the Cherokee and the Scots-Irish. Even if you don't believe in ghosts, you have to love a good story."

Nikki frowned. No doubt her father—and apparently Jack as well—would enjoy spending an afternoon swapping stories with this man, but today they needed to concentrate on finding Bridget. "Where were you working yesterday afternoon, Mr. Cooper?"

The older man turned his attention back to her. "I was out fixing one of the cables that had snapped up at one of the backcountry sites."

"Besides the broken cable, did you see anything else unusual in the area?"

"No. Met the usual folks along the way. Most of them are just looking for a quiet place to get away from their busy lives for a little while."

"Did it appear that anyone was staying at the campsite where you were?"

"I'm not sure if anyone was registered or not, and I didn't see anyone. But most people were probably on that trail at that time."

Nikki made a note to check out the registry. According to park regulations, anyone who planned to stay overnight had to not only reserve a campsite or shelter but also carry a permit.

"I guess this isn't the first time you've been

asked to be on the lookout for someone who's gotten lost up in the mountains," she said.

"Hardly. A couple dozen go missing each year. Most are found within a few hours, thankfully. Others, well . . . there are a few who aren't quite so lucky."

Nikki set the ring on the table. "Tell me about the ring you found."

Cooper clasped his hands in front of him. "Didn't think much of it when I found it, to be honest. I planned to drop it off at the lost and found, figuring some girl would be missing it. By the time I got back, though, I'd completely forgotten about it. Until I watched the news this morning. Sent shivers up my spine when I saw the description of the girl, including the ring she was wearing. Then when the name on the ring was the same . . . well, I could be fairly certain it was hers."

"And you did what with the ring after that?"

"I took it straight to the police station. They told me they'd make sure the detectives investigating the case—which I presume is you—would get it."

"And you found this ring near one of the shelters?"

Cooper nodded. "After I fixed the broken cable, I decided to clean up a bit. That's when I found it."

"Where, exactly?"

"Near the fire ring. At the time, I figured the

owner must have been cooking over the fire and it slipped off. They were lucky it didn't fall in the fire."

The ring didn't guarantee that Bridget had been there, but it was the best lead they had so far. "Can you take us to the place where you found this?"

"Of course, but I'm not sure that's the best idea." Cooper glanced out the window. "There's a pretty severe storm moving in. Last I checked, it was predicted to hit in the next few hours. The weather tends to be a bit temperamental up here."

"Which is why we need to go now. Rain will wash away any evidence. How long to get to the site?"

"A couple hours on horseback."

Nikki caught the flicker of concern on Jack's face. Two hours could be too late.

"What about the helo?" Jack threw out. "We could arrange one with the highway patrol, if there's a clearing nearby."

"That shouldn't be a problem," Cooper said. "There's a clearing about a hundred yards or so from the site."

"Perfect." Nikki tossed her empty coffee cup into the trash and stood up. "Jack, I need you to make the transport arrangements. We'll leave as soon as possible. And, Anderson, I'd like you to come with us along with at least one other ranger. If there is any evidence at that campsite, we need to get it before the storm hits."

20

Nikki studied the terrain from the helicopter as they headed toward the clearing northeast of the visitor center. Below them, endless miles of trails weaved their way between mountainous forests, waterways, and vegetation. In the distance, dark clouds closed in on them. The weatherman's predictions had been right about the impending bad weather, but taking the time to search the scene was a chance they had to take. If there was any evidence that Bridget had been in the vicinity, they needed to find it before the rain washed it all away.

Nikki's mind drifted as they flew over a field of white trillium. Before Katie had met Tyler—long before Liam had come along—she and Katie had spent their days off hiking and rock climbing. One year they'd spent eight days hiking through Springer Mountain in Georgia, and another year ten days through Virginia's Shenandoah National Park. They'd even made plans to hike the entire Appalachian Trail that snaked its way for over two thousand miles through fourteen states. It would be the ultimate outdoor adventure. Anything to push them both physically and mentally.

And Tyler had managed to fit perfectly into Katie's life.

But marriage slowly changed things for Katie, especially after Liam came. Days off hiking the great outdoors had come farther and farther between. And while Katie relished being a mom, Nikki's focus had shifted to her career and finding Sarah.

They'd still managed to get together, but with Tyler gone overseas for months at a time, Katie was more often than not a single mom trying to juggle a part-time job as a cake decorator along with play dates, birthday parties, and soccer games. Their dream of escaping for six months to hike from Georgia all the way to Maine had been put on hold indefinitely. Instead, three or four times a year Nikki would show up with a date—or on her own—and they'd head out before dawn to hike, rock climb, or spend a day on the *Isabella* while Tyler's mom kept Liam. Somehow she'd believed that staying in shape would keep them young forever. None of them ever imagined Katie would die doing something they all loved.

Five minutes later, their pilot, Patrick Reynolds, landed the bird safely in the clearing and shut off the engine. Nikki climbed out of the helo behind Tyler, Cooper, and the rest of the crew: Ranger Anderson and Ranger Simpson; Reynolds and his copilot, Christian Lopez; and of course, Jack.

Their pilot checked his watch before addressing the group. "At the speed the storm's coming in, I want to be up in the air and out of here in the next forty-five minutes. And even that's pushing it, so no one wander off too far."

"Then we need to go directly to the campsite, Mr. Cooper," Nikki said.

Nikki plunged through the spongy ground cover behind their guide, absorbing her surroundings while the blades of the helo came to a stop. Her father had been the one who'd given her a love for the great outdoors. And shown her that there was always something new to discover.

Nikki ducked under a broken branch, scraping her shoulder, while battling her own bad memories. If Bridget was nearby, Nikki needed to be completely present. Any memories hovering in the shadows of her mind would have to be dealt with later. Their intent was to find evidence, then get back to their command post as soon as possible.

"Watch your footing," Cooper said. "This trail's also a horse trail, so it's muddy and slippery."

Nikki studied the thick forest surrounding them, wondering if the abductor had brought Bridget here. Wondering where she was now.

"I am so glad we chose to take the helo up here," Jack said beside her.

His eyes were still red and watery, and while the swelling had gone down where the wasp had stung him, the spot was still red and irritated. She should have left him and brought Gwen instead, but part of his background included specialized training in forensics. Which meant she needed him here.

"I'm assuming you're not fond of horseback riding either?" she asked.

"When I was twelve, I fell off a horse and broke my leg in three places. It's another bad memory." Jack shook his head. "Though I have a feeling you would have enjoyed it. You've probably even thought about hiking the Appalachian Trail."

"I have, actually," she said, watching her step.

"Why am I not surprised? Two thousand-plus miles of trekking through the wilderness for five or six months, battling the weather, bad food, no running water, hot showers, or flushable toilets . . ."

"And that doesn't appeal to you?"

"You have to ask? My nephew's planning to hike it next year, though. He's going with a couple buddies. You wouldn't believe all that they are doing to prepare over the next few months. Boots, waterproof clothing, first aid kit, flashlights, portable stove and a way to purify water, tent, sleeping bags, and food. And then you've got to lug those forty-odd pounds eight-plus hours a day for weeks."

"I should have left you back at the command center."

"Just because I grew up in the city doesn't

mean I can't do my job, even if it does include a stint through these woods."

Trees were thicker here, then slowly thinned out again as they approached a mountain stream with its little waterfalls. They crossed a footbridge that extended over the creek. The sound of rushing water surrounded Nikki, reminding her that the woods were never silent. Pinecones dropping. Branches rubbing against each other in the wind. Squirrels foraging . . . Even in the quiet moments, there was activity. And normally, beauty. But today, the sounds sent eerie chills up her spine.

"Welcome to a bit of paradise," Cooper said when they finally reached the campsite.

The setup was simple. There was a table and bench for cooking and eating, and a fire ring. The rustic lean-to shelter consisted of three walls and a roof plus a metal, bear-proof gate in the front. Inside were bunk beds with a skylight above them and a fireplace with a tarp to help keep the rain out.

Nikki glanced at Tyler and caught his somber expression. Apparently she wasn't the only one fighting not to dredge up memories everywhere she turned. He and Katie had spent their second anniversary camping not far from here. Katie had assured him that as long as they were together, the intoxicating night sky and a warm fire were all she needed. He'd promised her a Caribbean cruise once money wasn't so tight.

Unfortunately, that trip had never come.

Nikki reined in her thoughts. "We don't have a lot of time. Let's break into teams and divide the area into a grid. Look for anything that we might be able to tie to Bridget, and let me know the minute you find something. Mr. Cooper, Jack, you're with me. I want to know step by step exactly what you did here."

Nikki turned to Cooper while the others split up. She'd camped in the park dozens of times from the time she was a kid, but she'd never really thought much about what went on behind the scenes. "What exactly were you doing when you found the ring, Mr. Cooper?"

"Like I told you, I came here to fix a cable for the food storage system. The park provides cables so backpackers can hang their food and gear off the ground and away from the bears. It not only protects the campers but keeps the bears from learning to depend on human food."

"Walk me through your steps."

"Okay. I had several campsites in this area to check out. This one was my fourth." He stood in the middle of the open space and pointed toward the south. "I arrived on horseback from that direction and went straight to work. I fixed the cable, picked up a few scraps of trash, then left."

"Tell us about these campsites," Jack said. "Who maintains them and how do you get to them?"

"There are ten locations for developed camp-grounds where you have restrooms with running water, flush toilets, and picnic tables. These backcountry campsites are different. There are almost ninety backcountry campsites, and fifteen backcountry shelters. Backpackers have to hike in, either to a campsite or a shelter. Each one has to be maintained, most of the time by volunteers who have adopted a specific site. Volunteers agree to visit the site regularly. There are also ridgerunners this time of year."

"Ridgerunners?" Jack snapped a photo, then slipped a candy wrapper he found into an evidence bag.

"Think of them as concierges. They talk to the backpackers who are hiking the Appalachian Trail and going through the park, and the day hikers. They make sure people have backcountry shelter permits, handle problems among the hikers, and even take care of the outhouses along the trail."

"I think I'd want to skip that aspect of the job." Jack chuckled and continued photographing the scene. "So the ridgerunners are like . . . ambassadors."

"Exactly."

"Which means volunteers like you, and the ridgerunners, know this park well."

"It's our job to know the park."

If Bridget's abductor had brought her into the park, it made sense that not only did he know the park but he would want to keep her off the grid, not bring her to a campsite where they were liable to run into people. Mid-March to mid-May was thru-hiking season when most hikers made their way through the Smoky Mountains while hiking the Appalachian Trail. Backcountry camp-sites, like this one, tended to fill up quickly by midafternoon. Especially with a storm on the way.

She looked up at Cooper, her mind still working through the questions she had. "I spoke to Ranger Anderson yesterday about how people go missing here each year. What do you think? If you wanted to disappear in the park, how hard would it be?"

"To disappear?" Cooper's gaze narrowed. "I'm not sure I understand."

"Just humor me."

The older man rubbed his chin. "I suppose it's possible, depending on how well you knew the area, though this time of year it would be harder."

"So if you, for example, wanted to disappear inside the park, what would you do?"

"Me? I can't say I've ever thought through this, but when you're looking at hundreds of square miles of land, there would be plenty of places to hide. That's why hikers are advised not to hike at night and to stay on the trail. There would be no way to search every square inch of this place."

"So if you wanted to disappear, you'd want to avoid the campsites."

"That's where your chances of running into other hikers, campers, or rangers would be the greatest. And besides that, to stay at a campsite, you have to have a permit. More than likely someone would find out if you didn't. So if you wanted to stay off the grid, staying at a campsite wouldn't make sense. Though camping anywhere other than designated campsites and shelters isn't permitted."

"Then why would her abductor bring her to this campsite?"

Cooper shrugged. "I have no idea."

She stopped in front of the shelter. Except for a layer of dirt and a few leaves that had blown in, the place was empty. "Is this campsite one of your responsibilities?"

"Not officially. I was simply doing general repairs."

Nikki considered the two standout options. Either someone had brought Bridget into the park and they had camped here and she'd managed to escape without him knowing, or like Hansel and Gretel, her abductor was simply playing games and leaving bread crumbs.

Or there was a third option. Bridget was already dead. Acres of forest and mountains were the perfect graveyard to hide a body. People had vanished here. Planes had gone down, their wreckage never discovered. How much easier to dispose of a body in the park?

She shivered at the thought.

Cooper brushed her arm. "You okay, Agent Boyd?"

Nikki pulled away with a start. "Yes . . . I'm sorry. After you fixed the cable, you said you cleaned up."

"Yes, most hikers try to comply with the park's 'Leave No Trace' principle, but there are always some who don't listen. The place wasn't bad, though. I decided to go ahead and clean out the fire rings and make sure all litter was disposed of properly since I was already here. That's when I found the ring."

"And the trash?" Nikki asked. "What do you do with the trash?"

"All trash is hiked out of here."

Which meant anything else Bridget had left behind was probably already gone. "Show me exactly where you found the ring."

She and Jack followed him across the camp-site to the fire ring.

"Right here. It was as if someone had been working on the fire and it slipped off."

Or if their abductor wasn't leaving a trail, Bridget had dropped it on purpose when he wasn't looking.

Nikki knelt beside Cooper. "Were the coals hot?"

"No, but most campers leave in the morning and arrive in the afternoon."

Nikki started moving in a spiral pattern away from where he'd found the ring. "What did you do next after finishing up here?"

267

"This was my last campsite. As soon as I was finished, I headed back to the visitor center."

Nikki frowned. Finding the ring might be encouraging, but it wasn't solid proof that Bridget had been here. Nor did it point to where she was now. Dozens of campers passed through these campsites every day, all encouraged to make as little impact on the environment as possible. It would be easier to find a needle in a haystack than the footprint of one young girl.

Nikki stood in the center of the clearing and stared at the shelter. Winds were picking up and the sky had darkened considerably around them. She glanced at her watch. Fifteen minutes had passed, and so far no one had found anything. As good a lead as this could have been, without something else, it was going to turn into another dead end. No more solid than chasing ghosts, like Cooper's legends.

"Agent Boyd?" Anderson shouted from outside the open area. "You need to come see something."

Nikki jogged toward where Anderson and Tyler stood in the middle of a second small clearing not far from the campsite. "What have you got?"

"You're not going to like this."

Nikki looked past them. A dozen feet away, within the shelter of a grove of trees, was a fresh grave.

21

Nikki felt the last sliver of hope she'd held on to for the past few hours slip away. Wind whipped against her hair as the fickle April temperatures continued to drop, especially at the higher altitude. Storm clouds churned along the horizon, but all she could see was a fresh grave where more than likely they'd find Bridget's body.

"We've got a compact shovel for emergencies in the helo," Reynolds said. "I'll go grab it."

Nikki nodded as the fading hope morphed into despair, then full-blown anger. She knew the odds of finding Bridget had been diminishing with each hour that had passed, but finding her here . . . this way . . . She blinked away the tears. She'd prayed. Begged God to guide them to her.

But apparently—the same as with Sarah—her prayers had gone unheard.

Her temples pulsed, while the lingering head-ache she'd fought the past two days continued to grow.

This isn't right, God. We should have been able to stop him.

But they hadn't. And now Bridget was, in all likelihood, dead.

"We don't know for sure that she's in there."

Tyler moved beside her, his fingers gripping her arm. "This could be another game. Just like he's been playing you all along."

"Maybe." She wanted desperately to believe the abductor was simply trying to get to her, and wouldn't hurt Bridget. But she knew she had to be realistic as well. He'd already proven he knew how to get to her. Toying with her emotions was like dragging her toward the edge of a cliff. Killing Bridget would push her over—and force her to relive Sarah's abduction afresh.

"Maybe he brought me here because he wanted me to find her? He told me how disappointed he was that I didn't find the clues he'd left for Sarah. To him, he's giving me another chance."

She could still hear his voice, playing over and over in her mind. Just like she'd seen him in her dreams for the last ten years. She knew his MO from every detail in the police reports. Knew how he stalked his victims. How he took their photos. Dug a fresh grave . . .

Was that the only reason he'd lured her here? To drag her into the scenario? This time it was another girl missing. Another family devastated. And she was left knowing she hadn't been able to stop him. Nikki felt the hairs on her neck prickle. She turned around slowly, staring into the dense forest surrounding them. A chipmunk scampered up one of the trees. Was *he* out there? Watching her?

Nikki glanced at Tyler. "No matter how many times I see what people are capable of doing, I'll never understand how anyone could do something like this to another person."

Reynolds returned to the site with the shovel and started digging up the freshly turned mound of dirt. Nikki's lungs compressed, forcing her to fight for each breath. Tyler stood silent beside her, because they both knew there was nothing to say at this moment. This was her worst nightmare. The ending she'd prayed against over and over. She knew the horror Bridget must have gone through to get to this place.

Sunlight pierced through a small opening in the clouds. Nikki felt a shiver slide up her spine. He *was* out there. Watching her. Smiling. Feeling the power he believed he had over his victims.

The power he believed he had over life and death.

The power she feared he now had over her.

The pile of loose dirt grew beside the unmarked grave. Somehow, she couldn't let him win. She needed to take everything she'd learned and figure out a way to use it against him. Because not finding Sarah's grave had become a two-edged sword. On one hand it had stopped the chance of any closure. If she was dead, her family still had to wait in order to move on. But if Sarah was alive, Nikki knew that ten years in captivity would change a person completely.

Which meant that even in those moments when she was able to cling to the lingering hope that Sarah was still out there, she couldn't help but wonder if it wouldn't be better if she wasn't suffering any-more.

At least if they managed to find Bridget alive, she'd have a chance to get her life back together with fewer battle scars.

She watched Reynolds continue to dig, praying with each scoop of dirt that Bridget wasn't here. Shovelful by shovelful, the pile expanded. Sweat beaded on the man's forehead. Reynolds wiped his hands on his uniform, then handed the shovel to Lopez, who took over for him.

Nikki held her breath, waiting. Jaw clenched. Heart racing. If he *had* buried Bridget, was there a chance she was still alive? Or was she simply grasping at straws again? There had been no evidence that any of his other victims had been buried alive. But so far, there was nothing. No body. No sign of Bridget.

A minute later, Lopez rested. "I don't think there's anything here, Agent Boyd."

Nikki let the air from her lungs out in a whoosh. Nothing in this case made sense. An unmarked grave with no body meant he *was* playing with her again.

"Dig deeper. Please. Just a few more minutes. There has to be something." She moved forward and knelt beside the grave.

Nikki grabbed a handful of loose dirt and clenched her fingers together. They'd found the bodies of four of the girls he'd killed. If there was no body this time, what was he trying to tell her? The beanie, the photo, the phone, the ring, the grave . . . none of them were a coincidence. And at this point, she had no option but to play along.

A minute later, the shovel hit something hard.

"Be careful." Nikki slowly stood back up, the loose dirt in her hand falling to the ground. "What is it?"

"I don't know, ma'am," Lopez said, still digging. "Give me a second."

She watched as Lopez dug around the item. A moment later, the officer pulled out a small metal box and handed it to Nikki. Her breath caught as she brushed the dirt off the top. Eight inches square. Three inches deep. The hinges creaked open as she lifted the lid.

Nikki felt the air sucked from her lungs as she pulled out the contents. "It's him."

Another photo. Another Polaroid.

But this time it was personal. Her finger ran down the familiar yellowed Polaroid photo. Her mouth went dry, nausea spreading through her, as she stared at the photo of her sister. Sarah looked back at her with fear in her eyes. She'd known what was going to happen to her. And Nikki hadn't been there to save her.

"How did he get this?" Nikki's voice cracked as she thrust the box back into Lopez's hands. "It's supposed to be locked up in police evidence."

Her mind fought to sort through what she knew. This wasn't possible. She'd looked through Sarah's case file dozens of times over the past ten years. Page after page, looking for something she'd missed. Never removing anything from the files. That photo had been there six months ago. But now it was here? How was that possible?

Tyler grasped her arm, keeping her steady on the uneven terrain. "Nikki, you can't let him get to you. Not now."

He was right, but she still couldn't move. Could barely breathe.

"It also means there's a good chance Bridget's still alive," Jack said. "It's the one thing that gives him leverage in this situation."

Nikki blinked back the tears, still unsure. Why would he need leverage? He already had the girl. Anger trumped the fear fighting to take over. Whatever game he was playing, she wasn't going to let him get away with it.

"I want this entire area swept again, this time perpendicular to the first search. Bridget might not have been here, but her abductor was. Which means we had to have missed something. Be thorough but as quick as possible before everything washes away. We need to find that one clue that will trip him up. I don't care how small or insignificant it might seem. We need to find him before it's too late for Bridget."

Their pilot didn't move. "I understand you want to find him, but this storm isn't slowing down, and I don't think any of us want to be stuck here all night. And I'm not flying this bird out of here if it's not safe."

"One more grid search," she said. "Twenty minutes. That's all I'm asking."

Reynolds hesitated, then nodded. "Twenty minutes, and we're taking off."

Tyler stepped beside her while the others spread out again for another search. "Nikki—"

"I'll be okay. Go search with them." She forced a smile. "I need to get some information from Gwen."

"You sure?"

She nodded, then watched him jog to catch up with his team. She waited for Gwen to answer while she automatically searched the secluded terrain around them.

"Nikki?"

"Gwen, can you hear me?"

"Barely, but yes."

The signal was poor, but at least she'd been able to get through. "Did you receive the boxes of files I asked for on the Angel Abductor?"

"Yeah. They were here when I arrived at the precinct in town."

"Great. What about my sister's files? Do you have those as well?"

"I haven't gone through them yet, but I'm sure they're here somewhere. Why? What's going on?"

"I'll fill you in later, but right now I need to know if there's something missing from Sarah's file."

Gwen let out a low groan. "That's going to take awhile. I haven't had a chance to organize them—"

"This is important."

There was a pause. "Okay. What am I looking for?"

"The Polaroid photo of Sarah. Just like the one that was left of Bridget. I need to know if it's still there. It will be filed on the day of her disappearance with the evidence from the crime scene. May 17, 2005."

"Okay."

Nikki closed her eyes and drew in a breath while Gwen looked, trying at the same time to calm her jagged nerves. Next month would be the ten-year anniversary of Sarah's disappearance. Funny how she could still see Sarah, still a teenager, as if it were just yesterday.

Memories clouded around Nikki, pulling her back to those last moments she knew she'd never forget. The week before Sarah had disappeared, Nikki had taken her shopping for a dress for her birthday. Her parents had offered to close the restaurant for her and her friends for a private party, and Luke had volunteered to play the DJ.

Finding the perfect dress hadn't proved to be quite as easy.

Sarah had tried on dozens of dresses in just as many shops until they finally stumbled into a boutique in downtown Nashville. She'd known the moment Sarah walked out of the dressing room in a pink chiffon dress with a full skirt that they'd finally found *the* dress.

"What do you think?" Sarah asked, twirling around in front of the three-way mirror.

"I think it's perfect."

Sarah's grin broadened as she clasped her hands in front of her. "Me too."

Nikki laughed. "And I think Brice is going to love it."

"I don't even know for sure if he's coming to the party."

"He'll be there."

Sarah had been *that* sister. She'd never been interested in following the crowd. She loved mixing vintage with funky modern prints, read the classics, preferred watching an original season of *Hawaii Five-0* over Jack Bauer, and listened to everything from '90s boy bands to '50s big bands. Her father had always said she was his flower child, and Sarah had been perfectly happy with that assessment. Comfortable in her own skin, she'd never been the typical teen who preferred spending every minute chatting with her friends.

"Nikki, are you still there?" Gwen asked.

"Yeah, I'm here."

"Good. I found the photo. It's here. Does that help?"

Nikki felt her chest constrict. What it did was prove that they were now looking for the same person who took her sister.

"Nikki . . . what's going on?"

She drew in a jagged breath, then gave Gwen a quick update of what they'd found.

"But there wasn't a body," Nikki said. "Just a photo of Sarah."

"I don't understand how he could have gotten it. I'm looking at the photo of your sister that was found at the crime scene."

"I don't know. He must have taken more than one picture."

And kept one for himself.

Her heart pounded. Up until now, she'd continued to hope they were simply looking at a copycat. As much as she wanted to find her sister's abductor, she didn't want to imagine he'd run free all these years.

Rain had started a light sprinkle across the clearing and the sky was continuing to darken. Time was running out. "We can't know for sure if Bridget was here or not, but he's been here."

Had to still be here. Somewhere.

Nikki hung up, then hurried to catch up with Jack. The other teams were slowly working the grid. Searching for that one piece of evidence that would help tie everything together. "Tyler was right about this being a game. A trail of clues. But I don't understand why." She brushed a strand of hair from her face. "Why go to all this trouble—luring me up here with Bridget's ring? So I'll find a picture of Sarah? And why did he take the time to bury it?"

"Because it's personal," Jack said.

It was the only thing that made sense. "Personal toward me. Okay. But why?"

"I don't know, but after the phone call last night, he clearly found a way to track down personal details about you and knows that you're looking for him."

She kept moving, searching the ground around her. "Why now, after all these years? Something would have had to trigger him to strike again. And this game he's playing? That was never a part of his MO. The authorities concluded he didn't seem to want the attention."

"Which points more to a copycat," Jack said.

"But he had this picture. Who else but Sarah's abductor would have it?"

"What if it isn't a game? What if he's trying to throw you off? Distract you."

"So maybe Bridget's not even in the park?" She stopped and rested her hands against her hips. "He could be on his way to Alaska or Florida, or Canada for that matter."

"He might have been planning it for a long time."

"Which means we could be following a ghost." But while the theory was plausible, she didn't buy it. He called her last night to hear her reaction. For whatever reason, he wanted her involved, which meant he was somewhere nearby, observing her. "I still think he's here. People like him enjoy seeing the reaction of those they want to hurt."

He'd told her he was disappointed she hadn't found the clues he'd left for her ten years ago. He wanted her to have found his handiwork. And they were missing something now. Just like they'd missed something all those years ago.

"So he's here, nearby, wanting to see how I react."

"It makes sense," Jack said.

So far he'd stayed in control of the situation. That had to change if they were going to find Bridget.

Cooper headed toward them. "Agent Boyd. Agent Spencer."

"Find anything else?"

"No . . ." He stopped and looked past them. "I need you both to stand still and don't move."

Nikki hesitated midstep, then put her foot down slowly. "What's going on, Cooper?"

"There's a black bear at your six, moving this direction."

22

Nikki froze. Full-grown black bears were nothing to mess with. They could weigh up to four hundred pounds and measure six feet in length. She'd heard of a number of trails and campsites currently closed due to encounters with aggressive bears, but you could have a run-in with a bear anywhere in the park. Even, apparently, in the middle of a criminal investigation.

"You've got to be kidding me," Jack whispered.

"I don't think he's kidding," Nikki said. "At two bears per square mile, our chances of running into one are actually pretty good."

Cooper took a step toward them. "I want you both to turn around slowly and face him. Then no sudden moves, but start walking backward with me."

"Most people would think we're lucky," Nikki said, doing as she'd been told. "They come hoping to run into one of these."

"As lucky as being stung by a yellow jacket and suffering from a stream of allergies. I should play the lottery when I get back home."

"Funny." Nikki glanced at Jack, who looked anything but amused. Clearly her attempts to lighten the moment weren't working.

"Keep walking," Cooper said. "Slowly."

She'd seen bears in the park before but never at such close range. At the moment, she'd have to agree with Jack and wished she were anywhere else but here. Not only were bears good tree climbers, but they could swim, and run up to thirty miles per hour. As long as the bear didn't see them as prey, they should be fine.

"How many people have died from bear attacks in these mountains?" Jack asked, continuing to slowly move backward.

"Just a handful," Cooper said. "The real problem started with humans trying to get too close to them. The truth is that you're far more likely to die from a bee sting or a car accident than a bear attack."

"Somehow that isn't very reassuring," Jack said, stumbling over a rock.

"We need to stand together to make ourselves look bigger," Cooper continued, "then get as far away from him as possible."

"And if we can't?" Jack asked.

Nikki felt the hairs on her neck bristle. She'd had enough close encounters lately. A bear attack wasn't something she wanted to add to the week's events.

"Jack, don't run," Nikki said.

"I'm not, but he's not stopping."

"You'll be fine," Cooper said. "Just step behind me. They typically avoid close encounters with humans."

Typically? Nikki wanted to laugh. Nothing about the past twenty-four hours had been typical.

She walked slowly backward, knowing she should have paid more attention to her surroundings. She'd been so focused on looking for any evidence Bridget or her abductor might have left behind, she'd somehow missed the fact that they were being stalked by a bear.

"Nobody run," Cooper said. "Just move slowly."

"This is exactly why I shouldn't have come," Jack said, taking another step backward. "I have no idea why every visitor in this park wants to spot a bear."

"Because they're beautiful creatures," Nikki said.

The bear wasn't deterred by their presence.

"All he wants us to do is back off," Cooper said.

"Then why is he still coming toward us?" Jack asked.

"I don't know. Just don't turn your back and don't run. Just keep moving slowly."

Nikki watched the bear; head low, ears laid back. That couldn't be a good sign.

Cooper started shouting, then picked up a couple of rocks and threw them in the bear's direction. Ten seconds later the bear turned around and disappeared into the bush.

Nikki's heart pounded in her throat.

"This is the problem with people feeding the

bears," Cooper said, tossing down a rock he'd picked up. "They end up losing their instinctive fear of humans."

Which in turn made them dangerous and unpredictable.

"You're the kind of guide I want out here, Cooper," Jack said, still breathing hard.

"He's right," Nikki said. "You just saved our lives."

"Chances are he would have ambled off on his own eventually."

"You're sure he's not coming back?" Jack asked.

"I'll keep an eye out, but I wouldn't worry."

Nikki glanced at her watch, her heart still pounding over the encounter. "Crisis has been avoided, but we need to finish up our section."

Jack frowned. "Sorry if I've lost my interest in wandering through these bear-infested woods."

"Look on the bright side," Nikki said, as they continued along the grid. "You're not going to be bear food tonight."

"Oh, that's reassuring."

They hadn't come up with anything yet. Winds were kicking up, and Nikki had no doubt that Reynolds was watching the weather closely, ready to pull the plug any second and fly them out of there before it got too dangerous to leave. But if they missed a piece of evidence, it would be gone by nightfall.

She picked up a cigarette butt and slid it into an evidence bag, but there simply wasn't much to find.

A bolt of lightning flashed through the sky in the distance. "Find anything, Mr. Cooper?"

He shook his head. "Nothing. I suppose the park's motto 'Pack out whatever you pack in' can be a disadvantage sometimes."

"Jack? Anything?" Nikki turned around when he didn't respond. "Jack, what is it?"

"Nothing." But he was holding out his hands and frowning.

"Jack . . ."

He turned to her. His hands were covered by thick red welts.

"You must have gotten stung by something."

"You're definitely right about the stinging part."

Cooper only needed a second to study the welts. "Looks like stinging nettle. There's a creek just down that ridge. The cold water will help stop the itching."

Jack hesitated. "And the bear?"

"I'm sure he's long gone."

Jack crashed through the underbrush ahead of them. Nikki followed behind him. So much for leaving no trace. Jack balanced on a couple of rocks near the water's edge and submerged both hands.

"Better?" Nikki asked a minute later.

"Yeah, but if you ask me, this is my last out-door assignment. You can send Gwen next time. I hear she loves wildlife encounters."

"Lucky for you, our time's up," she said, hoping one of the other teams had found some-thing. "We need to get back to the helicopter and get out of here."

Jack glanced up at the sky. "I agree. This storm doesn't look as if it's going to let up, and I for one don't want to end up stuck here when it hits full force."

"For once, I agree with you," Nikki said, as they made their way back.

Tyler and Anderson were already back at the shelter, talking to a gray-haired hiker in his early fifties.

"Nikki," Tyler said, introducing them, "this is Michael Lambert."

Michael shook her hand. "Everyone on the trail calls me Mountain Mike."

"It's nice to meet you," Nikki said. "You spend a lot of time up here?"

"I've hiked the Appalachian Trail three times now. All 2,180 miles."

Jack let out a low whistle, clearly impressed.

A light rain had started to fall. The storm was picking up speed.

"How long have you been up there this time?"

"Just a couple of days. Got going this morning a bit slower than normal. I'm used to running into groups of hikers, but with the storm getting ready to hit, it's been pretty quiet. They were just telling me about a missing girl?"

"We're looking for a girl—sixteen years old—we believe was here earlier this morning." Nikki got out one of the flyers she had in her pocket and unfolded it. "This is a photo of her and a sketch of the suspect who abducted her. More than likely she was with this older man, late thirties, early forties, though we don't have a positive ID at this point."

The man studied the photo. "No. Sorry, but I haven't seen her or the man. Most folks are staying put for the day because of the storm coming in. I'm looking to hole up myself as well, if it doesn't pass quickly. These rains can easily signal flash floods."

"Have you seen anyone else out around here today?"

"Ran into a family of four heading north and a couple of single gals who are camping for a week. Overall, it's been pretty quiet. An occasional solo hiker. Many of the thru-hikers are already past this part."

Nikki handed him the flyer. "Keep an eye out for her then, will you, and if you do happen to see her or anything suspicious, be sure and call it in."

"You bet." Mountain Mike grabbed his pack and started back for the trail.

Nikki glanced around the group, then tried her

two-way radio for Lopez and Reynolds. "They're not answering, and we need to get out of here."

"They were searching west of here the last time I saw them," Anderson said.

"We're going to have to ride out the storm if we don't get out of here soon," Cooper said.

Nikki glanced at Jack. The welts on his hands were getting worse. "You all split up and look for them, while I run grab some allergy medicine in my bag in the helo. Let's try to be ready to leave in five."

Nikki ran toward the bird, praying that the storm would delay another ten or fifteen minutes. If they ended up having to ride it out in the shelter, that meant she couldn't look for Bridget. She needed to get back to the command post and find a way to put all these pieces together.

She'd started around the back side of the helo when something red caught her eye in the under-growth. Her breath caught. Reynolds lay half a dozen feet into the bush, motionless. She felt a wave of nausea sweep over her as she bent down beside him. Blood ran down the side of his head. Eyes stared up at her. She felt for his pulse. Nothing.

Their pilot was dead.

23

Nikki's stomach heaved. Patrick Reynolds's vacant face stared back at her. She pressed her hand against her mouth, muffling a scream.

"Patrick . . . Patrick . . . You're going to be all right. Please . . ." Nikki felt again for a pulse, this time in his neck.

Nothing.

No, God . . . please . . . no . . .

She picked up a stick the size of a bat and stumbled backward. The end of it was covered with blood. She stared into the woods surrounding the clearing where they'd landed. He had to be close by. Sarah's abductor. But why kill Reynolds? And what did he want from her?

A twig snapped behind her. Panic flooded through her as she whirled around. Someone grabbed her arm. She held the stick above her head and started to swing it at her attacker. He wasn't going to get her too—

"Nikki . . . whoa . . ." Tyler grabbed the stick before she could slam it into the side of his head. "What's going on? Didn't you hear me call you?"

Her hands were still shaking when he took the stick, and her knees threatened to give way.

Tyler tossed the stick onto the ground, then pulled her against him. "Nikki? What happened? We heard you scream."

She glanced at the others who were right behind Tyler and pulled away from him. "I found Reynolds. The pilot . . . he's dead."

"Dead?" Jack asked.

She struggled to focus. No matter how emotional or personal this case had become, she wasn't going to let herself fall apart. They still had to find Bridget. The ring had led her here, but why kill their pilot if this was about her? It didn't make sense.

She pointed to the bushes where he lay staring up at them. She'd seen dozens of dead bodies. Worked crime scenes. Watched the local ME perform autopsies. But this was different. She had no doubt that someone wanted her to be here. Wanted her to find the unmarked grave, and now, wanted her to find Reynolds's body.

"I don't understand why he would kill him. Or how all of this connects to the Angel Abductor," she said.

Tyler knelt down over Reynolds's lifeless form. "I'm no medical examiner, but it looks as if someone whacked him on the head from behind. More than likely he didn't even see the blow coming."

She pressed a hand across her mouth, wondering how in the world their missing person investigation had turned into a murder scene.

"Did you find Lopez?" she asked.

"No, but we didn't search long. We heard you scream and came running."

"Maybe whoever killed him was trying to sabotage the helicopter, and Reynolds caught him," Jack threw out.

"Why would someone want to do that?" Anderson asked.

"I don't know."

Chills swept through her as the wind picked up and the rain started again. A burst of lightning struck, followed by a rumble of thunder. The storm was moving in directly above them.

"What I do know is that it has to be him," she said. "The Angel Abductor. He's here . . . watching. Playing some game that I don't know the rules to."

She tried to stop the panic. He wanted her here. Just like he'd wanted her to see him last night.

"So what does this mean?" Cooper asked. "We're here, cut off from the rest of the world with a murderer on the loose?"

The group congregated in a circle next to the helo.

One dead.

One missing.

"So no one has seen Lopez since we split off to search the area," Nikki said. "Which could imply Lopez is somehow involved—"

"Or he's dead as well."

Nikki hesitated at Jack's statement. She wasn't ready to jump to either conclusion, but neither could they dismiss the possibilities.

She glanced at her watch. "Did any of you see anyone else out here while you were working the grid?"

"Just that hiker," Jack said. "Mountain Mike."

Nikki glanced off into the woods. Had their killer been right in front of them and they didn't even know it? Nikki knew they needed to proceed carefully. Lopez and Mountain Mike weren't their only suspects, but they were a logical place to start.

Nikki glanced at the rangers. "Do either of you know Lopez?"

Anderson glanced at Simpson before speaking. "We've worked with him on a number of cases, primarily ones—like this one—that overlap into the park. From what I remember, he's been on the force for over a decade, and he's got a wife and two small kids."

"Do you think he's capable of murder?" Jack asked.

"I certainly don't want to think so," Anderson said. "He's a fellow officer of the law."

Nikki looked from one man to the next. How well did they really know anyone standing right here? Anderson . . . Simpson . . . Cooper. She shook away the thought. She was seeing a killer behind every tree. And more than likely, the killer was still out there somewhere.

"So we've got a man dead and some sort of psycho on the loose now on top of this storm coming in?" Cooper said, pulling his jacket tighter around him. "I don't like this."

"I don't either," Jack said. "Because someone killed Reynolds, and it wasn't one of your ghosts."

"My vote is to get out of here," Cooper said. "Clearly this—Angel Abductor—is out there somewhere. This storm's picking up, and I don't intend to be another victim."

"I agree," Jack said, "but with our pilot dead and our copilot missing, I don't see us going anywhere anytime soon."

"We've also got a crime scene to process," Nikki reminded them. "If we leave now, there won't be anything to find once the storm dies out."

"So we stick around while he picks us off one by one?" Cooper asked.

"He's right," Anderson said. "We've got some serial killer in my park playing games with us. I don't know about the rest of you, but I don't believe in coincidences. We need to find this guy."

Nikki shivered. "I agree, but searching for him in this weather isn't going to be easy."

"So what do we do?" Simpson asked. "Stay

here and ride out the storm like sitting ducks?"

"I don't think we have a choice," Anderson said.

"We need to at least try to find Lopez," Nikki said.

"It's not going to be easy, like you've already said. Visibility's already minimal," Anderson said. "You've seen how thick this foliage is, and the storm's going to get worse before it gets better. We're going to have to wait for a break in the weather before we can even consider getting out of here."

"He's right," Cooper said. "Spring's always unpredictable. And it's been overly warm the past few days, which means most if not all of those creeks we passed on the way here are going to flood."

An uneasy feeling slithered through Nikki. Whatever was going on, they were on their own to find out the truth.

"I suggest we all move inside the shelter and wait it out," Simpson said.

"I agree, but first we have a murder scene to process and a man to find," Nikki said. "We need to split up into two groups. Simpson and Jack, process the scene as quickly as you can before this rain washes away all the evidence. The body needs to be wrapped up and put inside the helo. Anderson, Tyler, and Cooper, stay together, but search the immediate area for

Lopez. We need to find him. We'll meet back at the shelter in fifteen minutes."

"And you?"

Nikki didn't miss the concern in Tyler's eyes, but while she might be stretched to the limit emotionally, she wasn't ready to hold up a white flag. Not yet.

"I'll help Simpson and Jack as soon as I've given Gwen an update on our situation."

After three attempts, she finally got the call to go through. "Gwen? It's Nikki. Can you hear me?"

"Barely . . ."

"Listen, I don't have a lot of time to explain. The storm's hitting hard and the connection's horrible. But we've got a situation here. I need you to do a background check on Christian Lopez."

"Your copilot?"

"Yes."

"What's going on? Did you find Bridget?"

"No, but on top of this storm, we've got another problem. Our pilot . . . he's dead."

Nikki waited a few seconds for Gwen to absorb the information she'd just given her.

"Wait . . . you said your pilot is dead?" Gwen asked.

"Yeah, and because of this storm, we're not going to be able to go anywhere anytime soon. So right now, I've got a dead pilot and Lopez is missing. I want you to see if you can find a connection between them. And while you're at it, go ahead and check out the rest of the group."

"What am I looking for?"

"At this point, any red flags that pop up."

"Okay. But are you telling me you think Lopez killed Reynolds?"

"I don't know what to think. Just see what you can find out for me. Do a background check on a Mike Lambert as well. His trail name is Mountain Mike. We ran into him a few minutes ago."

"I'm on it, but, Nikki, there is one other thing . . ." The call cut in and out briefly. "I spoke with your mother a few minutes ago. She's been trying to get ahold of you."

Nikki pressed her fingers against her temple and felt the panic closing in again.

I'm not sure how much more I can take, God . . .

"What did she say? Please tell me Jamie and the baby are okay."

"I'm sorry, Nikki, but they've just taken Jamie in for an emergency C-section. The baby's heart rate dropped about twenty minutes ago. It's possible that the cord prolapsed. That's all she knew for now, but she promised to call again as soon as they get an update."

A moment later, Nikki ended the call, then slipped her phone back into her pocket.

"You okay?" Jack stopped snapping photos of the crime scene for a moment and looked up at her.

"Yeah."

Except she wasn't.

A numbness moved through her as she started helping the men sweep the scene. The familiar routine felt mechanical. Photographs of Reynolds's body were taken along with the surrounding area. Relevant notes were made, and all possible evidence collected. By the time they all met back at the shelter fifteen minutes later, the rain was beginning to slash against the side of the shelter. They weren't going anywhere at this point, but at least they'd be fairly warm if they stayed inside.

"There was no sign of Lopez," Tyler said as he sat down under the shelter beside her.

"I suggest we go through our packs and see what we have," Anderson said. "We could be looking at spending the night up here if the weather doesn't break, and it's going to get cold."

"Spend the night up here?" Jack frowned. "I don't know about the rest of you, but I've had about as much of the great outdoors as I can handle."

"If we stay together, we'll all be fine," Nikki said.

"I'm not sure Reynolds would agree if he were still alive," Cooper said.

Nikki stood up and moved to the other side of the overhang to call Gwen again. They needed answers if they were going to figure out what was going on.

"Do you have anything yet?" she asked as soon as Gwen answered.

"I had to do quite a bit of digging . . . ," Gwen said. The connection was breaking up. ". . . might have just come up with something . . . real name is Kenneth Waters. He was in the military for a couple years, trained as a satellite communication systems operator. He eventually left the military and went to work as a software engineer . . . later arrested on felony fraud charges. That must be why he changed his identity. If there's a connection to the Angel Abductor, I haven't found it yet . . . but I'll keep looking."

Felony charges?

"I don't get it," Nikki said. "How did those involved in the police hiring process miss something like that? If he had a felony—"

"I'm not talking about Lopez."

"Then who are you talking about?"

"Randall Cooper," Gwen said. "The park volunteer who's with you."

"Wait a minute—" Nikki's head spun at the news. He'd been here all along? But it made sense. He'd been watching her, and now he'd found the perfect way to stay even closer.

"Where is he now, Nikki, because you need to be careful."

"I know." She was right. The man was a murderer.

Nikki hung up the call and turned around. Cooper blocked her way.

"What did Gwen tell you?" he asked.

Nikki swallowed hard, refusing to allow him to see the alarm in her eyes. "She's still doing a background check on Lopez. Trying to find out why he might have killed the pilot."

"Lopez isn't the only one she's looking at, though, is he?" Cooper took a step toward her. "She's looking at all of us. Hoping to find a motive behind who killed Reynolds . . . and the girls."

Nikki reached for her weapon. "Yes, but she—"

Before she could pull her gun from her holster, he grabbed her and pressed a revolver against her head. "You can't fool me, Nikki. I can see the panic in your eyes. I wondered how long it would take you to figure out who I really am."

"Cooper?" Tyler stood up on the other side of the shelter. "I don't know what you think you're doing, but you need to put the gun down. You're outnumbered here."

"Something I've already anticipated."

Anderson, Jack, and Simpson pulled their weapons and pointed them at Cooper.

"I wouldn't do that if I were you, gentlemen," he said. "Nikki, drop your weapon onto the ground. Slowly."

"Tyler's right." Nikki's jaw clenched as she

did what he told her to. "You're outnumbered and will never get away with this."

"You don't really believe that, do you? Because you know how much I've already gotten away with. Of course, I'm going to have to change my plan now that you know the truth. I thought about picking you off one by one until only Nikki was left. You're the only one I really wanted up here. But you already know that as well, don't you?"

"You took my sister."

"Are you surprised? My plan ended up being so much easier than I thought. Just like Hansel and Gretel's trail of bread crumbs. I had you playing right into my hands each step of the way. Your emotional attachment is a handicap, Nikki, but I suppose you've figured that out as well by now."

"Put the gun down, Cooper," Jack said. "There's nowhere for you to run."

"I don't think so." Cooper held the gun against her head with one hand, then moved his other hand up above her head. "Because I always make sure I have the advantage. I suggest that everyone take a slow step back unless you want me to be the last thing you see."

"He's got a grenade." Anderson took a step back. "Do what he says."

A tangible fear swept through Nikki. The officers continued aiming their weapons at Cooper, but even a seasoned sniper would hesitate in this situation. If they shot Cooper, she'd be dead.

24

Nikki tried to stem the flow of adrenaline. She knew enough about frag grenades to realize that with the pin out, she'd be dead the second he let go. Along with anyone within twenty feet.

"Tyler . . . Jack . . . all of you need to move back."

Cooper laughed. "You're finally taking me seriously. That's good. Because not only do I have a grenade, I really don't care if I die with her."

"Where's Bridget, Cooper?" she asked. "Or should I call you Waters?"

"I'm used to Cooper after all these years, but Bridget . . . she's the least of your concerns at the moment. What you need to worry about is making sure these men do exactly what I say."

Jack held his weapon steady in front of him. "Then tell us what you want."

"We're going to walk back to the helicopter—the four of you ahead of me. You can start saying your goodbyes to Nikki on the way."

They hesitated, then started moving slowly in the direction of the clearing. Raindrops ran down Nikki's face. She blinked away the water as she struggled on the uneven terrain to keep up with Cooper while he held her against him.

"In case you forgot," Anderson said, "you killed our pilot, and our copilot's missing. Which means we're stuck here with you."

"Don't worry. Tyler knows how to fly a helicopter. Don't you, Tyler? It was a part of your advanced training."

"I took a few lessons, but I'm hardly a pilot. What I do know is that even a seasoned pilot wouldn't take off in this kind of weather. The wind's too strong."

Nikki caught Tyler's gaze, unsure if he was telling the truth or merely bluffing in order to take control of the situation. If anyone could get her out of this situation, he could.

"Then we'll wait until the storm passes," Cooper said. "I'm in no hurry."

"Why don't you tell us what you want," Tyler said. Any tension in his voice had dissipated. "Because I don't think you really want to die today. Not this way."

Cooper laughed as they neared the helicopter, the rain still continuing to fall heavily. "Don't play me like you did yesterday with Bridget's mom, because I already know all the tricks of a negotiator. You want me to talk and you'll listen. You'll do and say anything in order to defuse the situation."

"I just want to make sure we all get out of here without anyone getting hurt," Tyler said.

"It's a little too late for that, considering at least one of you is already dead."

"Did you kill Lopez?" Jack asked.

"He was out cold when I left him, though I assume he'll wake up eventually."

"If the temperature drops any more, and we haven't found him—"

"Forget about him," Cooper said, the weapon pressing deeper into Nikki's scalp. "Because I know who you are, Tyler, and how every fiber in your body is itching to take me down and save the girl. But take my advice. Don't even try to play the hero. You think you're capable of saving her, but you're not. Not this time."

Nikki watched Tyler's expression darken and knew he was weighing his options. Weighing whether or not trying to take Cooper down was worth the risk. Trying to determine if the man was really ready to die. But she knew there was no way he could move fast enough. Because stopping a grenade wasn't the same as stopping a shooter with a gun.

One split second. One quick release of the grenade, and they'd all be dead.

Cooper stopped a dozen feet from the helicopter. "Here's what you all have to understand. I didn't walk into this situation blindly. I've spent months planning this. Months studying Nikki, Tyler, and Jack in particular, because I expected the three of you to be here."

"What are you talking about?" Jack asked.

"Jack Spencer. Thirty-five years old. Single, though not for lack of trying, which makes me wonder if you're simply just afraid to tie the knot. I also know about your juvenile record. Barely escaped a half-dozen brushes with the law. Decided at eighteen to join the army, and that decision probably saved your life. You eventually retired from the military and became a police officer now turned detective for this task force. And apparently no longer the bad boy you used to be."

"You—"

"And, Tyler, you might not officially be a part of this team, but Nikki respects your input. I know you were part of an elite combat force that was ready at a moment's notice to fight for your country. You led countless missions across the Middle East and other undisclosed locations until a bullet slammed into your leg and forced you back home. Back to your wife and son. I tried to imagine what it must feel like for you now. You're trained in handling every possible scenario. Swimming, parachuting, surviving, hand-to-hand combat . . . and yet I know your weakness."

"None of that really matters," Tyler said. "All I want to do is help you put an end to this."

Cooper laughed, all signs of the warm fuzzy tour guide gone. "You don't want to help me.

You want to see me dead. But believe me, take a step forward and try me. I'll blow us all to smithereens. And it will be your fault. Just like the day you lost your wife."

Tyler's jaw clenched as he spoke, and Nikki didn't miss the flinch in his eyes. "Today has nothing to do with my wife."

Cooper was right. He'd found Tyler's weakness.

"It's a cascade effect," Cooper continued. "An unforeseen chain of events leading to this moment. Because today has everything to do with her, actually. If she hadn't died, you wouldn't be here today with Nikki on the one-year anniversary of your wife's death. That is the chain of events that put you here at this moment in these particular circumstances.

"Of course, if it wasn't you, it would probably be Ryan in your place. That's his name isn't it, Nikki? The rich guy you've just started dating. Flowers. Dinner. The symphony . . . Does he know you came here with Tyler?"

Nikki bit her lip. "That's none of your business."

"I suppose not."

How had she missed this? He'd clearly been stalking her. Following her. Just like he'd done with Bridget. He'd known ahead of time she was going to be rappelling with Tyler. Anticipated that she'd end up being the one who took the call when Bridget went missing. He'd discovered a way to find her cell phone number and he'd been there this morning at Sam's house while she'd been sleeping. He'd planned the whole thing out. Detail by detail. Leading them to this point, just like Tyler had said, and she'd followed him right into a trap.

"You see, I know about the accident on the *Isabella* with your wife," Cooper went on.

"I said leave my wife out of this."

"Why, Tyler? She's dead. Died aboard the *Isabella* one year ago yesterday. I read your story online, though I have to say I was surprised about what I read. Maybe it wasn't like today, though. Maybe there were things that were in your control. Maybe there was more to the story."

"What are you talking about?" Nikki asked.

"I know how quickly things can spiral out of control. Maybe you got in a fight over your son, or maybe she confessed to you that the baby wasn't yours. That she'd been seeing someone else. You lost your temper—"

"What—?" Tyler started.

"All it really takes is a moment of weakness. One moment when you lose control. She falls into the water. You hesitate . . . just a moment too long. And she dies."

Tyler's jaw clenched again. "I. Didn't. Kill. My. Wife."

"Temper, temper, Mr. Grant."

"Tyler, don't," Nikki said. "He's just trying to egg you on."

"I can't help but wonder how hard it's been for you, Tyler. Going back into civilian life. It's an adjustment, isn't it? If you think about it, there really isn't any equivalent job outside the military for what you used to do. I mean, I suppose you could settle for being a swimming instructor, but that doesn't exactly have the same adrenaline rush of being out there in enemy-controlled areas. I'm not even sure rappelling has the same adrenaline rush as that. But I'm done talking for now." A beam of sunlight broke through the clouds. "The storm's let up enough for you to take off, so I'll give you to the count of ten to board the helo and start the engine."

No one moved.

"You don't think I'm serious, but you don't have a choice. You leave, or I start shooting before I blow her up. Starting with you." Cooper turned and aimed his gun at Jack.

She felt her chest press against her lungs. She knew he wasn't just spouting words. And she didn't want to be responsible for someone else getting killed.

Tyler took a step forward. "Leaving Nikki behind isn't an option, Cooper."

"I have to say, I'm disappointed. Especially considering all you know about me by now. Do you really think this is nothing more than a game to me?"

"None of us think it's a game," Anderson said. "But it does need to end now."

Cooper shook his head. "No one ever takes me seriously, but maybe this time you will. One . . . two . . . three . . ."

"Let her go, Cooper. You can disappear into those mountains," Tyler said. "You know this park as well as any ranger. It would be easy for you."

"Four . . . five . . . six . . ."

"Tyler, go." Nikki didn't even try to fight the panic any longer. "All of you. Please."

"I'd listen to her if I were you." Cooper aimed the weapon at Jack and fired.

"Jack!" Nikki caught the stunned look in Jack's eyes as he stumbled backward.

A wave of raw terror coursed through her as blood spilled down his neck.

"Go . . . Tyler . . . now, please. Take Jack and get out of here. Do what he says. I'll be fine. If you leave now, before the brunt of the storm hits again, you should be okay."

"A smart lady," Cooper said. "I told you to take me seriously, but you refused to listen. Push me, and I'll shoot each one of you, one at a time, and I'll still win. You've got exactly thirty seconds to get that engine going and get that bird out of here."

She could see the conflict in Tyler's eyes as the men pulled Jack into the helo. She nodded. "Go. I'll be fine."

Except she knew she wouldn't be fine. But it wasn't just a choice between her and Jack. She'd seen the hate in Cooper's eyes. He'd kill them all before he let her go. And that wasn't something she was going to let happen.

She watched as Tyler looked at her for the last time, then climbed aboard the helo and turned on the engine. It roared to life as the blades began to rotate. Someone shut the door.

She was going to have to find a way out of this on her own.

25

A sinking feeling swept through Nikki as the sound of the rotating blades began to fade into the distance. She felt his gun pressed against her head, knew the grenade was right above her. She'd finally found him. The Angel Abductor. He'd killed half a dozen girls, maybe more, and she knew he wouldn't hesitate to kill her as well.

His lack of emotions wasn't his only advantage. He knew the terrain far better than she did. In a few hours, darkness would envelop them, and even with a map, she knew she'd struggle. The sound of the helo faded, taking with it any remaining seeds of hope. She shook away that thought. Tyler would come back for her. She knew he would. And in the meantime, she had to find a way to escape.

"Why are you doing this?" she asked.

"Sit down on the ground and don't move," he ordered, taking a step back from her.

She hesitated before complying.

"You still don't get it, do you?" His deep laugh sent a shiver down her spine as he jammed the safety back into the grenade and stuck it in the backpack he carried, along with her weapon.

Whatever game he was playing, he clearly had nothing to lose. "This—all of this—was never about Bridget or even your sister. It was always about you."

"I don't understand." She caught the darkness in his gaze. If she didn't find a way to escape, he would eventually kill her. "What does all of this have to do with me?"

"You can save your questions for later. We need to get out of here. There's a group of hikers planning to stay here tonight, and I don't want to run into them." He jutted his chin toward her, his gun still aimed at her. "Give me your phone."

She hesitated again.

"Let's get something clear." His icy stare met hers. "You're not in control anymore. I am."

She counted to five slowly, then handed it to him. He threw it into the trees beyond the clearing, grabbed her arm, then started walking the opposite direction.

"Where are we going?" she asked.

"I have a feeling your friends will be back before long, and I don't plan to be here when they do. I've waited too long to have my plans messed up."

"They know it's you. How do you expect to get out of here?"

"They have to find me first, which won't be easy." He laughed. "I always warn people not to hike off the main trails. It's extremely easy to get lost. There are few if any other hikers to run into for help, and you can't even count on your GPS. I can't tell you how many hikers I've spoken to who have no sense of direction. Makes me wonder what they were thinking, actually. But it also goes to show how easy it is to get lost. Or to disappear and never be found."

They left the main trail as the rain started up again, the cloud cover making the dense woods even darker. Nikki hurried to keep up as the brush became heavier. She stumbled on the root of a tree.

"Watch your step," he said. "These mountains can be deadly. Stinging nettles, poison ivy, yellow jackets, and black bears for starters."

"Thanks for the warning."

Nikki pressed through the thick undergrowth of rhododendrons, ferns, mountain laurel, and magnolias. Past bear scat, salamanders, and moss. She knew he wasn't exaggerating about the dangers of leaving the trail behind. She'd once heard of these thick canopies described by those lost in them as "laurel hells." A terrifying place to discover you were lost.

But Randall Cooper—or Kenneth Waters— knew this area like the back of his hand. She followed him up the choked ridge and gazed down the gorge beneath the darkened sky. Praying that Tyler and the others were safe. Praying that Jack and Bridget were still alive.

That she wouldn't slip and fall down the deep gully. And praying someone would find her before it was too late.

But a fall wasn't what she was really worried about. She had no doubt Tyler and the rangers would return to look for her, but searching here, with darkness only a few hours away, would be almost impossible.

In some situations, darkness actually helped. Night vision amplified light sources, making a search at night easier than in the day. But the brewing storm above them added yet another complication. And Cooper knew it. She just needed them to find her before he killed her. If they didn't, they'd find her unmarked grave . . . or never find her at all.

He gripped her arm. "I'm assuming you're not planning on doing anything stupid. But just in case you are, the weatherman reported lower than normal temperatures tonight. You're going to need me."

"Just tell me where we're going and what you want from me."

Nikki tried to pull away from him, but he shoved her back against a tree, reached into the side pocket of his backpack, and tightly secured her hands with duct tape.

"All you need to know," he said, "is that we're going for a walk, but I don't think I can trust you not to try to escape."

She frowned. "You were right about one thing. Where would I go?"

Even in the daytime this terrain could be challenging. Six months ago a man had slipped not far from this very spot and later died from injuries sustained in the fall. That wasn't a chance she wanted to take. Lightning struck in the distance. A misty rain was falling. Already she was soaking wet and cold. If he didn't kill her, she could end up with hypothermia by morning if she didn't get warm.

They kept walking as the sun continued to drop toward the horizon. Before long, the only source of light was going to be the moon and the beam of her abductor's flashlight. There were rocks on the trail, a steep slope to her left. One misstep would send her plunging into the dark void below.

"Hurry up," he ordered.

She stumbled again, struggling to keep her footing. "How am I supposed to negotiate this trail with my hands tied up?"

"I've watched you climb." He gripped her arm tighter. "You're athletic. Stay right beside me, and you'll be fine."

She shivered, as much from his words as her fear of falling. "Where's Bridget?"

"Safe. For now."

A surge of hope seeped through her. If Bridget was still alive . . . "Where?" she asked again.

"Save your questions for later."

Nikki shivered again. For all she knew, he was taking her in circles. She'd never been off the official trails. Never hiked in a storm with black clouds swirling above them. Even her warm fleece wouldn't be enough protection. While the days this time of year were typically warm and pleasant, at night the temperatures dropped significantly.

"Do you really know where you're going?"

Cooper laughed. "I've spent years negotiating these trails. Why do you think I brought you here? I know it better than some of these rangers who work here."

She tried to move farther away from the edge of the trail. Refusing to believe that she would be another one of those who vanished, their bodies never to be found. No. Not if she could help it. But options at this point were severely limited. Without her own flashlight or warm clothing. Without a map or intimate knowledge of the terrain, finding her way out was going to be impossible unless she managed to stumble onto a group of campers. But even that came with its own risks. The man had a gun—and a frag grenade. She couldn't risk another person's life, especially with a man whom she knew wouldn't hesitate to shoot anyone who got in his way.

She needed his gun and his flashlight, and the

best she could hope for was to bide her time until an opportunity presented itself.

She also needed answers.

"Tell me how a computer engineer decides to leave behind his corporate world and become a volunteer in a national park."

"It was a process. I was being sucked dry. My boss didn't like me, the government was taking a huge chunk of my income, and commuting made for a twelve-hour-plus day. I didn't have a life anymore. Or at least one I wanted."

"And prison? Was that a part of that process?"

"I was wrongly accused by a co-worker."

Right.

Her foot slipped on a patch of rocks. He grabbed her arm and pulled her away from the edge. "Be careful. You could fall and kill yourself."

"Would it really matter?" She didn't even try to bite back the sarcasm. "I thought that was your plan."

"Not yet."

"I told you I was going to have problems negotiating the trail tied up. Besides, there isn't exactly anywhere I can go."

"Nice try."

Her mind drifted to Sarah. Was this what Sarah had gone through? Was this what she'd felt like, knowing she was going to die?

She tried to ignore the fatigue laced with panic.

She needed to think clearly if she was going to find a way to escape, but even if she had a cell phone, reception was poor in most places up here. Help could be nearby, but she had no idea where the nearest trail was.

Nikki felt her foot slip again. This time she screamed, breaking the relative quiet of their surroundings. Her feet slid out from under her, and she plunged off the steep embankment. Unable to use her hands, she tried to dig her feet into the ground but couldn't stop herself from crashing through the thick undergrowth and rolling down the steep slope.

Seconds later, her back slammed against a tree at the bottom of the darkened incline. She stopped suddenly. Pain shot down her shoulder. For a moment, all Nikki could feel—all she could hear—was the pounding of her heart. She lay still, knowing he was coming after her. She could hear him making his way down the slope, a volley of pebbles falling in his wake. If she got up now, she might be able to get away, but pain engulfed her body while a fog engaged her brain.

Adrenaline flowed. Her body screamed at her to run, but her legs and arms wouldn't move. She glanced up at the top of the ridge that she'd fallen from. He would be here any second . . . She forced herself to sit up. As far as she could tell, nothing was broken, but she was going to be black and blue come morning. Ignoring the pain, she managed to push herself up without the use of her arms and stumbled to her feet. She had to run. Now.

She spun around slowly, with no idea which way to go. The overhanging clouds blocked any patches of sunlight, leaving it hard to see in the thick expanse of trees hovering beneath the storm's shadows. Back up the incline wasn't an option. To the left, the trees seemed to thin out, and she could hear the sound of rushing water.

By the time she started running, he was almost to the bottom of the ravine. She kept moving, her shoulder burning as she tried not to worry about what else might be out there. The sounds of the forest seemed amplified around her. She knew bears weren't the only animals that lived in the park. Wolves, copperheads, timber rattlers, cougars . . . But that wasn't what terrified her the most. She could hear his footsteps crashing behind her. He was getting closer. She struggled to catch her breath and forced herself to keep moving. He had two guns and at least one grenade. And clearly no qualms in using either.

Strings of spider silk stuck to her face and hair as she ran through a web, but there was no way to brush it off. She kept running straight ahead as fast as she could, but here—unlike on the main trails—the path wasn't maintained. Swerving to avoid a thornbush, she barely missed tripping over a rotting log.

Help me, God. Please . . .

She glanced back, her heart pounding in her throat. She couldn't hear him behind her anymore. Had she lost him?

The orange flame of a campfire flickered in the distance. If she could just get to a phone and call for help.

She paused again. Listening for his footsteps. Maybe she *had* lost him.

She stumbled into the campsite. Two couples sat around a fire, warming up from the chill of the storm. A few college-age kids hung out under the shelter's covering playing a game of cards. She stopped, realizing what a mess she must look like with her hands duct-taped in front of her and spiderwebs in her hair.

"I'm sorry . . ." She worked not to sound hysterical. "I'm Special Agent Nikki Boyd with the Tennessee Bureau of Investigations, and I need your help."

One of the men stood up slowly from where he sat. "Are you all right, ma'am?"

"No. I need a phone, and if you have one, a weapon." She struggled to ignore the pain in her shoulder as she explained. "And I need someone to undo my arms. The rest of you need to get inside the shelter, quickly. There's a man after me. He's got weapons, and he's dangerous. I can show you my badge once my arms are free."

A redheaded man in his late forties slowly started toward her after motioning the others inside the shelter. "Are you hurt?"

"Just banged up," Nikki said. "Please. Hurry."

But it was too late. Cooper crashed into the campsite. Another man had grabbed a handgun from a backpack, but Cooper already had his drawn. She turned around slowly, realizing she never should have come here and put these people at risk.

"That was a stupid move, Nikki," Cooper said. "May I suggest that none of you try and do something foolish or heroic."

The man with the gun hesitated. "I don't know what's going on, but the woman's made it clear that she doesn't want you around. So if I were you, I'd turn around and walk out of here. We'll make sure she gets back to safety."

"And I don't know what she told you, but that isn't how this is going to play out."

"Carl, let them both go. Please," a woman pleaded from the doorway of the shelter. "Don't get involved in this. He's got a gun."

"I'd listen to her if I were you," Cooper said. "Because here's what's going to happen. She and I are going to walk out of here, and none of you are going to follow us. Is that clear?"

No one answered.

Cooper waved his gun in the air. "I said is that clear, because if it's not . . ."

The man with the gun took another step forward. "The problem is that the woman said she didn't want to go with you. I suggest you let her go."

"You suggest I let her go?" Cooper laughed. "This isn't your fight."

"Let her go."

"I warned you. Why does no one listen to me?" Cooper fired off a shot.

The man with the gun dropped to his knees. Blood pooled across the sleeve of his shirt as the weapon dropped to the ground beside him. The woman screamed. Nikki felt her knees buckle as several of the hikers rushed to help him. How had it come to this?

She walked toward Cooper. She wasn't going to endanger anyone else's life.

"That's more like it." Cooper grabbed Nikki's arm, wrenching her sore shoulder in the process. "Maybe that will teach you to listen to what I say. And for the rest of you, if any of you try to stop me or come after us, I will shoot again."

He pulled her toward the trail.

"You didn't have to shoot him," she said, as the shelter disappeared behind them.

"Did you think I was just going to sit back and let you go without a fight?"

"Why don't you tell me what you want and put an end to this before someone else gets hurt?

You haven't told me anything. Not about Bridget, or why you want me." Nikki stopped in the middle of the path and pulled her arm away from him. He grabbed her again, but she was finished playing games. Finished watching him win. "Tell me what's going on. Where's Bridget? Did you kill her like the other girls? And what do you want with me?"

Cooper hesitated. "You still don't recognize me, do you?"

"I don't understand. Should I?"

"You've been searching for your sister's abductor for ten years. And I've been planning this moment for nearly that long."

26

Nikki needed to find a way to get control of the situation. Seconds blurred into minutes as she followed him. Twenty minutes? Thirty? She was no longer sure of anything. Cooper still had the advantage. Not only did he know the terrain, but off the main trails, their chances of running into anyone again were slim. Even if she were able to get away again, she had no idea where the nearest trailhead or shelter was.

I've been planning this moment.

His last statement played over and over in her mind. But he'd refused to answer any further questions. Clearly he wanted her to believe that he still had the upper hand.

The rain had finally stopped by the time he led her into a small clearing and pointed to a large rock. "Have a seat."

"You still haven't answered my questions."

"Patience." He moved aside a few thick branches, his gun still in his hand, and pulled out a large backpack. "Leaving corporate America was the best thing I ever did. I've learned to stay prepared no matter where I am. With all of the economic downturns, government shutdowns, war in the Middle East—and more recently

Ebola—one can never be too careful." He unzipped the pack with one hand and pulled out a down vest, while still keeping his eye on her. "Most people don't realize how very little it would take to bring down the highly fragile power grid we all rely on. And out here, you never know, for example, when the temperatures might drop, which is why you have to always be prepared."

Nikki tried to interpret the nagging feeling that wouldn't leave her alone. Something was still wrong. The basic physical evidence of the Angel Abductor and Bridget's case—in particular the similarities between the Polaroid photos —was strikingly similar. And clearly Cooper— even if he wasn't the Angel Abductor—wanted her to believe he was that person. But beyond abduction of a blond teen and the photo, the similarities in the cases ended. Cooper didn't fit the psycho-logical profile the police had come up with, nor did he fit her own evaluation of her sister's abductor.

The man who had abducted Sarah had managed to stay under the radar for years, careful never to get caught. In contrast, Cooper had left obvious clues he wanted Nikki to find. And for what-ever reason had led her here.

She watched him slip on the vest, then zip it up. "You're not the Angel Abductor, are you?"

He laughed as if he'd finally gotten the punch

line to a good joke. "I never actually said I was."

A swoosh of air escaped her lips. "Then if you're not him, tell me who you are."

He smiled. "I was wondering when you'd figure it out. Your problem was you wanted to see what you wanted to see. You wanted *him* to be behind all of this so you could find your sister's abductor."

"Why the games?"

He shook his head and dug back into his pack. "You know, you disappoint me, Nikki, because you still haven't figured out who I am. Especially when I know everything about you."

"How does Bridget fit into all of this?"

"Bridget was bait. Nothing more." He pulled out a Clif Bar and fumbled with the wrapper before taking a bite.

"Were you telling me the truth when you said she was safe?" she asked. The more information she could get out of him the better.

"Don't worry about Bridget."

As if that were possible.

"Just tell me where she is." Nikki's voice rose a notch. "If this is all somehow about me, then there's no reason to hurt her."

He took another bite of his bar. "Shouting won't get you anywhere."

"Then just tell me why. Make me understand."

"I plan to tell you everything before this is

over, simply because I want you to know. And I want to see your reaction." He chuckled again. "Sending you on a wild-goose chase . . . do you know how easy it was? The beanie. Her cell phone. The photo and the ring." His laugh sent chills down her spine.

"She was never even in the park," Nikki said.

"Of course not."

Sunlight trickled through a small break in the clouds, leaving a whitish glow across the late afternoon skyline.

"Then where is she?"

He took the last bite, then crumpled up the wrapper before shoving it into the side pocket of his bag. "One thing I've learned over the years is patience. You should learn the same thing."

"If you won't tell me where she is, then at least tell me if she's alive."

"She's fine, actually. Like I said, this was about you, not her. Do you know how easy it is to make a sixteen-year-old girl think you're some tall, dark, and handsome hero? If I had a daughter, I wouldn't let her near the internet. It's frightening how easy it was. If they find her soon, she should be okay. For now, though, I'd be far more concerned about yourself."

"Here's something I don't understand," Nikki said, ignoring the implications for the moment. "You might not be the Angel Abductor, but you had the photo of my sister. The photo that her abductor left is still in her file. Her abductor must have had a second one. How did you get it?"

"Bravo." Cooper slowly clapped his hands. "Well done, Special Agent Boyd."

"What do you know about him?"

"We met a few years ago in prison. Everyone called him the Coyote. Never knew his real name. Never asked." Cooper rested his forearms against his thighs, still holding the weapon pointed at her, apparently finally ready to talk. "He inspired me. Helped me form my own revenge plot. You're right. He kept photos of all the girls. When we discovered the connection between him and Sarah and you and me . . . It was what I'd been waiting for."

"And my sister?" Nikki's breath caught. Ten years with no solid leads. Had Randall Cooper become the closest connection she had to her sister's abductor?

"Sarah Marie Boyd." He shook his head. "I don't know what happened to her, actually. He refused to tell anyone—even me—the details of his crimes."

She stood up. Frustration ripped through her. "You're lying. You have to know something. He gave you her picture."

"Yes, but I don't believe you're in a position to accuse me of lying." He held out the gun, then motioned for her to sit back down.

Nikki hesitated, then obeyed. "You'll never get away with this."

"Why not?" He pointed to the thick brush surrounding them. "Look around you. There's nothing but miles and miles of wilderness. If I want to disappear, no one will be able to find me. But you know that as well, don't you?

"And I know what you're thinking," he continued. "That they'll come and find you. Except that it will be dark soon, and a nighttime rescue is never easy. I've seen them work and know how they do it. They call the search and rescue coordinator for the park. Bring in Anderson. Set up a conference call with local law enforcement in order to make a rescue plan. They'll appoint section chiefs, logistics, and someone to handle the media. It will be an all-out manhunt as they try and find one of their own. The storm will be an inconvenience, but they're lucky it isn't snowing. If it was, they'd have to pack zero-degree sleeping bags, long johns, pads, tents, and military meals. But none of that will matter, because I'll always be one step ahead of them."

Nikki refused to let panic set in. She heard a whistle nearby, and she recognized the small songbird her father had dubbed the preacher bird as it sang short-whistled sermons all day long. A coyote howled in the trees, sending eerie chills up her spine.

"Ironic, isn't it. But don't worry," he said, watching her. "They sound closer than they really are."

"Who *are* you?"

He stood in front of her and started pacing. "You really don't remember me, do you?"

"No." She searched his features for a glimmer of recognition. The scar across his cheek. Dark eyes. Narrow brow . . . She waited, but there was nothing. He could be anyone. From someone she arrested, to a relative of someone she'd sent to jail. A decade of law enforcement had put her at odds with dozens of people. And all it took was one person with a vendetta . . .

"It's been just over eight years since you saw me last. I've changed, I suppose. Lost some weight. Took on a few gray hairs. Got this scar on my face from a car accident."

"So we've met."

He had to be someone she put in prison. Someone who believed he was innocent and who blamed her for his incarceration.

"How about I give you a clue?"

She was tired of the games, but escape at this point was unlikely. She had no supplies, and besides that, she'd never find her way out of here. Anyone with any sense was hunkered down in a shelter, prepared to ride out the next wave of the storm.

He squatted down in front of her. "You were a

lowly beat cop back then, working with your partner. Miles Fisher."

Nikki's mind churned as she tried to organize the facts he was giving her, but she was still not sure where he was going.

Miles was her first partner. She had been new on the force. Still focused on finding Sarah, but determined that others wouldn't go through the horror she and her family were going through. In the meantime, she paid her dues working traffic stops and handing out tickets to offenders.

"There was a call one afternoon that you and your partner responded to," he continued. "A robbery in progress. Someone was attempting to hold up the local convenience store. Do you remember yet?"

Nikki searched her memory. Over the past decade she'd responded to dozens of robberies.

"This time was different." Any hint of a smile he'd had earlier had vanished. "This time you killed a man."

The accusation felt like a bullet hitting her own chest. She drew in a mouthful of air. That had been the first time she'd ever killed a man. And all these years later it still haunted her.

He sat back down across from her. "So you do remember, after all. They say when you take a life, especially the first time, it's imprinted on your mind forever."

He was right. It had been raining that day, just like today. And every second of that call had been imprinted on her mind. The layout of the store as they'd walked in. The store owner. And the face of the boy she'd killed as they zipped up the body bag and put him in the back of the coroner's van. She and her partner had responded to what she'd assumed would be simply another routine call. Instead it had made her question everything she believed in.

"You knew the man who was killed?" she asked.

"You say that like you weren't responsible for his death."

"He robbed the store, then pulled out a gun and threatened to kill the store owner. Threatened to kill me and my partner."

"So noble. But the truth is that you killed my brother that day. Brian didn't deserve to die. He wasn't even supposed to be there. And I . . . I ended up burying him. I think about that afternoon. Every. Single. Day."

Her breath caught. It had taken a long time for her to learn that she couldn't take responsibility for another man's sins. Though even that hadn't been enough to stop the nightmares that followed. "Your brother pulled a gun on me."

"You didn't have to shoot him. He was eighteen years old."

"Old enough to know there are consequences

for threatening to kill a police officer while holding a loaded weapon. Which was exactly what he did."

"Do you remember what he stole that day? A pack of cigarettes. He panicked, but it wasn't worth his life."

"I agree it wasn't worth his life," she said. "But you can justify the situation all you want, and it won't change anything. I can't change what happened that day."

Six months of counseling had helped to ease the guilt, but the weight of taking a man's life had never completely faded.

Cooper stood up again, his boots crunching on the damp undergrowth while he paced. "Unfortunately, the judge agreed with you. But for me, it's given me eight long years to plan what I wanted to say to you. Eight long years to finally confront the person who took my brother's life and ruined my family. My mother was never the same again. She died in a hospital room, still grieving the death of her baby boy.

"Within six months I'd lost both my mother and my brother, and not too long after that, my boss accused me of fraudulent practices," he continued. "Do you know how hard it is to get a job—a decent job—when you have a felony on your record? I always wanted to be a ranger, but with my background they wouldn't even look at me."

"So you found a way to change your identity."

He nodded. "It's amazing the people you meet in prison. I knew I'd never go back to the corporate world. A new identity gave me the freedom I needed to do what I wanted."

"You met the Angel Abductor while you were in prison?" she asked.

"We became friends. Interestingly enough, he wasn't in for what you might think. With all of his previous crimes, he was caught for fraud, like me. Crazy, isn't it?"

Nausea swept through her as he spoke. This was the closest she'd ever been to her sister's abductor, and yet she still hadn't found him.

"He confessed some things to me one day. Told me things he said he'd never told another soul. That's when I found out his connection to you. Eventually, he helped me plot my revenge." Cooper rubbed his hands together, as if the cold were beginning to affect him. "I lost track of him eventually. I was transferred to another prison and he . . . I'm honestly not sure what happened to him."

He scooped up a fallen branch and tossed it into the trees before turning back to her. "It must be a horrid feeling, not knowing what's happened to someone you care about. Not knowing if she's alive or dead. Or what he did to her. I suppose I'm lucky in that way. At least I know what happened to my brother."

Nikki pressed her hands against her temples. "Tell me what you want from me."

"For now? I want you to understand what I went through all these years. Suffering the way I did. I thought you deserved to remember what it's like to lose someone. To remember how it felt when you first saw that Polaroid of your sister. It was a nice idea he had, I thought. Leaving a bit of a personal touch behind at every crime scene."

"Do you actually think I have to be reminded of how I felt that day? I think of Sarah every single day."

"I know." He pulled a Polaroid camera from his backpack. "I bought this on eBay a few months ago. They don't make these anymore, you know, but I thought you would appreciate the touch."

"You're planning to take my photo, then kill me. Just like he would have."

Cooper aimed the camera at her and pushed the button. The flash went off. A few seconds later, he pulled the photo from the camera and dropped the blackened card into her lap. The image of her face slowly emerged. The determination in her eyes . . . and the fear.

"That," he said, dropping the camera back into his backpack, "depends on you."

27

Nikki could see it in his eyes as he grabbed her arm and pulled her up. Pain shot through her shoulder. Only one of them was going to get out of here alive. If she was going to make a move, it would have to be now, before darkness settled over the mountainside.

"We need to keep moving now that the weather has cleared up a bit," Cooper said.

"Where are we going?"

"You ask too many questions." He reached for his backpack, still holding his weapon.

Nikki didn't stop to consider the risks. While he turned away from her to pick up the backpack, she raised her hands above her head as high as she could, ignoring the searing pain in her shoulder, then slammed her bound hands downward as hard as she could, her elbows on either side of her hips.

The duct tape snapped in two.

Before he could react, she reached for his gun. He tried to stop her, but she was quicker this time. She grabbed the barrel of the gun and pushed it toward him, rolling it against his thumb and twisting his wrist. Cooper groaned in pain as she forced him to his knees. The weapon was now facing him. She wrapped her fingers over the bottom of his hand, but he wasn't done fighting. He jerked her toward the ground in one swift movement. The gun fired. Cooper slumped over onto his side, a frozen look of surprise on his face.

No . . . no . . . no . . .

Ears still ringing, she removed the magazine and tossed the gun aside while blood seeped through his clothes. She unzipped his coat and pulled it back from where the bullet had struck. Tears slid down her cheeks. She'd expected him to fight back. Hadn't she? Knew he believed he had nothing to lose. But it wasn't supposed to have come to this. Her life over his.

Just like with his brother.

A light rain began to fall again as she breathed in the smell of gunpowder. She reached for his backpack, unzipped it. She found a wool blanket in the front, pulled it out, and pressed it against the wound to stop the bleeding.

"Funny how nothing has changed." Cooper's voice broke as he spoke. "Special Agent Boyd, I was wrong. You win. Again."

She shook her head. "No one won today. And none of this brings back your brother."

He grabbed her hand, his fingers tightening against her wrist. "It was never about that. It was always about revenge. About making things right. But I ended up being the fool, didn't I?"

"All I know is that none of this had to happen," she said.

He choked, and blood ran down his chin. "Yes, it did."

But it didn't. She hadn't taken this job to take lives. She wanted to save them.

"I never meant to kill your brother," she said, praying for a miracle as she pressed harder against his side, but the blood had already soaked through the blanket and was beginning to pool against the hard earth. His face paled. Breath was rapid and shallow . . . She was losing him.

I'm so sorry, God . . . so sorry . . .

"He never would have shot you or your partner." Cooper coughed. "He just . . . he just made a mistake."

A mistake that cost him his life.

But while Cooper might not make it, there was still a chance for Bridget. If she was still alive, they needed to find her.

"Cooper . . . Tell me where Bridget is. She doesn't need to die."

His eyes had shut, and he wasn't responding.

"Cooper, I need you to listen to me." She shook him. "Tell me where Bridget is. Please."

He groaned, then opened his eyes. "I planned to kill her. To . . . bury her like the Angel Abductor, but I . . ."

"Tell me . . . please . . . Where is she?"

He closed his eyes again. "Find her, because my brother . . ."

She was losing him . . . the only link she had to finding Bridget.

Nikki sat back on her heels as his head slumped to the side. She checked his pulse. It was too late. He was gone, and the information to save Bridget had gone with him.

She slumped onto the ground beside him. Revenge had cost him everything . . . including his life. She zipped up his vest, then stopped. The grenade was still inside his backpack. She drew in a quick breath. If someone or something happened to stumble upon it before the authorities came . . .

Slowly, she reached inside the backpack and pulled it out. The pin still held the safety lock, stopping the trigger lever from opening and detonating the fuse. She set it down carefully beside her, then reached for the duct tape in the side pocket of the backpack where she'd seen him put it. Pulling off a large piece, she wrapped it around the grenade, firmly securing the pin in place.

Deciding that the safest place to keep the grenade was off the ground, she dug into his pack again until she found a scarf. A minute later, she'd secured the grenade to the branch of a tree, high enough off the ground, she prayed, that no animal or person would find it. Hopefully, she'd be able to lead the rangers back to the site to find Cooper's body as well, but she couldn't think about that right now.

Wind whipped around her, chilling her through her wet clothes. Lightning danced across the darkening sky. Cooper might be dead, but for her, this night was far from over. The storm still hovered above her, but even if the weather let up, finding her way in the dark was going to be impossible. And with the temperatures dropping, she could easily be at risk from hypothermia. It didn't have to be freezing to suffer from the effects of exposure, even at fifty degrees Fahrenheit or higher in wet and windy weather. And this time of year, the temps could easily drop below that.

But most importantly, she needed to find a way to let someone know Bridget was alive.

She unzipped Cooper's pack completely and began taking an inventory of its contents, not only for anything that might help her stay warm but also for any more weapons. She laid the items out beside her, searching first of all for a phone, a radio, or anything that could help her contact the authorities.

He'd implied he planned to disappear. Which meant there was no cell phone to trace. And he knew these mountains, which meant no need of a GPS.

What do I do, God?

She kept pulling out items. He'd clearly been prepared to stay in these mountains. A Swiss Army knife and a first aid kit. A flashlight, a slim mummy bag, and a packet of trail food. A raincoat, extra socks, gloves, and a fire starter kit. And her service weapon. She checked to ensure the safety was on, then slid it back into her holster. A minute later, she'd finished repacking the bag. But she had no idea where she was. Or where to go.

Rain pelted against the side of her face as the wind picked up. The sun slid behind the horizon while the last light of day was swallowed up by the forest surrounding her. Something rustled behind her. Nikki jumped at the sound. It could be anything. Bears, coyotes, wolves . . . She flipped on the flashlight and shone the beam into the darkness. But there was nothing there. Only her nerves playing tricks on her.

She turned around and took a step away from Cooper's body. The adrenaline rush of rappelling down the side of the cliff had always exhilarated her, but this—everything that had happened today—had brought with it feelings of pure terror. She shivered, turning around 360 degrees while wondering which direction she should go. Or whether she should simply stay there. The trees would provide shelter. She had the sleeping bag and an extra raincoat. She was so cold . . . and so tired.

And heading out into these woods only risked getting more lost. Her father used to tell her *a clear head will find itself*. And that if she ever got lost while they were hiking, she needed to stop, stay calm, and stay put.

She reached for her holster. She had a weapon. She had what she needed to start a fire. Which meant she wasn't completely out of options. Five minutes later, she'd gathered as much dry wood as she could find and had started a fire beneath the shelter of a tree. She pulled out the sleeping bag, trying to ignore the coyotes' howls in the distance, slid inside, and started praying. For Bridget, for her own safety, and for the numbing diversion of sleep.

Nikki woke up to darkness. Someone was shaking her shoulders. Calling her name. She fought to escape the heavy layer of sleep that had settled over her and the fingers gripping her shoulders. She pulled away, then tried to scramble backward in the confining sleeping bag. She reached for her gun beside her. She needed to run. Needed to get away from the scent of death that clung to her. What if Cooper wasn't really dead? If he found her again, this time he *would* kill her.

"Nikki . . . Nikki, stop. It's Tyler. Give me the gun."

Tyler? How had he found her?

She stopped fighting when she caught sight of his face in the beam of a flashlight. Flickers of memories surfaced. Cooper with a grenade. Chasing her through the woods. The gun going off. Cooper dying . . .

"He's dead," she said, looking into Tyler's eyes. She couldn't make herself care. The only thing she felt was numbness.

"We found his body," Tyler said, taking the weapon from her, "but I need to make sure you're okay. There's blood all over you."

She unzipped the sleeping bag and wiped her hands against her clothes, still trying to find her equilibrium. She was covered with blood. How had she not noticed?

"It's his blood." Her voice broke as the numbness began to fade. She looked up. Cooper was moving toward her in slow motion. Grenade in hand. A smirk on his face. He was going to kill her.

"Nikki?"

Cooper's image vanished.

"I shot him," she said.

"You did what you had to do," Tyler said. "Everything is going to be okay now. Can you get up?"

She nodded. "I think so. Bridget's alive. We've got to find her."

"Cooper told you that?" Gwen asked.

"Yes."

"He could have been lying," Tyler said.

"No. He was telling the truth."

"Do you know where she is?"

"I know she was never in the park, but he would have had to hide her nearby. If he has a piece of property, a close friend . . . We need to find her."

"Okay," Gwen said. "I'll radio in the information and get a couple officers searching for that information right now."

She let Tyler help her up. Gwen was standing in front of her, holding a warm blanket. Anderson, Simpson . . . they were all there, along with a couple more uniformed officers she didn't recognize.

"It's good to see you alive, Special Agent Boyd," Anderson said. "Though I've decided you're as much a magnet for trouble as Jack is for yellow jackets."

She shot him a weak smile. "All I know is that it's good to be alive." She pointed to the scarf in the tree, where she'd hung the grenade, the ends of the red strip blowing in the gusty wind. "The grenade. I put it up in the tree. I didn't want anyone to stumble across it . . ."

Tyler pressed his hands against her shoulders. "They'll take care of it, Nikki. They'll take care of everything."

"He's right," Anderson said.

"We're just all glad you're okay." Gwen

wrapped the blanket around her shoulders. "We came in by helicopter. Do you think you can walk out of here? It's not too far."

"Yeah. But what about Jack?" she asked. If he was dead . . .

"It's a miracle," Gwen said, "but that boy's tougher than you think. He's already out of surgery, and the doctors believe he'll make a full recovery."

"And Lopez?"

"Some hikers found him disoriented but alive, with a huge goose egg on the back of his head," Tyler said.

They started back through the darkness by the light of their flashlights. Officers were processing the scene. Taking photos and gathering evidence at the place where she'd killed a man. No matter what Cooper had done, she hadn't wanted to take another life. Maybe there hadn't been any other options, but that didn't stop the collision of her moral beliefs and the reality of what had happened.

"Do you have any idea why Cooper killed Reynolds?" she asked, still not feeling completely steady on her feet. Thankful for Tyler's arm around her. She was cold, her clothes still damp, but all she could think about was finding Bridget.

"I did some more checking," Gwen said, "and found out that Reynolds was Cooper's arresting officer about seven years ago for felony fraud charges. Under the name—"

"Kenneth Waters," Nikki said.

Somehow it was all beginning to make sense. "He met someone in prison who gave him a new identity."

Gwen nodded. "Reynolds must have recognized him, then confronted him. Cooper was afraid his plan was about to evaporate into thin air."

"So he killed him."

Nikki pulled the blanket tighter around her shoulders, wondering if she'd ever be able to warm up again. She told her part of what had happened as they walked. About Cooper's confession. The Coyote. And the other man he'd shot. "Did they find him?"

Tyler nodded. "It's been a busy night for the search and rescue teams, but the shot was superficial, and he's going to be okay."

"What about me?" she asked, finally catching sight of the helo in the clearing. "How did you find me?"

"That was a miracle as well," Gwen said. "Do you remember Mountain Mike?"

"Yeah . . . The thru-hiker we interviewed earlier."

Already it seemed like a lifetime ago.

Tyler pointed to the other side of the clearing. She hadn't noticed the man standing there. He was at the edge of the clearing, his backpack slung across his shoulder, talking to one of the officers.

"He found me?"

Gwen called him over, then instructed the pilot they brought to get ready for takeoff.

"Special Agent Boyd," he said, walking up to her. "You don't know how happy I am to see you alive."

"I hear I owe you a big thank-you, but I still don't know how you found me."

"There's not much to tell, really," Mountain Mike said. "I started back down the trail after I spoke to you at the shelter. Ten minutes or so later, I realized I must have dropped my iPod. With the weather picking up, I debated whether or not I should go look for it but finally decided to double back to try to find it. When I arrived at the edge of the clearing, Cooper was putting a bullet through one of your men.

"I saw the grenade, knew he had a gun, and knew as well that I couldn't take him down. But I did have a phone. I called in my location to the park dispatch and told them what I'd seen. They patched me through to Agent McKenna. I told her I was going to follow you in order to keep her updated on your location. I lost track of you once it started getting dark, though I heard the gunshot."

Nikki's breath caught, realizing that tonight

could have ended so differently. For all of them.

"The last location he was able to call in narrowed down the area enough for us to find you with our night vision goggles from the helo," Gwen said as the helicopter's rotor started to turn, accelerating slowly.

Nikki shook her head. "I don't know what to say except for thank you. You took a big risk, following a man you'd already seen shoot someone."

"It wasn't a hard decision." Mountain Mike's expression softened as the helo powered up beside them. "I have a daughter about your age. I hope someone would do the same for her if she were ever in trouble."

"Let's get you out of here," Gwen said, now having to shout above the noise of the helo's engine. "We need to go find our missing girl."

28

Tyler's breath warmed the back of her neck as she leaned against his shoulder.

"You're shaking," he said.

"I'm just so cold."

"It's over now." He pulled the blanket tighter around her. "We'll have you home and warmed up before you know it."

Nikki closed her eyes for a moment as the rest of the response team filed onto the helo and the pilot took the bird into the air. But it wasn't over. Not yet. Not until they found Bridget. And then she'd find time to sleep for the next forty-eight hours.

"There will be an ambulance waiting for you—"

"I don't need to see a doctor," Nikki interrupted Gwen.

"We figured you'd pull that argument again, but it's not up for discussion."

"All I've got is a few scrapes and bruises. We still need to find Bridget—"

"We will," Tyler said. "But I'm also going to make sure you're okay."

An hour later, she had her medical clearance and a cup of hot coffee someone had handed her. Sleep would have to come later.

"We're looking for properties under his name—both names," Gwen said inside the mobile command post, "but so far we're coming up blank."

"Where did Cooper live?"

"The address on his volunteer application is an apartment building in Gatlinburg. I already sent a team there, but they didn't find anything. Landlord said she hasn't seen him for a couple of days."

"Keep looking. She has to be nearby."

Nikki was convinced he would have kept Bridget close. Somewhere convenient to the park.

"I got a call from your mom while you were changing," Gwen said. "She's been trying to get ahold of you. I told her you'd lost your phone."

Nikki's breath caught. It was a question she'd been afraid to ask. "What did she say?"

"The baby was born just after nine thirty. Jamie's going to be fine."

"And the baby?"

Gwen caught her gaze. "Your mom seemed upbeat, but she's clearly not out of the woods. She's in ICU under close observation right now. It sounded as if they would know more in a few hours."

"She . . . so it's a girl?" Nikki couldn't help but smile. Matthew and Jamie had decided to wait until the baby was born to find out, but Jamie had told her she secretly wanted a girl.

Please, Jesus . . . heal that sweet new baby.

"What did you tell them about me?" she asked.

"That you would call as soon as you could. I didn't want to tell them anything without having some answers. We've managed to keep the story off the news channels, but that luck's not going to last much longer."

"Thank you." Nikki felt a trickle of relief wash through her, but the night still wasn't over. "And Kyle?"

"He's back at his hotel, asleep. I haven't called him yet either. I'm not ready to get his hopes up again."

"That was the right call. For now anyway."

Tyler stepped into the vehicle and handed her a bottle of juice and a Snickers bar from the vending machine. "Anything yet?"

Nikki thanked him, then shook her head.

"I know you want to find her alive," Gwen said, "but he might have been lying to you."

"No. I believe he was telling the truth when he told me she was alive. She's still out there. Somewhere. And it makes sense. He would have needed her as leverage if things went wrong. He never planned to leave the park in a body bag."

"Okay, so if you're right, then we need to think this through. He had to have told you some-thing before he died. Given you some clue as to where he might have taken her."

She worked to push back the exhaustion that

had been hovering over her the past few hours. Nauseous over the reality she'd killed a man. Because the emotional impact was interfering with her thinking.

"He told me she wasn't inside the park, but there are hundreds of cabins and places outside the park where she could be."

"Okay. Then start slowly, from the beginning, and walk me through what happened. You've always told me that even without a good lead, you can utilize logic, and that's what we need right now." Tyler brought her mind back into focus. "What did the two of you talk about?"

Nikki drew in a deep breath and felt herself begin to relax. "He spoke about how I'd killed his younger brother, and he'd found a way to revenge his death."

"What was his brother's name?" Gwen asked.

"Brian Linford. They were stepbrothers."

"I'm looking it up now."

It might have been a long time ago, but she'd never forgotten Brian's face or his name. She'd taken a man's life, and that moment had almost signaled the end of her career. Some days, if it weren't for Sarah and her need to find her, she was convinced she'd have quit the force years ago.

"What about the Coyote?" Tyler asked. "He couldn't tell you what happened to him?"

"Cooper got transferred, and they lost touch."

"Which only means he's out there somewhere."

"I know, but I've also realized I can't keep clinging to some false hope that my sister's story is suddenly going to have a happily-ever-after ending. I've lived on those hopes for ten years."

She wanted to believe Sarah was still out there. But she also knew Sarah's abductor was a calculated killer. And Randall Cooper was no different. He'd made it clear he'd get rid of anyone who got in his way. Bridget might have been leverage, but she was also disposable.

"Wait . . . I think I've got something," Gwen said. "Take a look at this. A property on the outskirts of town was registered to a Brian R. Linford. Looks like a small cabin located on a couple of acres."

"Bingo." Nikki jumped up and slid in behind Gwen at the computer. "Get us a nighttime search warrant. That's got to be the place."

Tyler studied the map. "Location would be right. He picked her up in Obed, then drove her there on the way into the park before setting the rest of his plan in action."

"Giving us just enough bread crumbs to follow along the way."

It was still dark when they pulled up on the property. A chain-link fence marked the front boundary of the area where a one-story cabin sat tucked away from the road. Overgrown grass swallowed a few old cars in the moonlight.

Tyler hung back as Nikki and Gwen, along with a team of officers, made their way quietly in the dark toward the front porch.

One of the officers knocked on the door. "This is the police. We have a search warrant for these premises."

Five seconds later, they opened the door with a battering ram. The smell of cigarettes hit Nikki as they filed into the house. The yellow light shining in the living room did little to illuminate the room. Blinds were closed. There was a worn floral couch in front of the TV. The living room opened up to a kitchen that hadn't had a proper cleaning for weeks. A couple of empty takeout boxes still on the table.

They split up to search the house. Nikki made her way down a musty hall into the one bedroom. A wooden dresser sat beside an unmade bed. There was no sign of Bridget.

She's got to be here, God. Show us. Please.

"Clear."

"Clear."

"Clear."

She joined the others back in the living room.

"There's no sign of anyone," Gwen said.

"We're missing something," Nikki said, thinking out loud.

"What about his personal life?" Gwen said. "Anything that stood out when he talked to you?"

"I don't know . . . He'd thought through every scenario he could think of. He had a backpack full of supplies stashed. I'm pretty sure he was planning to disappear after killing me."

"Where was he planning to go?" Gwen asked.

"He never mentioned a specific place." Something clicked. "But he sounded a bit like a prepper."

"A prepper?"

"You know. One of those people who worry about the end of the world coming."

He'd gone from a computer wizard with a high-paying job to a man wanting to disappear off the grid.

"There's nothing in this house that I saw that would point to that," one of the officers said.

"A basement?" Nikki asked.

Gwen shook her head. "According to the floor plan, no."

"Maybe it's not in the house," Nikki said.

She ran back outside, her heart pounding as she took the front porch stairs two at a time. Wind whipped around her as the sun began to rise, but she barely felt the cold. She stood in the middle of the lot. A couple of old rusty cars sat in the driveway. Beyond that, there was a grove of trees. Gwen and the rest of the team were right behind her.

She spun around in a slow circle, trying to jog her memory on anything he might have said. "What about a storm shelter?"

"It would make sense. Preppers often hide their stash and don't want others to know about what they've got."

"So it wouldn't necessarily be in the open, like in the house."

"And he's got a couple acres here," Nikki said. "Plenty of space to hide someone."

Plenty of space to bury a dead body.

Nikki dismissed the thought.

"Let's spread out now. We'll clear the property quad by quad."

Ten minutes later, Nikki's flashlight reflected off something metal. "I think I've found it."

The door was secured with a padlock. She called the guys with the battering ram.

Let her be alive if she's here, God, please. Let her be alive.

Once the door was open, Nikki started slowly down the stairs, the light of her flashlight illuminating guns, ammunition, and enough food rations to last through the apocalypse.

"Bridget? Bridget, are you down here?"

Something moved just past the light of her flashlight.

Nikki saw her a moment later. Sitting in the corner of the darkened room. Hands tied behind her back and a gag in her mouth, eyes wide open in terror.

"It's okay now, Bridget. It's going to be okay."

She sobbed as Nikki knelt down beside her

and pulled the gag out, using her coat to wipe her tear-streaked face before freeing her hands. A well of emotion balled in the pit of Nikki's stomach. For a moment, it was Sarah's face she saw. Ten years of waiting for her sister.

"You're going to be okay, sweetie. Everything's okay now. I promise." Nikki shook off the illusion and pulled Bridget into her arms. "I'm so, so sorry you had to go through this, but it's over."

Bridget's chest heaved as she began crying harder.

"Bridget. Hey . . . you're going to be okay. My name's Nikki Boyd. I'm a special agent with the Tennessee Bureau of Investigation. We're here to take you home."

Relief swept through her as the girl gave her a weak smile. Six other girls hadn't been so lucky. But this one was.

Thank you, Jesus. Thank you.

Nikki brushed a strand of Bridget's hair behind her shoulder. Forgetting the past couple of days was going to take a long time . . . for both of them. But for the moment, all she cared about was the fact that Bridget was alive.

"Are you hurt anywhere? Do you think you can stand up?"

Bridget nodded as Nikki helped her to her feet.

"You're safe now. We're going to get you out of here."

Someone handed Nikki a blanket. She wrapped

it around the girl's shoulders. "Did anyone hurt you?"

Bridget shook her head, still trembling. "He just . . . tied me up and left me here alone."

So Cooper had told her the truth. She'd never even gone into the park.

The girl's eyes darted across the room. "Where is he?"

"He can't hurt you anymore, sweetie. He's . . . he's dead."

Bridget's body shook as she started crying again. "I was so stupid. He told me his name was Sean. Showed me pictures of him with his friends and sisters. We talked for hours. I thought . . . I thought he loved me. I just wanted to meet him in person. When I found out it had all been a lie, I thought . . . I thought I was going to die. I was so . . . so scared. He just left me here."

"It's over now, Bridget. I promise. You're safe now."

They helped her up the stairs and into the early morning sunlight. Someone handed her a water bottle.

"We're going to get you to the hospital, get you cleaned up, and make sure you're okay. They're calling your brother right now. He'll meet you at the hospital. He's worked hard to make sure you were found."

"He's going to be so mad at me." Tears were back again, flowing down her cheeks. "If he found out why I asked to come here this weekend . . ."

"He loves you. And he's not the only one. Your mother came as well."

"She came?"

"I know there's been a lot of hurt, Bridget, as well as a lot of loss, and this experience isn't going to fix everything. I also know that life isn't like it was when I was your age. But maybe this is a chance to start over."

"I was just so scared."

Nikki wrapped her arms around the girl. "I know, sweetie. I know."

Paramedics took Bridget to the waiting ambulance.

"Do you think she's going to be okay?" Tyler asked.

"I hope so," Nikki said. "She's been through more than most people experience in a lifetime, but it could have ended so much worse."

"She's not the only one." He looked down at her with those deep brown eyes of his, stirring something—not for the first time—somewhere in the depths of her heart. "It's time to get you home."

She nudged him with her shoulder, then winced. "Time for that breakfast you owe me."

"We can arrange that as well."

"Actually, all I really want right now is a long shower and my bed." She watched the ambulance drive away. "I hope Bridget understands

358

that there are people out there who love her. Her brother, her friends, her mother."

"I'm sorry in a way that Cooper didn't end up being the Angel Abductor. I know you didn't find the answers you're looking for."

"I have a name. Maybe the Coyote will end up being the one clue that changes everything."

And give her and her family closure.

Gwen walked up to them and handed Nikki her phone. "It's your mom."

Nikki smiled as she took the phone. "Mom?"

"Nikki? Are you okay? I've been worried. I haven't been able to get ahold of you."

"I know, and I'm sorry. But everything's okay now. Tell me about the baby. Is she going to be okay?"

"She's beautiful, Nikki. So beautiful. The last few hours have been touch and go, but she's stabilizing. The doctors believe she's going to be fine. And they named her Sarah. Sarah Ruth Boyd."

Nikki smiled. Sarah for her sister. Ruth for her mother.

"What about Bridget? Did you find her?"

"We found her, Mom. She's going to be all right."

"I'm so glad to hear that. And what about you? Are you coming home?"

Nikki glanced at Tyler and smiled. "As soon as we finish up here, I'll be on my way home."

29

Nikki sat on the edge of the grassy ridge, wind tugging her hair as she stared out across the valley framed by the majestic Smoky Mountains. The dark clouds from the storm had begun to dissipate, leaving rays of sunshine across the valley still holding a hint of mist.

It was a place like this where they'd scattered Katie's ashes—a hill with a stunning view. Twelve months ago, six days after the accident, she'd stood behind Tyler in the small ceremony that attempted to celebrate Katie's life as much as accept her death. But at the time, the words of the minister had rung hollow. And she'd felt the aching pain that had seared through Tyler as she'd watched him try to explain to Liam why his mother wasn't coming back. He'd lost his best friend, wife, and lover, and Liam had lost his mother.

She'd watched the wind catch Katie's ashes, wishing life wasn't so fragile. Hating how in a matter of seconds, everything in life could change forever. Sarah had vanished. Katie had slipped into the water. Bridget had trusted the wrong person.

One fatal moment.

Everything changed.

And life would never be the same again for any of them. She'd never be able to capture the sweet smile of her sixteen-year-old sister. Never laugh over coffee with Katie.

She let the sun warm her face, knowing she should feel grateful, and really, she was. She'd managed to make it out alive, and Bridget was safe. Along with the bad, so much good had happened. Bridget was back with her brother. Her mother was getting the help she needed. Hopefully, they'd be able to start again as a family, though only time would tell if Loretta Ellison would be able to lay her demons aside and embrace her role as the mother she'd never been able to be.

"Can I join you?" Tyler asked.

She looked up at him and nodded.

"I didn't realize you'd slipped out of the command post," he said as he sat down beside her.

"I snuck out. I needed a few minutes to clear my head before we head back to Nashville."

"I just spoke to Gwen. They'll be ready to leave in about ten minutes."

"I'm ready."

She caught the shadow of darkness that settled over his expression. One she'd seen before. When she arrived at the marina after Katie's accident.

Then again on the day they scattered Katie's ashes.

Lost. Alone.

"Tyler?"

"I haven't been able to get it out of my head."

"What?"

"Yesterday, when Cooper stood there, holding you with a grenade in his hand, threatening to kill you. Our flying away and leaving you there with him. If there was anything I could have done differently. Anything, Nikki. You know I would have. I thought I'd lost you."

"You did the only thing you could do. He was bent on destroying me, and I truly believe he would have killed all of us, himself included."

"Maybe. But I should have found a way to stop him—"

"How? There was nothing you could have done. Nothing, Tyler." She reached out and grasped his hands. "You can't carry that guilt. Just like I can't carry this guilt over Sarah anymore. And like you can't carry your guilt from Katie's death. You know what else I've learned?"

"What?"

"That sometimes there truly is nothing you can do to change your circumstances. Sometimes all you can do is hold on for dear life and pray that God will help you find a way through the storm. Sometimes he shows you a way to escape, and sometimes he walks through the fire with you. But I'm starting to realize that as much as I've battled with God, nothing that happens here on this earth changes who God is."

"Maybe there was some good that came out of this. A girl's life was saved. A man won't hurt anyone else. And you're one step closer to finding what happened to your sister."

"I hope so." She hoped he was right. She was afraid to grasp the glimmer of hope that they could find closure over her sister. "I thought I'd found her abductor, Tyler. Wanted so much for it to be him. And while I'm glad we found Bridget —truly I am—I thought I was going to find answers to Sarah's disappearance as well."

She felt as if the last few days she'd been caught in the destructive path of a tornado. It was something she hated about her job. She arrived right when a family was being ripped apart. But finding just one person made it all worth it.

"I can't even imagine your frustration, but you helped save a girl's life. Bridget's family won't have to go through what you all have gone through."

"I know." She knew that should be enough. Wanted it to be enough. "Life still leaves me wondering why sometimes it's so hard. Loss is so deep that there are times I'm not sure I'll ever find my way out of the darkness."

"Katie once told me she planned to live to be a hundred, because there was so much she wanted to experience," Tyler said. "She never got that chance, but she did manage to teach me to capture each day. Or at least try to. Which is what I keep trying to do."

Nikki ran her fingers across his knuckles, then traced the blue vein along the back of his hand. They'd both lost and loved, but maybe that's what life was about. You couldn't feel the pain of loss if you hadn't already felt the joy of love.

"Katie did love life to the fullest," Nikki said. "That's one of the things I remember most about her."

"And she loved this place. Do you remember the first time we came here? Katie and I. You and . . . what was his name? Brett?"

"Ben. Now, there's a guy I prefer to forget, though the setting was perfect."

Tyler laughed. "I remember how he bragged about how much he loved hiking, and I don't think he made it half a mile before he was about to pass out. Blamed it on allergies."

"And whined like a baby," Nikki said. "Katie had good intentions, but she never could butt out of my love life."

"I might have a confession." He shot her a wide grin. "He was my idea."

"Yours? You were the one who suggested I go out with him?"

"I'm sorry." Tyler laughed as he pulled her

against him. "I didn't know you as well back then as I do now."

"And you apparently didn't know Ben either."

"She wanted you to be happy. We both did."

"I'd rather live out my days in a nunnery."

They'd spent the day hiking, and despite not clicking with her date, they ended up having a good time. So much had changed since then. Tyler had gone off to war. She'd joined the police force. They'd lost Katie . . .

He drew his arm tighter against her waist until she could smell the familiar scent of his aftershave as she looked up at him. "Did you know she was planning a trip to Africa?"

Nikki's eyes widened. "I knew she was wanting to travel as soon as the kids got a little older, but I don't remember her mentioning Africa."

"She told me she wanted to go on a safari in Kenya and go shark cage diving in South Africa."

Nikki laughed. "I'm not surprised." Her smile slowly faded as the memories surfaced. "I miss her, Tyler."

"So do I." She heard the longing in his voice. He might have accepted the reality of her death on one level, but that acceptance didn't erase the pain.

She pulled back and caught his gaze. "Where are you now in all of this? With losing Katie?"

Katie would have wanted her to ask him.

Would have wanted her to help pull him out of the dark tunnel she knew he'd stumble into after her death. Nikki studied his face in the sunlight as she waited for him to continue. Studied the flecks of brown in his eyes.

"It depends on the moment, to be honest. This morning I realized I'd made it through a year without her. A whole year. I can hardly believe it's been that long in some ways. At other times, I feel like it's been a lifetime."

He swallowed hard. "Sometimes I think I might be okay again, then something completely unexpected pushes me under until I'm left gasping for breath and unable to function. How can I be a father when I can't even find the energy to fix a box of macaroni and cheese for dinner? But I have to. For Liam. He's the one thing that seems to make everything okay. He's the reason to get up in the morning, even after all this time."

"And God?" she asked.

"I can feel him calling me back. Sometimes I still want to run like the prodigal son. At least my head knows. It's my heart that's having a harder time trying to let go."

"Give it time. There is no formula for grief. No timeframe that says where you need to be by a certain date. This is your journey."

He shrugged. "So maybe it's okay to just keep

getting out of bed every morning. Loving my son. Being determined to be the best dad I can be for him."

She nudged him with her shoulder. "Which is exactly what you are. An incredible father."

"I'm trying. As long as I can keep holding on to memories of Katie. Her laughing at my lame jokes. My hands against her stomach, feeling the baby kick for the first time. Watching Liam lick lime frosting off the beaters in the kitchen while they made cupcakes. And funny things like how she hated mayonnaise because it was too gooey, but loved running barefoot in the mud. Because I worry about the things I'm slowly forgetting. The moments I don't think about her, I feel guilty. I can't feel her presence like I used to.

"But the memories I do have remind me that I'm alive. They help me celebrate the fact that Katie was once a part of my life. And no matter how bad I feel, I would never want to change that. She'll always be a part of who I am." He smiled down at her. "But enough of the past. You impressed me these past couple days with your incredible balance of empathy and professionalism. You know what it means to lose someone you love, and yet you can also get a handle on the details of what needs to be done."

"Thanks." She felt a blush creep up her cheeks at the compliment. "I like to think that Sarah would be proud of me for helping bring back other girls."

"Do you still think she's out there? Alive?"

"If I quit looking, it means I've given up hope. If she is out there, I have to find her." She glanced at her watch. They needed to leave. "You ready to go?"

"Yeah. I guess we should."

He grabbed her hands to help her up, and once again she felt the intimacy of the moment with his nearness as she caught his expression. And an unanticipated longing coupled with it. This time she didn't even try to fight her heart. Because somehow—at least for her—their relationship had changed. And she had no idea how to take it back to the point where it used to be. Where Tyler was simply the husband of her best friend.

"Tyler?" She searched his face, at a complete loss for what to say.

"You okay?"

"Yeah . . . I . . . I'm ready to go." Because there was nothing she could say. Not yet.

But the unexpected feelings were suddenly clear. She was falling in love with her best friend's husband.

Epilogue

One week later

Nikki watched Sarah Ruth Boyd sleep in her arms another minute before handing her back to Jamie. "She's so beautiful."

"The doctor told me she's perfect." Jamie brushed the baby's dark bangs across her forehead, then looked at Nikki. "You should have one."

"A baby?" Nikki sat back down on the round ottoman across from her sister-in-law and laughed.

"Don't you want one?"

"Of course, maybe even two, but—"

"But what? You've always known exactly what you wanted in life and gone after it. I've always admired you for that. Now you've got that hunky boyfriend in the wings who's definitely marriage material. *And* I understand looking to get married."

Nikki squirmed at the comment. "I'm not sure I'd call him my boyfriend, and I'm certainly not ready to say I do."

Jamie fingered the tassel on Sarah's pink bootie, then leaned forward. "If you want my advice, you better start claiming him as your own. Or someone else will. I'm just sayin'."

"Auntie Nikki!" Liam bounced across the living room floor of her parents' downtown condo, formally dissolving the awkward conversation with her sister-in-law on love and marriage.

"Liam . . ."

He threw himself into her arms. When he was born, Tyler and Katie had officially made Nikki his godmother. At the time she never considered the possibility of losing either of them.

"Daddy got me a new fish yesterday," Liam said, his brown eyes wide with excitement.

She pulled him onto her lap before tousling his hair. Liam was all boy, preferring a pile of dirt to watching TV. Katie had struggled to keep him out of mischief, but it was that angelic face of his that got her every time.

Nikki moved his wiggly body away from the sleeping baby across from them. "What did you name it?"

"Jonah."

Nikki laughed. "Well, that's . . . appropriate."

"Feeling rested yet?" Tyler walked up to her with two plates of raspberry cheesecake.

"Hey . . . Yeah, I am, actually. I'm feeling much better. Partly thanks to you and your movie therapy last night."

A week later, and she was still treading on thin ice with no idea how to sort out her feelings. Or how to move forward to the place her heart wanted to take her.

"I grabbed two slices of cake. One for me and one for you. Your mom says it's going fast."

She laughed as she took one of the plates. "I haven't eaten lunch yet."

"So start with dessert."

She smiled at him, then took a bite. "How'd you know this was my absolute favorite?"

Tyler winked at her. "Ryan isn't the only one who knows your favorites."

"Nikki."

Nikki turned around, then cleared her throat as Ryan walked across the room toward her. With his refined plaid shirt, jacket, and hint of a five-o'clock shadow, Jamie was right about one thing. He was a hunk. But she also knew she had to find a way to tell him the truth.

"Ryan. Hi. I didn't know you were going to be able to come. You know Tyler Grant, don't you?"

"Actually I don't think we've met." Tyler shook Ryan's hand, clearly sizing him up. "But I've heard a lot about you."

"Really?" Ryan said.

"Tyler's a longtime friend of mine, and his son, Liam . . . well, Liam's probably back at the dessert table."

"Then Liam must be a boy after my own heart."

Nikki shot Tyler a you-better-behave look,

then smiled back at Ryan. Somehow she hadn't imagined feeling quite so . . . awkward when the two of them finally met.

"Have you seen the view from my parents' balcony?" She needed to get the two of them apart before things got even more awkward. "I could show it to you, then you can grab some of my dad's barbeque. It's the best you'll find this side of the Mississippi."

"If it tastes half as good as it smells, I won't be disappointed."

She told Tyler they'd be back, then grabbed Ryan's arm and pulled him toward the balcony door. "Just tell my father that after you've tried it. The whole southern barbeque thing is my daddy's baby. He might end up talking with you the rest of the night, but you'll be his friend for life."

"Not a bad idea."

They stepped outside and she waited for the reaction that always came.

"Wow. The view is stunning."

"It was what sold my mom on the property. Dad was looking for a place closer to the restaurant with all the kids gone. She finally decided not having a garden to worry about wasn't such a bad idea after all."

He ran his hand down her arm, then pulled back. "Listen, I know these past few days must have been horrible for you. I saw the local news report covering the story. What a nightmare. You should have called me. Let me know what was going on. Let me know that you're okay."

"I'm sorry I didn't communicate more." She caught the disappointment in his eyes and fiddled with the drawstring of her red tie-dyed maxi dress. "But you're right, it was a tough week."

She hadn't purposely avoided his calls. She'd just needed time to sort things out. Not just about Cooper and everything that had happened inside the park, but about her own feelings toward Ryan and Tyler that she was still trying to sort through.

"Everything happened so fast, and then when I got back, I took a few days off."

"But you're okay. That man didn't hurt you?"

"Physically, no, though I can't say the experience didn't affect me. But I'm okay. Really."

She'd had nightmares the past few nights but knew they'd eventually fade. Hopefully the memory of Randall Cooper would fade as well.

"And the girl you were looking for, she's okay?"

"She will be. It was extremely traumatic for her, but her friends and family are rallying around her."

Ryan shook his head. "All I know is that I used to think it would be fun to trade in my desk job for some high-adrenaline career, but honestly, after hearing about some of the things you've had to face, I don't know how you do it. I think running my slice of the world from behind a computer screen is more than enough adventure for me."

"I'll admit I thought about switching careers a few times over the past few days." She felt the awkwardness that passed between them and looked down. She was still holding the uneaten cake Tyler had brought her. "You ready for some barbeque?"

She tried to steady her emotions. It was the wrong thing to say. She needed to tell him the truth, but had no idea how.

"Yes, but first . . ." Ryan hesitated for a moment. "I have no idea what you're going to think about this, but my parents called last night. They plan to be in town for Memorial Day, and while I know it's a bit early in our relationship, they'd really like to meet you."

Nikki felt her pulse quicken. She looked up at him, knowing she had to tell him the truth. Everyone was after her to get engaged. Get married. Have a couple babies and live happily ever after. That was how it worked in the fairy tales and the romance novels. Why was real life so messy and complicated?

"I'd like to meet your family, but . . ."

She turned and looked back inside the condo to where Tyler stood talking with her mother. Liam stood beside him eating what had to be at least seconds on desserts. There was no denying it anymore.

"Listen, if you're not ready, I understand. And I'm sure this past week must have been completely unsettling. Forget I asked, okay?" He started toward the door, then paused. "Though I do have one other question for you."

She needed to tell him the truth.

"He's in love with you, isn't he?"

Nikki felt her heart tremor at the question. "I'm sorry . . . who's in love with me?"

He couldn't be talking about Tyler. Tyler was still in love with Katie. And it was going to take time before he was ready to move on.

"Tyler. Your friend. The man I just met inside."

"No . . . he's always been like a brother. Even a best friend, but he's not in love with me. His wife died a year ago. She was my best friend since college. We've been through a lot together, especially this past year."

"Then you're in love with him."

Nikki paused. She wasn't ready to confess her feelings toward anyone—especially not to Ryan—but neither could she deny it. "I think I am. I didn't even know until last week when we were up there in the mountains. I thought I was going to die and I realized . . . I realized I was in love with him. I'm so sorry, Ryan."

Disappointment shone through his smile. "So I wasn't just imagining that look in your eyes when you were with him. It's the same look I always hoped you'd give me one day."

She shook her head. "I never meant to hurt you, or—"

"Fall in love?" He dropped his hands to his sides. "Sometimes we don't have control over what our heart feels, do we?"

"I really am sorry."

"Don't be. You're still quite a catch, Nikki Boyd." His gaze shifted inside where Tyler was still talking to her mother. "Once he realizes—what I'm pretty certain he already feels—he's going to be one very lucky guy."

"Ryan—"

He shook his head. "Don't worry about it. I had just hoped that you might be the one."

Jamie had been right. He was ready to put a ring on her finger.

He kissed her cheek. "If you do happen to realize you picked the wrong guy, call me, okay?"

She laughed, blinking back the tears threatening to spill. "Okay."

"I'll see you around, Special Agent Nikki Boyd."

Nikki nodded, then watched Ryan go back into the house, say goodbye to her mother, then head toward the front door. She turned back to the railing and stared out over the city. Confessing her feelings toward Tyler had only managed to make them seem all that more real. She'd never meant to hurt Ryan. Never meant to fall in love with Tyler. But she had. And now she had no idea what to do about it.

"Hey." Tyler walked up beside her.

"I didn't even hear you come out," she said, shooting him a nervous smile.

"Everything okay?"

"It will be."

"Why is Mr. Perfect leaving?"

"We're not going to be seeing each other anymore."

"Was it something I said?"

"No. You were fine, for once." She glanced down at the tiled flooring, wondering if she'd somehow gone completely crazy letting Ryan walk away. But knew it would be more of a mistake to lead him on.

"So everything isn't okay."

Nikki looked up at him, then brushed an imaginary piece of lint off the collar of his striped shirt and hesitated. "I think he's nice, and we have a lot in common, but . . . I don't know . . . we're at different places in life. He thought . . ." She paused.

"Thought what, Nikki?"

He thought you were in love with me.

But she knew he wasn't. Still, Tyler was everything she wanted in a man. More perfect even than Mr. Perfect. But he'd belonged to her best friend and was still nursing a broken heart.

"Nothing," she said, turning away. "He's just . . . he's not the right one for me."

"I'm sorry." He reached down and brushed a kiss across her forehead, making her heart swoon. "I know I teased you about him, but only because he seemed to make you happy. If you want to talk . . ."

"No, I'm fine." She flashed him a smile and slipped her hand into the crook of his arm, wondering if Ryan was right about Tyler. Wondering if he'd suddenly realize, like she had, that he was in love with her. And willing, in the meantime, to wait for him. "I'm okay, because I'm here with the people I love and care about the most. My friends and family . . . and you."

A Note to My Readers

I loved researching this book! Over the past few months, I've read a firsthand account of hiking the Appalachian Trail and another book written by a ranger who worked in the Smoky Mountains. I devoured information on the park and surrounding area and turned to a couple of experts in hiking and rappelling and police work for their input into my story. I also tackled the more difficult side of research about what happens when a child goes missing, and how families and friends often respond, along with local authorities.

While this book is a work of fiction, I have tried to realistically show the heartache that goes along with having someone you love disappear, both from the point of view of the family and from the response of the law.

I have also taken some liberties, including creating the newly instated Missing Persons Task Force team for the sake of the story. Those who are familiar with this part of Tennessee will be able to recognize many of the beautiful landmarks I've included, like the stunning Smoky Mountains Park, but will also notice that I have created certain settings as needed for the story as well as characters—rangers included—who don't exist in real life.

During the writing of this book, I came to greatly admire the rangers and law officers who work diligently to make our world a better place. They put their own lives at risk for the sake of saving others. To them, I salute you for your hard, tireless work!

Acknowledgments

I'm always so grateful to those who work alongside me in the writing of a new story. It truly takes a village. Thanks to my wonderful editors, Andrea, Barb, and Ellen, for helping me take my stories to the next level. To the team at Revell . . . you all rock! Thanks for everything you do to get the word out about my books. A huge thanks to Eric and Janet for helping me with the rappelling scene and ensuring my police procedure is accurate. Any mistakes are all my own! And lastly to my wonderful family, who stands by and supports me while I write. Love you guys!!!

About the Author

Lisa Harris is a bestselling author, a Christy Award finalist for *Blood Ransom*, Christy Award winner for *Dangerous Passage*, and the winner of the Best Inspirational Suspense Novel for 2011 from *Romantic Times*. She has sold over thirty novels and novella collections. Along with her husband, she and her three children have spent over twelve years living as missionaries in Africa, where she homeschools, leads a women's group, and runs a nonprofit organization that works alongside their church-planting ministry. The ECHO Project works in southern Africa promoting Education, Compassion, Health, and Opportunity and is a way for her to *"speak up for those who cannot speak for themselves . . . the poor and helpless, and see that they get justice"* (Prov. 31:8–9).

When she's not working, she loves hanging out with her family, cooking different ethnic dishes, photography, and heading into the African bush on safari. For more information about her books and life in Africa, visit her website at www.lisaharriswrites.com or her blog at http://mybloginthe heartofafrica.blogspot.com. For more information about The ECHO Project, please visit www.theECHOproject.org.

Center Point Large Print
600 Brooks Road / PO Box 1
Thorndike, ME 04986-0001 USA

(207) 568-3717

US & Canada:
1 800 929-9108
www.centerpointlargeprint.com